JENS BJØRNEBOE (1920-1976) was one of the most controversial figures of his day; outspoken and anarchic, he clashed with most institutions in his determination to challenge repression, censorship and authoritarianism. Novelist, poet, playwright, journalist and essayist, he poured forth a steady stream of works which were as provocative in their subject matter as they were innovative in their form and which attacked the establishment's most sacred cows: a repressive school system, a hypocritical Christianity, an inhumane prison system, power-seeking politicians, corrupt police and depraved moral guardians. His most significant work is generally considered to be the trilogy The History of Bestiality (1966-1973), where he turned his attention to a more general problem, namely the evil inherent in the human race itself. *The Sharks* (1974), a thrilling story of mutiny and shipwreck, was Bjørneboe's last major work.

ESTHER GREENLEAF MÜRER is a freelance translator, who has also translated Jens Bjørneboe's trilogy The History of Bestiality, consisting of the novels *Moment of Freedom* (*Frihetens øyeblikk*, 1966), *Powderhouse* (*Kruttårnet*, 1969) and *The Silence* (*Stillheten*, 1973). All three volumes were published by Norvik Press.

Some other books from Norvik Press

Kjell Askildsen: *A Sudden Liberating Thought* (translated by Sverre Lyngstad)

Johan Borgen: *Little Lord* (translated by Janet Garton)

Jens Bjørneboe: *Moment of Freedom* (translated by Esther Greenleaf Mürer)

Jens Bjørneboe: *Powderhouse* (translated by Esther Greenleaf Mürer)

Jens Bjørneboe: *The Silence* (translated by Esther Greenleaf Mürer)

Hans Børli: *We Own the Forests and Other Poems* (translated by Louis Muinzer)

Peter Fjågesund: *Knut Hamsun Abroad: International Reception*

Arne Garborg: *The Making of Daniel Braut* (translated by Marie Wells)

Sigurd Hoel: *A Fortnight Before the Frost* (translated by Sverre Lyngstad)

Jonas Lie: *The Family at Gilje* (translated by Marie Wells)

Amalie Skram: *Fru Inés* (translated by Katherine Hanson and Judith Messick)

Amalie Skram: *Lucie* (translated by Katherine Hanson and Judith Messick)

Amalie and Erik Skram: *Caught in the Enchanter's Net: Selected Letters* (edited and translated by Janet Garton)

THE SHARKS

The history of a crew and a shipwrek

by

Jens Bjørneboe

Translated from the Norwegian by
Esther Greenleaf Mürer

Norvik Press
2016

Originally published in Norwegian as *Haiene* © Gyldendal norsk forlag 1974.

This translation © Esther Greenleaf Mürer 1992

The translator's moral right to be identified as the translator of the work has been asserted.

A catalogue record for this book is available from the British Library.
ISBN: 978-1-909408-12-8

First published in 1992 by Norvik Press, University of East Anglia, Norwich NR4 7TJ. This edition first published in 2016.

Norvik Press
Department of Scandinavian Studies
University College London
Gower Street
London WC1E 6BT
United Kingdom

Website: www.norvikpress.com
E-mail address: norvik.press@ucl.ac.uk

Managing editors: Elettra Carbone, Sarah Death, Janet Garton, C. Claire Thomson.

Cover illustration: Detail of ship wreck on Burnham beach at low tide, Somerset, 2008.

Cover design: Elettra Carbone

Printed in the UK by Lightning Source UK Ltd.

To
Marianne, Therese and Suzanne

Contents

– from birth to death the shark is driven by one unquenchable desire, by hunger.

Prologue

On the twenty-first of April in the year 1900, the office boy Eugene Henderson stood outside the door to the shipping firm Malcolm & Malcolm in Glasgow. It was a wet, grey morning, and Eugene was a very young man with a high collar, reddish-blond hair and a disposition to freckles, thin sprouting whiskers, and a certain tendency to fat. He carefully wiped his shoes on the doormat before entering. With hat in hand he greeted the clerks behind the counter with the greatest politeness and modesty. One or two looked up and nodded back before returning to their stamp boxes, ledgers, and correspondence. There was no warmth in their greetings.

The trouble was that young Henderson had a pronounced taste for lying in his warm bed, and today he was late again. He looked around from one to another. Something in the atmosphere was different from usual. Just one of the salaried employees laid down his pen and looked up at him, over thick steel-rimmed spectacles on a long, thin nose. It was Benson, after Henderson the firm's junior employee, and the two were, each in his sluggish and phlegmatic way, friends of a sort; now and then they drank a glass of stout together. Benson cast a gloomy look at the other, and slowly, reproachfully shook his head. Henderson divested himself of his greatcoat and umbrella, went behind the counter, and bent over him.

'What's the matter?' he whispered: 'Is something wrong?'

'The boss arrived earlier than usual today. You were unlucky.'

'Damnation.'

Henderson looked around the office. When all was said and done he was, in his unshakable sluggishness and despite his inclination to oversleep, a clever and most hard-working office boy. And since his somnolence was, as it were, of a bourgeois and relatively balanced sort, and never entailed more than a few minutes' tardiness, his superiors accepted it with ironic indulgence. He was a useful young man who took his earthly calling seriously, almost solemnly.

'Did Mr. Malcolm say anything?' he asked in a low voice.

'No,' replied Benson. 'He didn't need to. He just looked at your place — *hard.*'

Now the office boy seemed to have finished waking; he scanned the room yet again. Then he said:

'Something's happened. What's going on?'

'It's six months ago today.'

'Six months since what?'

The clerk took off his spectacles and looked at him gravely.

'It's the twenty-first of April. Exactly half a year since the *Neptune* sailed from Manila, and four months since she was reported missing. Mr. Malcolm reminded us of the fact before you came; he said that now the ship will be presumed lost and will finally be written off.'

'Well,' replied Henderson, gazing out the window: 'Will there be any trouble with the insurance?'

Benson had no time to answer. The door to the inner offices had opened, and Mr. Algot, the office manager, appeared with a stack of papers in his hand. He was still wearing galoshes; the round, milk-blue eyes in his healthy pink face stared at the office boy in astonishment.

'Well, well, well, Mr. Henderson!' he said, as if thunderstruck: 'You have deigned to make your appearance, sir!'

'Excuse me,' said Henderson, 'it won't happen again.'

'What won't happen again? That you make your appearance? You surely don't mean to say, sir, that we shan't have the pleasure of seeing you again?'

'I shan't oversleep again,' said the office boy, hanging his head.

'All right, Henderson,' replied the manager, handing him the papers: 'We have a bank errand for you.'

'Thank you, sir.'

Algot cast a look toward the outer wall. Between the windows hung an aquarelle of the bark *Neptune*. He shook his head.

'With all hands,' he said softly.

Book One

The Mate

Sailor, beware, sailor, take care . . . .

My name is Peder Jensen, born in Hammerfest in Norway in 1866. I was second mate on the *Neptune,* and I shall relate what happened.

I shall record it as well as my uncommon memory and modest writing ability allow. Only the Gods in heaven know what was the meaning of that terrible, insane voyage. But as sure as the Southern Cross stands in the firmament, just as certain it is that everything has a meaning. It's just that our defective human reason lacks the power to grasp it. But this voyage began more absurdly, more meaninglessly, than any other journey I know of. It was as if the vessel were soaked through and through with hate — built, welded, rigged, and riveted with hate. It's as if she were possessed by Satan.

And she was one of the loveliest creatures I've seen; a white-painted bark, somewhat overcanvassed. Now, a bark is always the noblest and loveliest, the most graceful and beautiful thing afloat on the sea. For me a bark is the topgallant of the shipbuilder's art. But even for a bark she was improbable: wild, fast, moody, difficult to sail, and a dazzling beauty. If I myself had christened her — from her appearance — I should have named her 'Venus', for the goddess of beauty and love and for the wondrous planet in the evening sky.

And yet all this well-nigh sensual loveliness was possessed by the devil.

But I've heard like things of human beings, of women, beautiful and wild, mysterious, inscrutable, magnificent, driving men to frenzy: that they themselves were victims of demon possession. Tales of love, madness, and death.

As I said: *Neptune* was possessed by Satan. When I think of her it strikes me as sick, wicked, and perverse to call such a vessel by a man's name. Neptune is to the highest degree a male deity as he pursues his fruitful veneries in the ocean's bottomless, enigmatic deep. It was simply indecent to name this vessel after him — after such a pronounced he-god. At the sight of her I would have christened her 'Sancta Vénere' — Holy Venus. And she was perhaps the fastest sailer I've had under my feet.

In short: I was wildly in love with her when I went aboard in Manila. That was why I signed on. I boarded her with a sea chest and a violin case, with my trembling heart and fevered brain: all I own and possess in this singular world. On the twenty-first of October, 1899, we sailed out of the harbour, duly laden with cordage and hemp. There I stood on her planks, with the sky above me and the sea below. Great God, what a situation! Upward, the endless space of heaven; downward, the dark, bottomless sea. A third of the crew, plus the steward and the third mate, were dead drunk. The carpenter lay senseless after a fight with one of the hands. It delayed our sailing, but we sailed.

Once I had settled into my cabin, I went through the medicine chest. As second mate I was also the ship's medicine man, and I had an unpleasant foreboding that we should find a use for our medicines. The chest contained the usual nautical pharmacopoeia: quinine, opium, morphine, ether, chloroform, etc.; dressings, splints, and a small array of relatively simple but modern surgical instruments. It's rather tiresome that I'm inclined to spew at the sight of blood, but that's the way of it: it is my fate, and I must bear it.

16

It is also my fate to be a seaman. For of all things on earth, it is first and foremost a seaman that I am. That means that I'm afraid of the sea. I hate the sea. I despise the loathsome, malicious roar of the surf. Indeed I have a kind of hydrophobia, both bodily and spiritual. The thought of the deep, that realm of twilight and darkness where so many men of my calling have rotted, fills me with genuine terror. All sailors are afraid of the sea. They know what it is.

At least six generations of my forefathers have been seamen. I hate the ocean, the bottomlessness, the depth, but I can never escape it. The sea is the incomprehensible: fathomless as the starry sky, as the human heart.

From terror of the ocean I've tried to live on land, with firm ground under my feet. At such times, when my dread of the sea had become too strong to bear, I earned my daily bread by giving instruction. I've taught chiefly mathematics and geography, and French and English as well, but also music. Still, after a time on land, it was the sea again. Always. That is my fate and my curse: to love what I hate.

What more is there to tell? I'm five feet eleven inches tall and a rather straightforward man. At the time I signed on in Manila I was thirty-three years old.

Then *Neptune* set out on her last, meaningless, incomprehensible voyage, on a southeasterly course, by way of Cape Horn, bound for Marseilles. The voyage of death which was to mark me for life. That autumn of 1899 I thought too of another journey, soon to begin: the voyage into a new century. I did a great deal of thinking back then — on the deck planks or in my cabin on board that lovely accursed ship. She was so beautiful that for me to this very day her name is still *Sancta Vénere* — Holy Venus.

The Carpenter

After the towing hawser had been cast off and the sails set, it was not my nautical duties which claimed me. That is: not chart, dividers, straightedge, compass, or sextant — but still it was nautical work. A seaman must be equal to anything. Often you're cut off from land for months at a time, and you must know how to splint a broken arm or leg, pull a tooth, amputate a crushed finger; indeed you must be able to milk a cow — or to act as a midwife and deliver a child, should the birth occur on the high seas.

Once we were under sail and heard the clear, almost transparent lapping of water and waves around the ship's bow and along her sides, I had to bury myself in the medicine chest again. The carpenter was still unconscious, and aside from his breathing displayed no sign of life. The half-open eyes were lifeless, showing only an enamelled white. His face was pale as lime, his pulse slow and irregular. They had laid him supine on the battened-down hatch, and as the ship heeled under her full spread of sail he lay there with his head lower than his feet. Blood from his mouth and nose had spread down over his face to his neck. On his forehead, just below the hairline, was a three-inch open wound. The blood had first run down into his eyebrows and eyes; then it had run back, down into his hair.

How or why the scuffle began, I don't know — but judging from what I saw, it was a purely animal fight. They were out to kill each other.

The fight's savagery and brutishness — I could almost say insanity — filled me with deep revulsion, a well-nigh sickening dread, and seemed to paralyse the crew as well. They stood mute and motionless, watching, with no visible sign of sympathy or support for either party. The crew? But there's no other word for that strange assemblage of folk from every corner and edge of the globe, of every colour and race, denizens of the whole world's docks and ports, foregathered on the bark *Neptune* for her last voyage — straight across the Pacific from Manila to Cape Horn, calling at Rio, then across the Atlantic and through the Mediterranean to Marseilles.

Already as I stood watching the passive, sullen crew and the two men rolling like beasts of prey on the deck, I felt a hopeless longing for Marseilles — a deep sadness, an impotent feeling that I should never see that part of the world again. Strange to say I thought too of how good dinner would taste at La Poulette after months of monotonous ship's fare. But this went through me in a flash, in a fraction of a second.

What was happening between those two deranged men on the deck was much too terrible to permit of other thoughts. I heard the loathsome sound of fists against flesh, and saw that both their faces were smeared with blood.

The carpenter was a brawny, middle-sized man in his thirties. He was — as I later learned — a Javanese, but a bastard of partly Dutch descent. His opponent was a lean, muscular South American — a Peruvian signed on as ordinary seaman.

The first thing I saw was the carpenter striking the other across the mouth with such force that the blood literally spurted. The other fell backward and rolled several turns over the deck. But he was back on his feet almost instantly. Like a cat he sprang on his foe, bringing him down; and, raising his trunk, let the carpenter have it, time after time — then they both rolled sideways. The

Javanese got his arms around the ordinary's neck and pulled his face toward his own. It looked as if he were kissing him, and all at once a wild, piercing scream came from the Peruvian. The carpenter was biting his cheek; with a violent effort he tore himself loose, the blood streaming down over his neck and chest. Both were on their feet again almost at once. Twice the carpenter hit the Peruvian in the face, then the latter brought up his knee and kicked him full force in the crotch. As he doubled up screaming, the ordinary hit him over the nape. He fell, but got hold of the other's legs, sending him backward. Again they rolled on the deck, and when they came to rest the ordinary was back on top. He seized the carpenter's throat with his left hand and with his right rained blow after blow on his mouth and nose. The carpenter got hold of the other's long hair, pulled down his head, and set both thumbs in his eyes. The Peruvian screamed like crazy and tried to get the other's hands off his face, but the Javanese held on: four fingers of each hand gripping his hair, the thumbs firmly planted in his eyes.

The crew stood as before — motionless, silent, watching. The only sound was the wild, heartrending screams of the ordinary. By twisting onto his side he freed himself at last; he rolled a couple of turns on the deck, then came to rest on his knees, face down, his hands over his eyes. He was no longer screaming, but jerked convulsively.

Slowly the carpenter rose and spat out blood over the deck. Then he walked up to the other, paused, then kicked him in the crotch from behind. With a bellow the Peruvian rolled onto his side. Twice more the other kicked him, now in the stomach.

It was clear that the fight was over. But suddenly he was up again, reeling, wild as a tiger from rage. His skull rammed the mouth of the Javanese, who staggered backward, his hands over his face. He stood thus for a moment, then sprang on the other. The blow caught the Peruvian on the jaw, and he fell backward toward the hatch. Beside him lay a plank, two inches thick and about four feet long. Quick as lightning he grabbed it and jumped up. The carpenter, unable to avoid the blow, merely threw back his head.

20

The other raised the plank high with both hands and struck. It rammed the carpenter there where the temple joins the forehead, and he collapsed as if shot.

With two of the men I laid the lifeless body up on the hatch. Then followed all the activity requisite to getting a vessel under sail and out to sea. The Peruvian tottered forward and down into the forecastle.

When I was free I had the carpenter carried aft, down to the narrow sick bay. I must confess that at first I had no idea what I should do with him. After taking his pulse I undressed him, sent the cabin boy for some boiled water, and began washing the blood off his neck, face, and head. Outside, under the porthole, the water rippled and splashed against the planking. The vessel was heeling quite strongly now; she was making good headway.

The carpenter was utterly lifeless from the looks of him. Under the half-closed lids I saw only the whites of his eyes. At best it was a severe concussion — at worst a fractured skull, possibly with internal bleeding. When I had washed away most of the blood, I saw what a beating he had taken. His mouth and nose seemed like continuous wounds, and the open gash in his forehead still bled profusely, as head wounds always do. As I washed it out I could see the frontal bone between its gaping lips. From the left corner of his mouth ran a long, deep gash toward his ear. Two of his front teeth were destroyed.

I examined his jaw to see if it were broken, but found no indication that it was.

Then I washed his face with vinegar and spirit, but he gave no sign of life. I poured a glass of brandy into the half-open mouth; it had no effect. On the whole he didn't look as if he would survive the next few hours. There was nothing more I could do but to sew up the wounds on his forehead and next to his mouth. I don't like to sew, and there's not much point in basting together a man who is about to leave this world forever; but should the miracle happen — should he in fact one day return from his lethargy to our waking,

21

conscious, living world — then at least this patchwork would be done.

I took along two curved needles, catgut, clamps, and two pairs of tweezers to the galley and boiled them for several minutes. Then I went back and began the loathsome work.

By the time I had taken the first stitch and was about to knot the gut, I was on the verge of throwing up. In all I took eleven stitches in his forehead and seven from the corner of his mouth. In a cut under his right eye I took four. As I was sewing up the wound below his hairline, something happened: at the two final stitches he gave two distinct groans or sighs. They were unmistakable signs of life. Otherwise he lay as before. Over the big gash on his forehead I laid a sterile compress, then wound a bandage like a turban around his head. The wound on his cheek could be plastered along the stitches. His nose and lips I treated with alcohol and then plaster.

He was breathing quite evenly now, but his pulse was still faint, irregular, and slow. I was fairly certain that he would die during the night, and it struck me how meaningless it was to work on this dying, crude, savage human brute. Of course it was a desperate and godless thought; only the powers which rule over life and death know what really dwells in the human heart. If the man should in fact pull through, it wouldn't be my fault; but it was nonetheless important that I do my best with his injuries.

Of the two destroyed incisors, one — that nearest the centre — was loose at the root; the other was broken. I looked at them and reflected that we had months of sailing before us with no access to a dentist, and that the teeth were sure to occasion him pain and discomfort — if, that is, he should defy my expectations and not go the way of all flesh in the next few days.

From the instruments I selected a forceps which I thought would do, and pulled the loose tooth with no trouble. Like all his teeth, it was flawless and white as ivory. The other was more difficult. For one thing, it was broken so near to the gum that it was hard to get a grip on it; for another, it sat almost unbelievably fast. Finally, after several minutes' work, it began to loosen, and I

22

wiggled and twisted it with increasingly greater effect. The carpenter groaned once. Then I had the tooth out, and put it aside with the other debris from my field surgeon's labours. The floor of the sick bay was strewn with bloody rags and cotton.

I began a prayer to the Lord that in future he might spare me further labours as a medicine man — something to which neither my brain, my nerves, nor my fingers were suited. But instead I just sat gazing at the bandaged head and the naked body. He was a very well-built man, and was doubtless equipped with greater physical resistance than white people are. And he'd need that toughness now.

But if — as was probable — he *did* have a cranial fracture, a real crack in his skull, after that awful blow; then what could I, a layman with only the most rudimentary knowledge of medicine, do for him? Surely one could do something beyond just letting him lie there, letting his tough, catlike, animal constitution fight against death. This mysterious life force — couldn't I come to its aid?

As I sat in my shirtsleeves, sweating, brooding over what I could do, I was yet filled with a great inner joy: I was on board my dearest, my own *Sancta Vénere*, the loveliest ship I had ever seen. The sick bay lay on her port side — the lee side at present; and as the salt seawater lapped at her planking, a wave would cover the porthole so that I saw into the water's pale, sun-filled blue. The thought of Holy Venus — of the beauteous, radiant Evening Star, east of the sun and west of the moon, to which I had consecrated her in my heart — of her lovely, outsized rigging, her slim white hull — all this made me happy. I felt like a god, or at the very least a prince, basking in the gods' golden favour. When I had done serving Asclepius here below in the cabin, I would go up on deck and consummate the blessedness. I would become one with her, I would take the helm and have her in my arms!

Ah, youth! Ah, the joy of life!

A sound from the dying man recalled my dreaming thoughts to the sickbed. It came from low in his throat and resembled a kind of faint gurgling. Was it a sign of life, or was it the first, inchoate death rattle? Was the Majesty already present here below the afterdeck? I didn't know.

Then it was quiet again.

On the shelf over the berth, between a bundle of stearine candles and an empty brandy bottle, stood Dr. Thiers' big, two-volume *Handbook of Ship's Medicine*, next to a catalogue of pharmaceutical preparations. I sat for a long time with the books across my knees, hoping to find something about how, in a case of emergency, one gives first aid for a cracked skull. Finally I concluded that the only thing I could do was to try to stimulate the heart-action. I gave him belladonna and then an injection of something whose name I've forgotten. (Fate, by the way, has heard my prayer: since *Neptune*'s last voyage I've escaped further service as a quacksalver/medicine man. But I must add that I myself have had a hand in the game of fate: now, whenever I sign on, I declare myself unfit to be an amateur ship's doctor; and in time I've forgotten what little I knew, not merely the name of the preparation which I injected into the carpenter.)

However, the treatment seemed effective; after a time the patient's breathing deepened, and his pulse grew more regular, faster, and firmer. That was encouraging, and I had risen to go on deck when suddenly I thought of the other fighting cock — the Peruvian ordinary who had been the Javanese's opponent. The black American cabin boy was sent forward to fetch him.

The sick bay was much too cramped to permit of treating another man there, and I resolved to use my own cabin as a first-aid station for him. When I had made ready with boiled water, dressings, and instruments, he came aft, his arm supported on the shoulder of another sailor. He was in miserable shape, terribly battered. Around his head he had tied a dirty scarf to stanch the bleeding from the bite on his cheek. But instead of stopping the blood, it had merely glued itself to his face, so that it caused him great pain when I removed it.

I sat him on a chair facing the weather porthole and began to examine him. Both eyes were bloodshot and heavily bruised. The left one squinted, and looked to be seriously damaged. The carpenter's Javanese fangs had left a ghastly wound, and in two places the lower teeth had gone clean through his cheek. His left hand was totally paralysed.

After washing off the blood, I rinsed his eyes. The right one wasn't so bad; over the left I laid a boric-acid compress and covered it with a leather patch tied firmly around his head with a string. For the pain I gave him 'aurum', a mixture of opium and alcohol.

Then I undressed him to the waist, laid a towel over my pillow, and bade him lie on the bunk. I washed and disinfected the wound in his cheek as best I could, then made a roll of a clean handkerchief, which I moistened with ether. He was instructed to hold it over his mouth and nostrils and breathe deeply. When he was sufficiently fuddled — barely conscious — I set about sewing up the wound. It was much harder to sew than the carpenter's two wounds, and I used a great many stitches. He must have felt pain during the operation, but no sound escaped him. Then I laid a sterile compress over the bite and plastered it well, covering half his face. I also took a stitch or two in his upper lip. The sun and the pure sea air, and God, would have to do the rest.

From his forearm out to the tip of his left little finger I laid a flat wooden splint, and bandaged the hand so as to immobilize the last two fingers. The damage was chiefly to the two upper phalanges, and whether the trouble was fracture or a severe sprain, the splint would be all to the good. (I hope to God that no doctor, I mean no real medical man, reads this. But the fact is that I did what I could — to the best of my judgment and poor ability.) Finally I gave the patient — who was if possible even more battered after my treatment — a tumblerful of brandy and helped him up to the afterdeck.

I went up to the helmsman, a small-boned Cuban with slender hands and a fine, chiselled face. He spoke English well, and I asked him to help the Peruvian down to the forecastle. I said I would take the helm till the watch changed; he could remain forward. The first mate was in the charthouse. It was just before sundown, and land was no longer in sight. On the western sky there burned the whole mysterious tropical magnificence of colour — but I didn't see it. I took no notice of anything.

I was standing at the helm of *Sancta Vénere*!

That first, physical contact with my beloved! I held her living soul in my hands — laid hands on her for the first time!

It's no exaggeration to say that I trembled as I first gripped the mahogany wheel. The deck sloped under me, the wind was from starboard, a little abaft the beam; but I was mindful of nothing but her. Carefully I eased her a quarter of a point off to windward, just to feel the contact, to feel how she minded her rudder. And I felt it, the faint quivering — she too trembled at my touch! A tall flame of happiness went through me, from my feet to my fingertips I felt the trembling of her, of this oneness of hull and rigging — of body and soul, of ropes and wind. It was a great, rushing music: the sea, the ship, and the wind.

Yes, I was standing at the helm of Holy Venus!

Slowly the sun sank into the ocean, the twilight was brief; and not long afterward the Evening Star grew visible as I stood there, dizzy with the happiness of love. I knew that it was *Sancta Vénere*'s soul I loved, and that she loved me in return. And what is earthly passion to loving a soul?

There was a light in the binnacle; the compass needle shook too. Everything quivered — hull and rigging, foremast, mainmast, mizzenmast. She had shown herself to be as I thought when I saw her from land for the first time, at the first glance. Now I was commanding her, *Sancta Vénere* — Holy Venus — the orb of love!

How long I stood there as helmsman I don't know, but the tropical night was black when the watch changed and my relief arrived.

I went below again, to resume tending the sick — this time not the carpenter, but the third mate and the steward. Both were still dead drunk. The mate lay supine in his bunk, open-mouthed, his face red and swollen. He was snoring heavily. There was somewhat more life in the steward. He had taken a bottle of rum to his berth

26

when he turned in, and it lay beside him on the pillow. He was drunk as an auk, but his swimming blue eyes were open. He seemed almost as moribund as the carpenter, and feebly attempted to speak. I surmised that he was talking about the bottle, and that he couldn't hold it up; so I filled a tumbler and carefully, patiently poured the contents into his mouth. Then, with endless trouble, I manoeuvred a glass of saline into them each, and had thereby done what I could for them. I later found out that the third mate — a big, burly young North American — was just an ordinary drunkard, while the steward — a Flemish Belgian in his late forties — was a true alcoholic, with cirrhosis and incipient dementia. (The very next morning I gave him a shot of morphine to quiet him down.)

After I had finished with those two, I went to sit in the sick bay. I was very tired, but I stayed. His breathing was shallower now, his pulse weaker and slower again. About an hour after midnight I gave him some more belladonna and another shot of the stuff whose name I've forgotten. Around three a faint quivering appeared in his eyelids, and he seemed on the verge of opening them. But then he was gone again. A little later I got a few tablespoons of brandy into him.

Toward five in the morning I heard a faint sound from the passageway, and turned my head. The door slowly opened; outside stood the captain in his nightshirt, his impenetrable round face utterly devoid of expression.

'Well?' he said: 'Mr. Jensen, how goes it with that blasted Javanese mutt? Is he going to live?'

'I'm beginning to think so, sir.'

Slowly the door closed after him. For him that had been a long speech.

Around six I went up to the officers' mess to get some food into myself. I was stiff with fatigue. The table had been rigged with fiddles to retain the tea, plates, and eating utensils. The little black cabin boy was drunk with sleep as he poured the tea and handed the toast and marmalade.

'Sleep well, my boy?' I said.

'Yes, sir.'

I drank two cups of tea and got down a few slices of bread. Then the captain entered. He had exchanged his nightshirt for the white tropical uniform, and again he looked at me with his stolid, expressionless face.

'Turn in, mister,' he said.

I got up and went to my cabin, which still bore the signs of having been used as a lazarette the day before. The instant my head hit the pillow, I was asleep.

Thus passed my first twenty-four hours on board the Sailing Vessel *Neptune*.

Poseidon — The Sea

> And the spirit of God moved upon
> the face of the waters . . . .

As I said: I'm a seaman. I'll go further: I will say that the Gods in
their wrath have made me a seaman; in every fibre of my body, in
every cell of my nerves and brain, I am a seaman. It's not of my own
free will; I was made thus. I mentioned that six generations of my
forefathers were seamen; all of them gained their meagre livelihood,
their poor bread, from the ocean — from Neptune/Poseidon's awful
realm. Six generations have sailed that stormy surface — I myself am
thus the seventh — and others have made their living from the deep,
from the blue twilight world under the water's crust, there where
the bottomless dark begins.

What is this 'Neptune's kingdom'? Many of my race have met
the death angel while pursuing their hard daily toil on the sea; an
uncle went down in the Arctic Ocean, and my grandfather was
sailing with the ship *Union* when she vanished without a trace in the
South Atlantic in 1847. A brother of his was on board the schooner
Stella Maris when she foundered in the Indian Ocean two years
later, and was numbered among the lost. We have rendered our
tribute to Neptune's cannabalic drives. It's not just Saturn who eats

his children. For it is Neptune whose sons we are — fry of Poseidon — and he swallows us. I am a seaman, and I won't marry. No grieving widow, no breadless children, shall remain after me.

As you sail southeast from the archipelago, you quickly get into deep sea. East of the Philippines' thousands of islands lies the Mindanao region, where the ocean depth has been measured at more than 33,000 feet. That's what I mean by 'bottomless' — for in practice it has no bottom or limit. So intense is the pressure down there, under millions of tons of water, that none will ever penetrate it. All would be crushed, flattened like tin cans. Ships which founder here never reach the bottom. And we have other such ocean deeps: Due east of the Mindanao trench, south of the Mariana Islands, there are depths of more than 36,000 feet. South of the equator — in a trench stretching all the way from Samoa past the Friendly Islands and down toward New Zealand — 36,000 feet has been measured in several places. In the Atlantic it's only east of San Domingo that we find comparable depths — at least with soundings of more than 30,000 feet.

It is deeps such as these that we have beneath our keel after putting out to sea from the Philippines: the world of mystery, of the fathomless, the irrational. If the ocean surface, in savagery and rebellion, in calm and storm, resembles human feelings — that sea on which we sail our little ships of reason and consciousness, in the violent but known world of the emotions — then the great deeps, the ocean's dark abysses, resemble the human heart's unknown, never-visited worlds: the inscrutable, inaccessible, night-dark, soundless underworld of the soul.

This is Neptune's kingdom.

We shall turn our gaze from the deep to look in the other direction — toward that unending space where the all-pervading forces bear and sustain planets and fixed stars, the solar system and the constellations. We shall look at that heaven of shining, distant worlds which lies above our masts while thirty-five thousand feet of depth and darkness stretch beneath our keel.

They've found a new star, a new planet within our own solar system. It was discovered by the astronomer Galle in 1846, fifty-three years before the bark *Sancta Vénere* set out on her last voyage.

This new star is Neptune.

It has two moons — Nereid and Triton — and a diameter four times greater than that of our own star, Earth. It is the outermost of the planets, and its distance from the sun is immense: our solar system's ultimate contact with the powers of unending space. Neptune is a great star and a great god. And his spiritual and physical influence is incalculable.

Who, then, is this virile, mighty he-god?

The Greeks called him Poseidon, and in very ancient times also Psyche, who only later became a goddess — the human soul, the higher, unearthly love, Vénere ennobled — I could almost say: Holy Venus. (It occurs to me that Sancta Vénere has been forced to lend her name to those diseases which medical science calls 'venereal', which in shipping offices the world over are referred to as 'self-inflicted' — and which were unfortunately not unknown on board our own lovely white bark.) But it's not Psyche or the sublimated Venus we shall discuss here; it is the violent, brutal, and mighty Neptune, lord of abysses and deeps, author of the passions.

We shall look a bit more closely at how mythology, the clear childhood dreams of humanity, describes him. Who says that our reason sees further into the abyss?

Now I must say at once that I hope the reader won't write me off as an impractical dreamer, a visionary and mystic. The fact is that I measure the sun's height, calculate positions, chart them with straightedge and pencil, and keep a log or a ship's journal just as carefully, accurately, and conscientiously as any ship's officer in the British merchant fleet. But, as I said, seven generations of seamen's blood flow in my veins; I believe in pictures, in stars and signs. And it is only I who have set down the history of the bark *Neptune*'s final voyage; so if you want to know what happened, you must accept me as I am. I write as I do, not from deficient reason, but from experiences not all have had. I'm a thoroughly empirical soul; it was in these waters that Darwin sailed on the bark *Beagle* seventy years ago, and I shan't disgrace him. To be sure, I've set my course in another direction; but we sail by the same stars.

I wish only to add that no one plumbs the human heart's abysses with the aid of a lead line.

Poseidon was the son of Chronos and thus the brother of Zeus — which says no little about his position among gods, Titans, and men. When Zeus allotted the underworld to Hades, he set Poseidon to reign over the sea, over all that globe-embracing liquid element.

But the original lord of the sea was the Titan Oceanus, son of the sky-god Uranus (whose star, found in 1789 by the astronomer Herschel, presaged the outbreak of the Great French Revolution) — sired on the earth-spirit, Gea. Oceanus was so mighty that only Zeus outshone him. He mated with his sister and begot three thousand sons — the Oceanids. But Oceanus grew old; the gods of Olympus conquered the earth, and finally the sea as well. Zeus drove Oceanus out; Poseidon/Neptune inherited his kingdom and became untrammelled master of the seas and streams. All the sea- and river-gods were forced to bow down and serve him.

Sometimes Poseidon appears on the ocean surface; but the depths, the submarine chasms, are his home, his palace. He reigns deep, deep down in the unknown, infinitely far below the sunlit, day-bright surface where the dolphins pursue their play. His fertility and potency are immense; though married to the Nereid Amphitrite, he has sired noble races of demigods on other Nereids, on nymphs, mermaids, and other half-conscious spirits of the deep.

In appearance he is an athletic, middle-aged god, with an enormous flowing mane and beard. In his right hand he carries his emblem, his dreadful trident. His brow is high and broad, his eyes blue and so vast that they mirror the sky. No mortal can bear to gaze upon him. Woe to him whom Neptune or his star hold in thrall!

And since Neptune lives in all that flows, he can also settle in the blood — as its hidden, sinful river-god, who calls the half-conscious powers of the night to unceasing, total rebellion. Neptune of the blood! Up from the abyssal unconscious, from the ocean deep as from the soundlessness of the human heart, his dreadful forces mount, driving folk to frenzies and prophetic dreams, to narcomania, alcoholism, chaos, unquenchable lust, treachery, lies, and incurable madness. Of course Neptune has much to do with the moon as well, with the tides and moon-sickness, with ebb and flow. And not only in the blood, but also in the body's other fluids Neptune and his trident are at work; in the moisture of the tissues and especially inside the skull, in the strange amniotic fluid in which the brain floats and hovers. He makes the nerves inflamed and the brain febrile, calls forth visions, and lets us hear the roars and the great, terrifying music of the Tritons' conch-horns. Of course he is in the hurricane and the water-spout, the cyclone — and above all in the calm, deathly centre of the typhoon.

Only a few, an extreme few people, only those who have endured the greatest trials, can comprehend and respond to Neptune's very highest, most spiritual emanations — from Psyche, whom I have mentioned: the redeemed, divine Venus. Neptune is likewise the demon of the poppy, of opium, morphine, and alcohol — and the mediums' protector and inspiration, both when they speak for the spirits and when they simply lie and cheat. Falsehood is half-brother to telepathy.

All the water gods and goddesses are Poseidon/Neptune's servants: undines, potamids, Tritons, mermaids, water sprites, Nereids, river-carls; Pontus, Glaucus, Phorcys and Proteus and all the sirens, Scylla and Charybdis, ocean spirits and monsters.

And likewise the beasts of the ocean: whales, mussels, sharks, snails, giant octopuses, plankton, crabs, and molluscs — all living things obey him.

Neptune also raises the storm, on the ocean's face and within the blood and in the brain's amniotic fluid: storms of feeling, typhoons of madness.

Is it strange that I'm afraid of the sea?

For the ocean, the sea itself, is one of those living things which are subject to him — for whoever has met the ocean whipped up in rage, in blind and hate-filled passion, knows that the sea is a living, ensouled monster — in its delirium of hate possessed by one devilish mania: to smash everything it meets. The carnivore Sea in its madness is the embodiment of all destructive lust — one of our globe's greatest manifestations of Evil.

All seamen suffer from the same terror as I; when I'm at sea — as I almost always am — when I have the ship's planks and the sea under me, be I standing at the helm or charting a position — always, always I feel a faint, shuddering dread.

Is it this dread which draws me to the sea, again and again? Is that why I can't live quietly on land, teaching mathematics and leading a peaceful life — is it the longing for this faint, permanent dread, this whiff of death and reality, which drags me forth?

Yes, it is strange to be on the ocean; only one out of billions of *Homo sapiens*, an infinitesimal human atom, yet great enough to mirror in his brain the riddles both of the firmament and of the ocean depths.

The Philippines too are born of the ocean, risen from the depths, with the China Sea to the west and the Pacific to the east. The insular kingdom is reported to comprise between seven and eight thousand islands, peopled by perhaps twenty-five million children of humanity; a few Spaniards and Chinese, a number of mixed race, but mostly Malays — who, like the islands, are born of the sea. As everyone knows, the Spanish-American War had ended the year before *Neptune*'s departure, with the Americans victorious; one result being that Spain was obliged to sell the Philippines to the United States for the price set by the victors: twenty million dollars. The island kingdom was purchased complete with rats, banana plants, and people; and if one assumes that the Americans got the islands gratis as part of the bargain, and paid only for the inhabitants, then the unit price was not quite one dollar per head.

To visualize the terrain, both on land and under water, you need only reflect that while the highest mountain on the islands is circa 10,000 feet high, the ocean to the east is over 33,000 feet deep. The total drop is thus 43,000 feet — 13,000 feet more than that of the world's highest mountain.

From Manila *Neptune* put out to sea heading due west; then she coursed northward through the China Sea, and thence to the east, down into the Pacific. We were laden with huge quantities of cordage and Manila hemp.

I write 'hemp' because that's what it's called; but Manila rope or 'hemp' hasn't the slightest botanical relation to true hemp. Manila rope is spun from the fibres of a banana plant which grows on the islands, and is far superior to the common, true hempen rope. The banana plant is called *pisang* by the natives, and belongs to the family Musaceae; one species — *Musa textilis* — yields the stuff for the noble Manila 'hemp', which is then used for finer cordage, the more expensive sacks, mats, and much else.

True hemp, on the other hand, belongs to the species *Cannabis sativa*, and is grown not only in the tropics, but even in Europe; it provides the raw material for coarser rope, sacks, and so forth. Since time immemorial this hemp has been cultivated in India. A related species, *Cannabis indica*, commonly known as 'Indian hemp', contains a mildly narcotic substance. This Indian hemp, smoked for centuries all over the Orient and today in Europe as well, produces in the smoker a nobler intoxication than liquor — less brutal, less coarsening, less harmful.

The resin which this plant yields is called in the Arabic tongue 'hashish'. When eaten or smoked it produces a contemplative, highly pleasant state which — though it can't compare with the sleep and the dream-images of opium — must nonetheless be assigned to the realm of narcosis, to Neptune's kingdom.

But one cannot talk of the sea with no mention of the Winds, the air, space.

To be sure, Poseidon's empire is vast; it covers most of the earth, and extends so far down that the entire Himalayan *massif* could be set on the bottom without causing the slightest ripple on the surface. But the domain of the winds is greater, for it envelops the globe, the entire star of Gea. Over this empire reigns Aeolus, son of

Neptune. Aeolus is the winds' keeper, but he is also their father and their god. He is the lord of space, of breeze, gale, and storm, of hurricane, cyclone, and typhoon.

But four of the winds have a different parentage: Astraeus and Eos — the firmament and the dawn — engendered the winds of the earth's four corners. They are Notus, the south wind; Boreas, the north wind; Eurus, the east wind; and Zephyrus, the west wind. In the Pacific and in the Atlantic the wind from the south meets the wind from the north — Notus embraces Boreas at the equator, and because of the earth's rotation, both are deflected to the west; thus arise the eternal, stable winds, the sailing vessel's friends, the trades; Boreas forms the northeast trade wind, Notus the southeast. The remaining brothers, Zephyrus from the west and Eurus from the east, are moodier, more gypsy-like, more incalculable. Only during the monsoons can they be forecast; they divide the year between them — Zephyrus blows for one half of every twelvemonth, Eurus for the other.

In May-June the monsoon shifts direction, and again in October-November. At these times, while Eurus and Zephyrus change watch, their kinsman, the god Typhon, looses his titanic powers; he is, as his name declares, the spirit of the cyclone, the hurricane, the typhoon — the most savage god of all.

In the Philippines these changes of watch are simply called the typhoon season.

It was on the twenty-first of October that *Neptune* put out to sea.

The Third Mate and the Ship's Boy Pat

When I turned out for the next watch, I first went amidships to the galley and asked the cabin boy Moses to bring my tea and toast up to the charthouse aft, or more precisely to the small saloon there.

Then I looked in on the steward. He was in a dreadful state, agitated in the extreme, with drooling mouth and running eyes. He was mumbling incoherently, and fixed me with a look of profound terror. Then he covered his eyes with his hands and screamed loudly. He screamed several times, then turned his face to the planking and sobbed heartrendingly.

I poured out a big glass of brandy and turned him in the bunk. His face was wet with tears, and he shook so much that he couldn't hold the glass. So I put my left arm behind his neck and held the glass to his trembling lips. Slowly, almost drop by drop, he got down most of the contents — while those blue eyes stared at me, wide and rigid with terror. Then he threw it all up. At seventeen I was cabin boy on a passenger ship, and I've learned to clean up vomit.

For a moment he lay still, groaning deeply; then he again covered his face and screamed with all his lung-power, wildly and piercingly. I took his keys from the hook on the bulkhead and sent the cook aft to the galley stores for a bottle of red wine — into half of which I then stirred sugar as I warmed it over the coals in the stove. All the while the steward screamed in his bunk like a madman.

I had to twist his hands from his face, and little by little I got him to swallow a big cup of the warm, sugared wine. He quieted almost at once; he closed his eyes, and his hands no longer shook so. Then he disgorged the wine in a long jet. I cleaned it up. Thereupon the sobbing resumed, and gradually went over into the same piercing cries as before. He was in Neptune's power.

There was only one thing to do, though I did it with extreme reluctance: I went aft and fetched what I needed from the medicine chest. Then I returned, got the cook and the little black cabin boy to hold him — and gave him a shot of morphine.

On the poop I met the third mate, who himself didn't look exactly morning-fresh. His bloated, swollen face was almost as red as his hair. He was wearing his blue uniform jacket, but his shirt was collarless and open at the neck. He stood with his head tilted back, looking up into the rigging.

'Good morning,' I said.

He didn't reply, didn't stir; just stayed as he was, with his gaze directed at the masthead. The wind was quite stiff now, and the waves were capped with lacy foam. Now and then a blob of foam would flake off and fly like a gull from the wavecrest: a fresh gale turning to strong. I took no notice of what the third mate was staring at, but just looked out over the sea; it was dark-blue and white.

At the helm stood the same Cuban sailor whom I had relieved the night before. We exchanged nods, and I glanced at the compass in front of him. He stood with his lips tightly pinched, and his slender, refined face bore a strangely sullen expression. His neck and head could have been cast in bronze. He too was looking upward. The ship was rolling strongly as I entered the charthouse to relieve the first mate, a rather tall, lean North American and (as I subsequently learned) a very religious man. He would later impart

38

to the tale of *Neptune*'s last voyage one of the most sinister portents we received during those first weeks. Now he went to turn in, and probably to read his Bible.

I checked our position on the chart; then I returned to the helmsman.

'Fall off two points,' I said.

'Fall off two points,' he replied. He was a seaman.

Sancta Vénere sailed like a goddess now. The wind force lay at the transition from fresh to strong gale. Both skysails had been taken in. Heeling strongly, *Sancta Vénere* shot through the seas like an arrow as the spray from windward swept in clouds over her deck. Lord, what a ship she was to sail with! Again I felt the same joy as had filled me when I took the helm the evening before.

On the table in the diminutive saloon next to the charthouse stood the toast, marmalade, and a steaming jug of tea. I was hungry, rested, and happy. The barometer held steady, a good distance from the strong-gale point. The world, the wind, the ship — all was functioning as it should. *Sancta Vénere* was probably doing about sixteen knots.

I chewed the bread with the tasty marmalade very slowly as I sipped my sweet, strong tea. Out on the main deck almost the whole crew stood clustered in three or four groups. They didn't seem to be talking, but something was clearly holding everyone's attention. Most were staring upward, at the rigging.

Striking as the aggregation was, I didn't react to it so consciously as I should have done. I was much too anxious, much too busy dreading the next of the day's duties: to see to the carpenter and if necessary continue my labours as samaritan and quacksalver.

Was he still alive at all?

When I had finished with the Javanese, I must then go forward to look at the Peruvian ordinary, who would also doubtless be bunk-ridden for several days to come. Truth to tell, this last made me shudder the most. The sick bay, where the carpenter was ensconced, lay safely under the poop — wall to wall with the officers' wardroom. But to reach the forecastle and the Peruvian, I would have to go across the deck and past those knots of men. And there was a compactness about them, a stillness — something unbudgingly silent and threatening.

The fact is that I was *afraid*.

With my last cup of tea I smoked a cigarette; then I went below to the sick bay. Earlier that morning, when I had gone in to get the morphine for the steward, I had barely glanced at the carpenter. Now I looked at him properly.

First and most important: the man was alive. But his pulse was weak, slow, and irregular. His breathing was uneven, and not deep.

Such of his face as could be seen amid the bandages, compresses, and plaster bore no resemblance to human skin-colour; it was dark-blue, violet, and yellow-green. He had big bruises on his body as well; in particular his chest, shoulders, and upper arms were covered with blue and yellow splotches. Moreover, he lay just as senseless, extinguished, as he had the day before — his eyes the same sickening, ghastly slits showing only the whites. Under the bandages, however, the bleeding had stopped.

Again I gave him belladonna and a shot of that preparation whose name I've forgotten; and now too I presently had the impression that it was working. Perhaps it was simply my imagination, inspired by my hope that perhaps this dying man might yet pull through. Quite apart from the annoyance of sailing the whole remaining journey with no ship's carpenter.

For some minutes I sat beside the bunk, gathering my courage to go forward to see the Peruvian — to pass the gloomy and for some reason agitated crew. Rough as the sailing was now, the portlight here on the lee side was almost constantly under water — and I looked into the beautiful, transparent, glittering world of green sunlit brine.

Then I rose and went up the companionway.

Even before I had reached the narrow passage between the charthouse and the first mate's quarters, I could hear that something was up. There was a sound of excited voices, of shouts and oaths.

40

When I emerged on the poop, the helmsman was alone there; the third mate had gone down to the main deck.

'What's going on?' I said.

The Cuban raised his left hand from the wheel, and I saw that he had two gold rings on his slim fingers; then he pointed up into the rigging, all the way up to the mainmast-head. My glance followed his direction: at the end of the skysail yard there hung a figure, clinging fast.

'Who's that?' I said.

'Pat.'

'Why doesn't he come down?'

'He can't.'

I knew the phenomenon from before: At that height terror can become so fierce that the novice doesn't dare to relinquish the grip he already has, and so can't take the new holds which he must in order to come down. The situation is approximately that of a cat stuck high in a tree. In panic you cling to the nearest object, and if no help comes you hang there until exhaustion numbs your arms and fingers and you fall down of yourself. Add to this that *Neptune*'s rigging was somewhat outsized, and her mainmast very tall; thus the boy was dangling more than a hundred feet above us, as from the cornice of a twelve-story building. Instantly I felt a stab of the terror which he must be feeling all the time.

'Who's Pat?' I asked.

'The smaller of the deck boys.'

'Has he never been aloft before?'

'On his first voyage he was signed on as cabin boy. This is the first time he's sailed on deck.'

'How old is he?'

'Fourteen.'

'Who sent him aloft?'

'The third mate.'

I am a peaceable man, but now something boiled over in me; I grew dizzy, almost senseless with rage. So I lurched over to the

41

ladder going down from the poop to the main deck, whence the yells, shrieks, and curses came.

The third mate was standing below, with his broad back and his damned idiotic pink bull neck toward me. Before him stood two men; one was a Malay, medium-sized and not especially brawny. The other was a mulatto of most uncommon dimensions: He was even taller than the third mate, and had the biggest shoulders I've ever seen on a man. Behind them stood a band of silent seamen.

'So you won't obey orders!' the third mate was shouting at the Malay: 'You devil's bastard, you dirty son of a bitch!'

'I only asked permission to bring him down,' replied the sailor.

'I told you to belay!'

'I ask the mate's permission to fetch him!'

'The boy will come down by himself! Devil wipe my arse if I don't teach him that this ship ain't no young ladies' finishing school!'

'He *can't* come down alone,' said the mulatto.

'Belay and lay for'ard!' yelled the mate: 'That's a damned bloody order! Ain't nobody going to stir from this deck!'

'Let me get him, mister — or else....' the Malay persisted.

The mate gasped.

'Or else!' he roared: 'Or else...?'

'Or else I'll go get him anyhow.'

Almost before he had finished, the mate struck him in the face, hard. The sailor staggered backward, then stopped. His face turned crimson, and from the corner of his mouth a thin stripe of blood ran down over his chin. The mate thrashed with his arms at the men surrounding him.

'Lay for'ard!' he shrieked: 'Go on! Get! Don't stand there like sheep! Lay for'ard!'

A few of the men stirred; most stayed where they were. The mulatto stood unmoving before him. Wild with fury the third mate raised a clenched fist under the other's nose.

'You damned nigger bastard!' he said softly, almost falsetto: 'You're asking for it!'

42

'If you strike me, sir,' said the mulatto, 'then I'm going to hit back.'

I don't know which had the upper hand in me: rage at the mate's idiotic brutality, or dread of the whole loathsome, hate-filled situation. But I went down the ladder; and now the men, catching sight of me for the first time, eyed me with the same mute hostility. For a moment there was perfect silence.

'How long has Pat been up there?' I said to the mulatto.

'Almost three hours, sir.'

I looked at the mate, but felt such a strong revulsion that I couldn't bear to speak to him. Instead I turned to the mulatto again:

'What's your name?'

'James Arrowsmith.'

'Arrowsmith,' I said: 'fetch the boy down from the rigging.'

'Thank you, sir!'

He turned and sauntered over to the rail. There he placed a coil of rope over one shoulder, across his chest, and under the opposite arm; then he grabbed hold of the ratlines and swung himself up. In less than a minute he was at the top, climbing out along the yardarm. He had to pry the boy loose, loosen his grip finger by finger.

With trembling heart I pressed through the group of men blocking my path; silently, with no visible reaction, they made way, and I went forward to see to the Peruvian ordinary. He was still among the living, but was almost as sick as the carpenter and the steward. His chest was more badly hurt than the former's, and the big sutured bite in his left cheek had become inflamed. It was dark red.

I felt a wave of ineffable weariness over it all, and I was dizzy when I came out on deck after the stink of sweat, filth, and petroleum from the forecastle.

It took the big mulatto a great deal longer to bring the deck boy down than he had needed to climb up to the skysail and out the yardarm. First, after loosening the boy's grip on the rigging, he simply tucked him under his arm like a bundle and carried him in

43

to the masthead. I repeat that this took place almost forty yards up, with a wind force midway between fresh and strong gale. With one arm and both feet on the footrope below, he lugged the boy in. Then he sat him on his back, where he clung tight; passed the rope around him; and so began the descent.

When I got back, only the last phase remained. The mulatto brought the boy down the ratlines and let him slide to the deck. The boy collapsed as if boneless, while the vomit flowed out over his face, neck, and chest. James Arrowsmith stood motionless beside him, pouring with sweat.

The boy Pat couldn't move; he lay in spasms beside the hatch.

'Mr. Arrowsmith,' I said; 'do you know where my cabin is?'

'Yes, sir.'

'Do you want to take him there? Mr. Arrowsmith?'

'No, sir.'

'Well, Arrowsmith, I'll take him myself. But I'll ask you to come along.'

'Aye, aye, sir.'

I took the boy in my arms. He was white in the face, the open eyes were blue, and his fair hair hung to his shoulders. Pat weighed scarcely more than ninety pounds, and it cost me no strain to carry him across the main deck, up the ladder, over the poop, and down to my own cabin. He was in such shock that one had to reckon on the boy's dying: utterly paralysed, with goose-flesh all over his white face and neck.

When I had laid him in my bunk I turned to the mulatto, who had followed me.

'Mr. Hammersmith,' I said.

'Arrowsmith,' he said.

'Mr. Arrowsmith,' I went on: 'I ask you to accept my thanks. The boy is alive.'

'You could have fetched him down yourself,' replied Arrowsmith.

'No,' I said, 'I couldn't have.'

'You *ought* to have fetched him down yourself,' Arrowsmith persisted.

I looked at him, considering it. He was pale under his tawny mulatto skin. The sweat still ran from him.

'I *couldn't*,' I said. He looked at me.

'You're strong enough,' he said.

'No,' I said.

'The little Malay was willing, and he isn't as strong as you, sir.'

'Listen, Mr. Arrowsmith: it's not just that I'm an officer; I'm thirty-three years old. I haven't been on a skysail yard for more than ten years.'

'You were afraid, Mr. Jensen?'

'Yes,' I said: 'I was afraid. And I still am.'

'Sir,' he said: 'If I hadn't been there, what would you have done? It would have been well for the crew if you had fetched him.'

The sweat still ran from his face, and not because of the heat. He was deathly pale under the brown skin.

'If you hadn't been there, Mr. Arrowsmith, then I would have brought him down myself. But it scares me to death just to think of it. Ten years is a long time.'

The mulatto turned and squeezed out through the cabin's much too narrow door. I called after him:

'Arrowsmith!'

He didn't reply.

Then I was alone with Pat.

The latter was a thin, rather unattractive fourteen-year-old — pasty-faced, with dark circles under his eyes and bad teeth. Pat was British, and it later turned out that he was — after the captain, the other deck boy, the steward, and myself — the fifth and last European on board the *Neptune*. The only appealing thing about him was the slender white hands and thin child's fingers with which he had clung to the skysail yard. Nothing in the world is so lonely as a young hand.

Pat showed all the signs of chronic malnutrition. He was as undernourished as only a British subject —white or coloured —can be. The world's biggest and richest land, the British Empire, can't feed her children in Whitechapel or Soho, Pat's world and home.

He was still vomiting, mainly gall and gastric acid. When I undressed his thin sparrow's body, I saw that not only nausea but diarrhoea too had asserted itself on the skysail. It had left a trail in his pants. Pat was still half-dead with fright, and I didn't know what to do. I began by washing him.

Then suddenly he raised his thin trunk and clutched me — his left arm around my neck, his right hand gripping my wrist.

'Don't leave me!' he cried.

All the woe of humanity seemed to issue from that scrawny throat. Then he repeated it:

'Mister, don't go!'

I laid my hand over his pale, hollow cheek:

'I won't leave you, Pat.'

'Don't send me forward!' he begged.

'You can stay here, Pat.'

He sank back again.

'Don't send me aloft any more,' he whispered.

'It wasn't I who sent you up.'

'No, it was the third mate.'

'It was Arrowsmith who brought you down.'

'James?'

'Yes.'

'I'm so scared of him. He's so terribly strong.'

He lay still for a long time, and I considered what I could do for him. Finally I gave him an aurum-mixture of a hundred drops of opium in a glass of rum. The opium, in addition to its sedative effect, might help the diarrhoea as well.

I looked at Pat's face.

In a way this fourteen-year-old was ancient. He had white hair down to his narrow shoulders; pale damp skin; and a gaunt, stringy neck. I spread the woollen blanket over his thin, pallid body — all the way to his chin. I held his hand throughout. He was afraid.

'Can you eat anything?' I said.

46

He didn't reply, just shook his head feebly.

'Soup?' I asked.

'Mister?' he said faintly; 'is this your cabin?'

'Yes.'

'It's so strange here. So quiet like.'

Slowly he began to cry. I stroked him over his long hair.

'Can I stay here, sir?' he faltered.

'Yes,' I said; 'you can stay here.'

Outside it was coming on to blow; we must be up to a strong gale by now. *Sancta Vénere* was heeling fiercely. I gave him another dose of aurum; he drank it slowly. The fingers which held the glass were thin and white like a little girl's.

'Mister?' he said.

'Yes?'

'Do you have any other children?'

'No.'

There followed a long pause. Then he turned his gaze on me, rather flat and veiled; and — halfway into sleep, a bit drunk —

'Can't I be your son?' he asked.

When I came out on deck, it was growing dark. I sent the helmsman forward and ordered the topmen to set both skysails again. She sailed like an angel. I was alone with her now; with the water over her lee rail and the spray blanketing the ship from windward, no one would remain on deck of his own accord. It was blowing up steadily, and the strong-gale point had been passed long since.

Now I was alone with her. The previous day I had touched her, felt her muscles, her nerves, the trembling in her slender body — but now, *now!* the hour was come! There was only she, *Sancta Vénere*, the wind, the sea, I. It was now we would hold our wedding! I was afraid, and it was glorious.

At times we heeled so much that the sea from leeward washed all the way over the hatches. God, it was lovely to be alone with her in this passionate embrace! We sailed, sailed, sailed! The spray from the weather bow came over the forecastle, over all the main deck, and beat on the quarterdeck — the poop was drenched with spray. She cut like an arrow through the waves, and I had never sailed such a vessel before. I was giddy, half-crazed, and senseless with joy.

Then a man stood beside me. Without a sound he came out of the darkness. The deck was sloping too much to allow of walking on it, so he had to keep reaching for a handhold. It was the captain.

His round, expressionless face was turned toward me, and I just barely recognized him in the dark. He spoke, but it was impossible to hear him because of the wind. I shook my head and cupped a hand behind my ear to show that the gale made me deaf.

He caught hold of the binnacle and laid one hand on the helm; then he roared with all his might:

'Mr. Jensen, are you thinking of dismasting the ship?'

'No, sir.'

He turned and lurched over to the starboard taffrail, where he read off the log. Then he stumbled back. With no change of expression he said:

'Mr. Jensen, are you *crazy*?'

'No, sir. According to Professor Bleuler's introductory textbook in psychiatry, I'm not crazy — just a bit nervous, sir.'

'Mr. Jensen. Are you aware that, apart from the ship and almost a thousand tons of valuable cargo, you're sailing with thirty people on board?' he shouted.

'Yes, sir.'

'Mister, I'll throw you overboard!'

At the top of my lungs I yelled back:

'Then you'll have only two mates left, sir. A drunkard and a Mormon. I'm not the one who's crazy, sir.'

For a moment most of the forecastle and waist lay submerged. It was smoking like a waterfall to leeward. The captain shouted again:

'Are you thinking of sailing her like that all night?'

'No, sir. Just till the next watch.'

'Mr. Jensen!' he roared: 'Aren't you *afraid*?'

48

'Of course, sir! I'm shaking in my boots, but I have to see what she'll take.'

He shouted back:

'Is this necessary, Mr. Jensen?'

'I *have* to, captain!' I yelled: 'Or I won't be able to rest.'

For a time he said nothing, just stared out into the darkness. Then he turned and roared:

'Well, Mr. Jensen. If it's essential to your peace of mind, you may carry her full sail so long as you are at the helm. But before the next watch you'll take in the foresail, the mainsail, and the fore- and main royals.'

'Foresail, mainsail, fore- and main royals,' I replied as loudly as I could.

He stood there yet awhile, shaking his head.

'Do you know what the log showed?' he shouted.

'No, sir.'

'*Eighteen* knots, Mr. Jensen!'

'Well, sir.'

Then he vanished into the night.

At the next watch I turned her over to the first mate in a gagged, reduced, and mangled condition, with a third of her sails taken in. She rode gently in the sea now.

'In God's name,' said the mate.

The wheel I gave to the helmsman, the same Malay whom the third mate had struck in the face earlier that day. I greeted him, but he didn't respond.

When I went below I was exhausted, limp in nerves and brain; but my happiness was complete. I had celebrated my wedding night with *Sancta Vénere*. She had received me and loved me.

Back in my cabin I had taken off my jacket and shirt, when I chanced to think of the carpenter. All at once I had a feeling that he was dead, and with bare chest I went down the passageway to look at him. He was lying as before, apparently lifeless, but with his breathing and pulse still in action.

I had counted out the drops of belladonna and was filling the needle, when I heard a sound. I turned my head to look. In the berth the carpenter lay with open eyes, gazing at me.

'Who the hell are you?' he said feebly: 'And where am I?'

'I am Peder Jensen,' I said; 'second mate on the bark *Neptune*. You yourself are carpenter on the same vessel, and you have been unconscious for almost forty-eight hours. We are now east of the north coast of the Philippines, bound across the Pacific for Cape Horn.'

He uttered a long moan of pain, and raised both hands above his head. To still the pain I gave him opium.

I returned to my cabin, filled with a strange joy and amazement that this carnivore of a human being had lived. I finished undressing. Only when I went to turn in did I see Pat — lying in the narrow bunk, thin and little and stark naked. For a moment my only wish was to jump overboard.

Then I came to my senses, squeezed in beside him, and lay down. My 'son' gave no sign of life. A moment later we were both asleep.

The Bark *Neptune*

C'est fou, pas être fou...

A peculiarity of *Sancta Vénere*: Over her clipper bow, under the
heel of the bowsprit like a kind of figurehead, hung two large
rosettes carved in wood. Seen at a distance and in profile the bows
thus looked like a symbol of manhood, taken from a shameless
Etruscan or Levantine past not given to blushing over its natural
fruitfulness as we do today in our British-dominated time. For just
as the previous century was ruled by the passionate, justice-seeking,
revolutionary French, so our own has been stamped by the brine-
soaked, money-grubbing Britons. But everything has its time; new
centuries will bring new empires and new world masters — and they
all shall pass away, while Orion's belt abides.

Can it be this strange masculine bowsprit with the two rosettes
which caused *Sancta Vénere* to be christened with a he-name —
Neptune? Can this have been her true secret: that in her innermost
she was a *man*? Was *Sancta Vénere* androgynous? Was she simply a
freemartin? A hermaphrodite?

No! *Sancta Vénere* was a woman from keel to truck; a proud,
self-willed, independent, wholly ungovernable woman, made for
that love which presupposes a like independence and strength in her

51

lover — a love which can exist only between equals, between free souls! She had masculine traits as well — just as every true man has feminine sides, though few are strong enough to show them. Oh, Lord! Only once have I loved thus, and she was a ship! She was built in Glasgow in 1866; hence both she and I were thirty-three years old when we put out to sea from Manila that fateful autumn. She was hence in her best years; a full-blown, mature woman, not to be subdued by any man. She knitted no mittens for the Zulu mission, she belonged to no sewing club; she looked up to no staid and sober husband, chair of the local county board. No, *Sancta Vénere* had her home in the long swells beneath the Southern Cross. There she was free, and there she found her lovers.

What I write here is the account of her last voyage, and not a textbook of nautical terminology or facts. I'm writing this for landlubbers who don't know what a royal is, who have no idea how many cable lengths there are to a league, or how many fathoms to a cable length. It's not a book about 'bells' or 'hounds' or 'perihelion' or 'centipede' or 'Beaufort scale'. It's a book about human fates and S/V *Neptune*. I shan't plague the reader with sea terms which in any case he won't understand. I shall use only those which are absolutely essential.

But *Sancta Vénere* was a bark, and the reader must know what a bark is. He must know how my beloved looked, who she was. He must know her outer person, as it were.

A bark is a vessel with three or four masts. I decidedly prefer the three-master; she is lovelier, more natural, more rhythmic and harmonious. The two forward masts are square-rigged: fitted with crosswise rectangular sails on yards. The third, the aftermast, has fore-and-aft sails; it is gaff-rigged, with a so-called mizzen between boom and gaff, and a mizzen-topsail between gaff and masthead. The mast is called the mizzenmast, after the sail.

The only difference between a full-rigged ship and a bark is that on a ship the mizzenmast has both fore-and-aft and square sails. To me the bark is more rhythmic, lovelier. She has the light, graceful mizzen rig, and it's that which gives her the bewitching feminine appearance. And she usually comes about more nimbly than a ship; though in much they are sisters, and are often cross-rigged: no great changes are required to turn a bark into a ship or vice versa. The ship demands a larger crew.

We shall look very briefly at *Sancta Vénere*'s hull and sails, beginning forward. The three masts were: foremast, mainmast, mizzenmast. Let us say that the rigging is the visible part of her soul, and the hull, the vessel itself, her ensouled but earthly body. The rigging bound her with Aeolus, with the spirits of space — the Winds; the hull had wedded her fate to Neptune, to the abyss and the passions within her — her own frightful Neptunian ego.

I think I've mentioned that she had a clipper bow — a sharp, protruding stem. The deck on her fore part was somewhat higher than the main deck; under it was the forecastle, the crew's quarters. Abaft the foremast was the first deckhouse, which held the galley and the steward's and cook's cabins. The afterdeck, or poop, was about seven feet higher than the waist; here the other deckhouse sat, containing the charthouse, a tiny saloon, and the cabin for the first mate.

Sancta Vénere was a composite bark: built with wooden planking, but on an iron frame — which was less bulky but just as strong as the usual heavy oak beams. She weighed 1090 tons net, measured two hundred thirty-six feet from rosettes to stern and a scant thirty-six feet across the beam. We had four lifeboats, and a ship's complement of twenty-seven men. There was also the captain's wife and their two small children. All in all *Sancta Vénere* was home, world, and coffin for thirty immortal human souls.

Her somewhat outsized mainmast reached one hundred twenty-five feet above the water line. In all she could set more than 32,000 square feet of canvas — the better part of an acre.

It was not seldom that we sailed her between two hundred fifty and three hundred nautical miles in a day — for an average speed of eleven to fourteen knots.

I myself had sailed her, with all her cloth spread during a whole gale, up to more than eighteen knots.

All her stays, backstays, and shrouds were of steel wire. But first I should doubtless explain what shrouds and stays and backstays are; it's very simple, but you must know it to understand what a staysail is.

The stays are stretched taut between masts and hull to brace the rigging—to strengthen the masts' ability to withstand the wind, and in the final instance to prevent dismasting in critical situations. The backstays slant upward from the sides of the vessel, the stays from the centre line forward of the masts; and along these fore-and-aft stays slanting up to the top are fitted a greater or lesser number of triangular sails, all cut like jibs, like the foresails on small sailboats. Between the bowsprit and the foremast and in each of the two spaces between the three masts — foremast, mainmast, and mizzenmast — there are three or four staysails, each with its own name.

The shrouds are the most important element of the rigging. They are a complex of lines running up from the side, forward of the backstays—formerly of coarse hempen rope, on modern vessels always of steel cable. The shrouds are connected by ratlines — horizontal wooden slats — so that they resemble a sort of rope ladder. To each mast run two sets of shrouds: one from port, one from starboard. Their function is a double one: not only do they greatly buttress the rigging, but the crew climbs aloft on them as well.

We shall look at *Neptune*'s rig. At the very fore, between the bowsprit and the foremast, she had four sails — beginning forward: the flying jib, outer jib, inner jib, and fore-topmast staysail. The foremast was fitted with six 'square' sails—six rectangular sails bent to yards. Reckoning from the bottom they are: the foresail — which, next to the mainsail, is the vessel's largest sail; then follows the lower fore-topsail, and above that the upper fore-topsail. Above them are the fore-topgallant sail and then the foreroyal. At the top sets the fore-skysail.

Between the foremast and the mainmast we had, also counting from the bottom: the main staysail, main-topmast staysail, main-topgallant staysail. Some vessels also carry a main-royal stay sail, but *Neptune* did not.

Like the foremast, the mainmast too is square-rigged, with the same six rectangular sails, but larger. From the bottom they are: the mainsail, or course; the lower main-topsail, and the upper main-topsail. Then come the main-topgallant sail and the main royal. At the very top, with its yard just under the mainmast head, sets the main skysail, the vessel's highest sail — where poor Pat had got stuck.

Between the mainmast and the mizzenmast were three more sails — again from the bottom: mizzen staysail, mizzen-topmast staysail, and mizzen-topgallant staysail.

The mizzenmast is fitted with triangular sails; that is, its canvas is fore-and-aft. There's the mizzen, or spanker — a large sail between boom and gaff spars. From the gaff up to the mizzenmast head sets the mizzen-topsail.

Of course there are a thousand things to tell about *Sancta Vénere*'s physical body; a bark is a monstrously manifold and complex world of wood, iron, steel, hemp, and canvas. The running rigging alone — the cordage, or tackle — I could almost call it the nerves in *Sancta Vénere*'s visible and earthly being — this rigging alone is such a complicated machinery that it would be impossible to go into it more closely, for it involves hundreds of names and designations. On a ship every single thing — every rope end, every screw, I could almost say every nail and every spike — has its own designation. But to go into these details would defeat my purpose vis-à-vis land-dwelling readers who haven't made the deck planks the crust of their earth; it would serve to confuse instead of to enlighten.

I shall merely add that if *Neptune* didn't carry a main-royal staysail, this was a virtue of necessity; the rig was outsized nonetheless. *Sancta Vénere* was not only white-painted, slender, and beautiful; she was also dangerous in mind and temperament.

What matters is to get a clear and discernible picture of her.

Just as the sextant has replaced the old octant from the beginning of the eighteenth century, so the taffrail log with its mechanical, automatic counting mechanism has replaced the common log, or what was formerly called the 'chip'. Since a craft is in every essential sailed by compass, chronometer, and these two instruments, I shall briefly mention what they are.

The octant was invented around 1730 as an instrument to measure the sun's height above the horizon and thereby determine the ship's position. It built on earlier constructions of Arabic astronomers and seamen, and looked like a big wooden pair of dividers, plus an arc-shaped piece inscribed with a scale of degrees. The sextant is a later simplification and improvement of the octant, and is based — as the name suggests — on a division of the circle into sixths instead of into eighths as formerly. Two small mirrors and a small spyglass are the only other technical equipment needed to measure *any* heavenly body's height above the horizon, and by this means to compute the ship's position in north or south degrees and minutes of latitude.

The east-west longitudinal position is found by calculating the difference between local and Greenwich time. Local time — ship's time — is determined from the sun's position at the zenith, and Greenwich time is kept by the chronometer.

The product of speed x time = distance traversed. The log is the instrument by which you measure the ship's speed. In earlier times they used the 'chip log' — a large slice of wood, weighted with lead along one side so that it would float upright in the water when thrown overboard. Because of its flat form it acquired the name 'chip'. To the chip was fastened a log line, provided with knots at fixed, regular intervals. The log line was wound on a light hand-reel; and when the chip went overboard it pulled the log line out, so that you could measure the seconds elapsed between knots as they left the reel. You could thus determine the ship's speed in meters per second, and since half a meter per second corresponds to one nautical mile per hour, it was a simple mathematical operation to find the velocity in miles. But of course this measurement can never be wholly accurate — among other things because the chip doesn't stand quite still in the sea, but is inevitably dragged along to some degree by the weight of the log line and the resistance in the reel.

On *Sancta Vénere* we carried one of these old-fashioned chip logs as a reserve, but of course we always sailed with the mechanical taffrail log, or 'patent log' as it is also called. A taffrail log doesn't stand 'still' in the water, but follows the vessel. It is a cylindrical piece of wood or metal, known as the 'fish'; it has obliquely radial wings as on a propeller, causing it to rotate at a rate corresponding to the ship's speed. The revolutions are transmitted via the log line to a mechanical counting mechanism screwed to the rail at the stern. From the number of revolutions per minute it is very easy to read how many nautical miles the ship is doing in an hour.

À propos of logs and speed: I've mentioned that I sailed *Sancta Vénere* up to between eighteen and nineteen knots. I'm fully aware that this sounds unlikely, but I can relate that with my own eyes I've seen on board a sailing vessel a log-book recording three hundred ninety miles traversed in twenty-four hours — which means an *average* speed of seventeen knots for a whole day running! *Sancta Vénere's* eighteen knots isn't so improbable as it sounds.

Finally the ship's journal ought to be mentioned — the vessel's recollection and memory. Into the journal — the log-book — are entered each day precise data concerning not only navigation, position, speed, miles traversed, wind, weather, sea, and other physical conditions, but also everything of consequence that may happen on board — accidents, sickness, good luck, bad luck, meetings with other ships, collisions or running aground. The journal is most conscientiously kept and is a great responsibility, since it may have to be produced in the maritime court as material evidence.

I've mentioned that *Sancta Vénere* — alias S/V *Neptune* — was sailing with thirty souls on board. Three of them were passengers: the captain's wife and their two children — a girl of six and a four-year-old boy. The twenty-seven others, then, were the ship's complement. We were:

Aft — *the officers*

Captain
Mate
Second mate
Third mate

Amidships — *the galley hands*

Steward
Cook

Forward — *the crew* (to the best of my recall)

Boatswain
Sailmaker
Carpenter
8 able seamen
4 ordinary seamen
2 apprentices
2 deck boys
1 galley and cabin boy (aft)
1 cabin boy (forward).

The crew was from the whole world, of every nationality and colour. We were five Europeans on board: the captain, the Belgian steward, the deck boy Pat, the other deck boy, and I. (The captain's wife was American, and both children were English-speaking, born in the United States.)

So far I have barely mentioned the captain, the first mate, the third mate, the steward, the Javanese carpenter, the mulatto able James Arrowsmith, the Peruvian ordinary, and the deck boy Pat. Later I shall dwell more fully on each, and on the rest who shared a common fate during this bark *Neptune*'s final voyage.

I may also mention here that both the captain and the fanatically religious first mate were co-owners and shareholders in the shipping firm which owned the vessel, and were thus interested both in a swift voyage and in cheap rations. Moreover, it's a well-known fact that, while men on American ships work hard and eat well, on a

British vessel they receive scant and bad food — although they're not so hard-driven in their work.

Thus — and with this crew: Africans, Asians, Americans, Australians, and Europeans — *Sancta Vénere* sailed southeastward, out into the long transparent swells of the Pacific. Every mile she left astern was a product of water and wind. But not of them alone; the voyage was also a result of human consciousness, of mathematics and slide rule, of sextant, compass, and log, of straightedge, pencil, eraser, dividers, and logarithm tables — of sublime mathematics. But don't think that I'm degrading the foremast hands into mere muscles for transmitting the activity of the charthouse — the brain — to rigging and tackle! No, it's of no use for a sailor to be a mountain of brawn if he hasn't the sea in his blood, if he can't hear the words to the song the wind sings in the backstays, can't understand the whispering of the waves around the ship's bow and along her sides, if he can't read the writing on the starry sky. In short: strong fists profit nothing unless all the humours of body and brain are akin to the brine, pervaded by this terrible element which is his hate and his love.

But did *Sancta Vénere* really sail? No, she glided, afloat between the air-sea over her and the water-sea below her. She glided — albeit in a mathematically definable fashion, on a course plotted by the convolutions of the human brain — glided through boundless space like a globe.

She was not without likeness to the globe we all sail with — Gea, the earth, which also floats in space. And whose voyage, course, speed, and trajectory can likewise be mathematically fixed and calculated in degrees, minutes, seconds — except that Gea's path and rhythm and velocity are products of a still more complex mathematics than that of the logarithm tables.

Who signed us on to her? What is her destination?

Who reads the compass and the log, who reads the sun's height and with what sextant? Who has plotted her course, determined her positions? Who uses the dividers and the straightedge?

And finally and most important: Who keeps the journal of the great voyage?

Where did we join her? Whither are we bound?

The Sharks

This is a damned unpleasant war,
but it's better than no war at all.
—Joseph Conrad

Once we had rounded the northernmost cape of the Philippines, we coursed to the southeast — and *Sancta Vénere* glided off like a gondola in her world of wind and sun and water, of swells and stars — with her precious cargo of Manila rope, banana fibres, one woman, six children, and twenty-three men. Under full sail we made good headway, and the quiet rhythm of life on board a ship underway began to manifest itself.

For a while one day was like the next, and at times I felt a great peace, a deep happiness. Still, there were things which troubled me. In the first place I had made an enemy on board — a real enemy.

The big, burly, pink third mate with the wet, water-blue eyes never spoke to me; he didn't return my 'good morning' and he didn't reply when addressed. But sometimes he'd send me a look, and it was a look full of mistrust and hatred. This emanation of hate was so intense as to cause me alarm and dread. I was afraid to turn my back to him. It wasn't the man himself whom I feared; he would scarcely do me harm, unless he found a chance to attack from the rear so covertly that he would never be found out. It would have to be some such thing as knocking me down from behind and throwing me to the sharks some night when we were alone in the darkness on the poop.

But such an opportunity he would never have. No, it wasn't the man, it was the irrational, stupid, idiotic hate itself which I feared.

It was most idiotic, this hate which the third mate bore me. It was a dumb, meaningless hate. The man — his name was Mr. Dickson — would never forget that I had caused him to lose face as an officer; I had undermined his authority and his status, not only in front of the Malay whom he had struck and James Arrowsmith, whom he hadn't struck — but also in front of the crew, who had witnessed the incident. To make matters worse, I had taken charge of the tortured, half-dead victim of Third Mate Dickson's lust for authority, the ship's boy Pat — first by letting Dickson's chief opponent, the mulatto, fetch the child down, and then by taking the boy aft. In the third mate's eyes I had thus destroyed his 'prestige' — or what he thought was his dignity. The result was this deep, ridiculous, feeble-minded hatred.

The world is full of such dumb, idiotic hate.

In reality I had saved what little 'dignity' and 'officer's honour' this uniformed cretin had left to lose. Had I not intervened as his superior, both the Malay and Arrowsmith would have gone aloft to fetch Pat down, without orders or permission from the command. That would have meant refusal of orders, an open break between officers and men: legally a 'mutiny'. But the third mate was too stupid to understand this.

Instead he hated all three of us: the Malay because he was yellow and refractory; Arrowsmith because he was a mulatto and a courageous man besides; both of them because they wouldn't be spat upon. Me he hated because I had demeaned him. He doubtless hated the men as well, since they had witnessed his loss of face.

But — as later became apparent — most of all and before all the rest he hated his scrawny little underfed victim, poor Pat from the slums of London.

As I've said, this wild, inarticulate hate scared me, it gave me a well-nigh sickening sense of meaninglessness and falsity and death.

It was likewise plaguesome to have to look after our wounded.

The ordinary seaman Carlos, the Peruvian who had almost killed the carpenter, was for the most part still bunk-ridden, and only rarely appeared on deck or up on the forecastle to take the air. The bite on his cheek was still inflamed, and I was obliged to clean and dress it daily. The wound caused him great pain, and his cheek was terribly swollen. The bruises around his eyes were no longer blue or violet; the carpenter's thumbs had left them literally black. And the left eye was gravely injured. His left hand was swollen to an almost incredible degree, leaving no doubt that one or two of his metacarpals were broken. All I could do was to leave the splint on and bind it well. I also made a sling for his arm — which at least reduced the pain somewhat, by allowing his hand to remain quiet.

Carlos was sulky and silent, and never concealed the fact that he regarded not only the carpenter, but me as well, as among the causes of the world's misery. When I tended his wounds, or laid a clean compress over his cheek, we never exchanged a word more than was needful. But one day he broke the silence:

'How's that damned corpse of a carpenter getting along?'

'Badly,' I said; 'you almost killed him.'

'He'll live?' Carlos went on.

'Yes.'

'That blasted swine,' he said slowly; 'I should have cut him up and thrown him to the dolphins, Mr. Jensen.'

'To the sharks,' I corrected him.

'Why is a man like that allowed to live, mister?'

'You'll have to ask your village priest about that,' I said.

'I piss on the priest,' he replied; 'just as I piss on that Dutch bastard of a carpenter. I'm just sorry I didn't cut open his belly — very sorry, Mr. Jensen,.'

'Would you so gladly go to prison for him?' I asked.

'I'd gladly go to hell to have seen his guts.'

I looked up into the Peruvian's face; his right eye, the one not covered by the leather patch, observed me with utter calm. It struck me that he beamed forth a hate which was more intelligent and more focused than the third mate's. In a sense it was more dangerous. From the looks of him the Peruvian was of Indian descent, but with some strands of Negro. And a few drops of Spanish or Portuguese blood might have straggled into his veins.

'What were you fighting about?' I said.

He didn't answer. For a while he sat silent and unmoving; then all at once he said softly, almost like a confidence:

'One day your turn will come too, mister.'

'What's wrong with me?' I asked.

'You're a damned gringo — an infernal *americano*. Isn't that enough?'

'I'm not American. I'm European.'

He didn't reply. And I could understand him; he had said enough. When I finished dressing his hand, I stood up:

'It will be awhile before you can kill anybody.'

From a samaritan point of view things were worse with the carpenter; it would be some time before he inquired after Carlos's health. He was still terribly weak, kept alive solely by his almost brute constitution. For hours at a time he would sink back into lethargy, later to open his black eyes anew and look dimly into the future. To talk to him was futile; at best the conversation would consist of a few monosyllables.

With great patience I got a little wine and a little soup into him, and it seemed to give him somewhat more vigour.

With the steward things were very bad indeed. Not even brandy could he swallow. He sweated and shook; now and then he cried or screamed. Once or twice, when the shrieking was at its worst, I gave him morphine again.

The first few days at sea we still had fresh meat and fresh vegetables on board, and I had the cook make bouillon for him. The cook was Chinese, as so often on British ships — and if anyone knows how to make soups, the Chinese do. Nobody in the world

can make such soups as a Chinese cook, and it's one of their proper-
ties that these soups are regarded as medicine: they are in fact
intended to soothe pains in ruined stomachs, and to restore health
generally. For the steward he made a light, clear soup to calm and
deaden the nerves behind the scorched, burnt-out mucosae of his
stomach and duodenum.

When the soup had cooled somewhat, I sat beside the steward's
bunk and cautiously began to feed him with a deep spoon. I did it
carefully and slowly; and in small sips, spoon by spoon, he got quite
a bit of it down. To give his stomach time to grow accustomed to
the alcohol-free nourishment, I often waited long between
spoonfuls. In perhaps half an hour I fed him almost a plate of it. The
Belgian seemed calmer now. Then he whispered:

'Give me a cup of rum.'

I mixed the rum with warm water and held the cup to his lips.
In tiny sups he managed to drink it down.

'Oh, Lord!' he mumbled: 'Lord!'

It was clearly an expression of content. But presently his face
grew whiter again. Then he disgorged everything, both the liquor
and the soup.

For the next two days he vomited blood.

The one who caused me the most concern, however, was my
new 'son' — the little deck boy Pat. Now and then he'd say things
which led me to think that the three hours on the skysail yard had
literally scared him out of his wits. But still I reflected that perhaps
he had been a bit strange from the beginning. In any case, he had
scarcely grown more clear-headed from sitting on the masthead. At
the same time I felt a growing revulsion toward the third mate. I
don't mean that I returned his foolish hatred, but I must own that
I disliked him strongly. Though I'm not disposed to violence, I
could feel that something inside me would not be averse to planting
a fist in that silly, bloated red face of his.

The day after the episode of the mainmast, I spent most of a free
watch in my cabin talking with Pat. He still lay in my berth, badly
frightened and uneasy. Two things in particular obsessed him, and

he begged and coaxed and pleaded: first, not to be sent aloft any more, and second, not to be sent back to the forecastle. He was afraid that the men would jeer at him because he hadn't withstood the height.

Neither of the two entreaties allowed of much deliberation. The first must be met; to send the boy up, with the terror now lodged in his bowels, would be tantamount to murder. To grant his other plea was out of the question; it was impossible to keep him aft. My berth was much too narrow for both of us, and because of him I had already slept once or twice on the little sofa next to the charthouse. He must be sent forward again. Of course Pat should never have gone to sea, never have set foot aboard a ship — weak, fearful, and asthenic as he was; but he was one of those who never have a choice. At sea at least he could almost eat his fill; he had never done so before.

It has often astonished me that England — the world's richest and mightiest nation, lord of an empire which spans the globe, ruler of the world's banks and stock exchanges, master of its seas — should care so poorly for her own subjects, her own children. I myself have walked around London while waiting for a berth, and I've seen the districts where Pat grew up; the poor sections, the slums — peopled by the jobless, by beggars, and by workers so underpaid that the line between them and the beggars is hair-thin. In this city a whole wandering world lives on the streets — a starving population which sleeps upon stairs and paving stones, a tribe of ashen, undernourished old folk and children. Their only alternative is the workhouses' water-soup, the jails, the reformatories, the children's prisons. I've seen them, the old, the still young but jobless, and the thin white-skinned children, walking the street with eyes fixed on pavement or gutter in the hope of finding something to stick in their mouths: orange peels, fibres or leavings of rotten, cast-off fruit — if they're lucky, part of a crust of bread. I've seen them fight like beasts over an apple core. And this miserable wandering nation of undernourished, homeless shadows is constantly growing, day by day, week by week. In these their haunts, where they beg, steal, and

66

kill — in Whitechapel, Soho, the East End — there Pat grew up, there he had his world, there arose that wretched little life which he so feared losing as he sat on the masthead. He was too small for his age, nervous, hollow-cheeked, almost without muscles; a trueborn child of the world's richest society, of our foul industrialized age — this stinking, carbon monoxide-poisoned, godforsaken world of machine shops, madhouses, prisons, morgues, and smokestacks.

The great turning point in Pat's life was his going to sea. The work was beyond his strength, to be sure, but he no longer walked about hunting rotten cabbage leaves in the gutter. As he clung to the skysail yard, puking and soiling his pants in terror, he already had much to lose: fixed mealtimes, a bunk to lie in. At the bottom of Pat's soul sprouts had appeared of something like a kind of happiness and zest for life.

How deep and lasting the damage left by his loneliness and terror up in the rigging would be, I couldn't know. But for life at sea he clearly wasn't strong enough, and now even the last vestiges of courage and will had been blown out of him: the tiny flame of vitality was quenched. The sole, absolutely sole possibility was to get him off the deck and back to the galley; washing potatoes, dishing up food, making tea, and mopping the floor he could doubtless manage. But *Neptune* had two cabin boys now.

I am not at bottom a sentimental man, nor signally tender-hearted; still, Pat affected me — his aura of endless misery filled me with compassion.

That day — after talking so long with my new 'son' — I next went up to the poop and stationed myself aft, at the taffrail. I would have preferred to go forward, or at least down to the main deck, and stand at the rail there to observe the sharp triangular dorsal fins which had followed us watch after watch for two days now. But such was the atmosphere amidships and forward that I shunned all contact with the crew. Something dark and unknown seemed to lie behind their silence — something I couldn't identify. On occasion they would form small clusters and talk softly among themselves, but their close, hostile silence was more striking. When they sent me a rare glance, it was fraught with an expectant, passive malice — something which really frightened me. Truth to tell, I felt unsure and ill at ease — actually afraid to leave the afterdeck.

In our wake and along our sides the sharks followed us; steadily, placidly, with limitless patience, they held the same speed as we and clove the long-stretching swells of the Pacific for mile after mile. The wind had abated, and the murmur of the breeze in the rigging was scarcely audible. Doubtless we would soon be becalmed, rocked by the waves, with the sails slatting against the masts and the sharks swimming in rings around us.

I leaned against the rail and looked down on the glorious bodies in the water. At our present low speed they could keep up by the barest movement of their tail fins. What was nature's aim in producing these beautiful monsters? In a sense, perhaps, the shark is the most complete, the most perfect creature in Neptune's kingdom. With its form, its strength, its swiftness, and its awful weapon it is the absolute carnivore — the highest nature could achieve in that direction. The shark has but one fault: it is always hungry.

A few yards off the port quarter swam a big hammerhead shark, and it struck me anew — as always when I see an example of the species — what a paradox is created by placing that strange misshapen head on that slim, steely body. Its head lies over the fish's nape like a huge crossbeam, short but very broad; it is often well over a yard, as much as five feet, between the outer edges where the eyes sit. This abnormal width of the head — five or six times as broad as it is long — makes the enormity of its dreadful gape architectonically possible; I've seen hammerheads with a gape more than three feet wide. It makes the hammerhead a great and deadly hunter, but aesthetically it spoils the magnificent lines of the svelte body with the huge fins. And this monstrous transverse snout with the diabolical jaws must offer a deal of resistance to the water during swimming.

Besides the hammerhead I counted five or six other sharks, of the usual shape and size: with pointed snouts and normal head-form.

They were smaller species: porbeagles, dogfishes, and what have you. Now and then a white belly glinted greenly through the clear water. In unperturbed majesty the hammerhead glided forward like the fixed midpoint among them; it was as if it had taken the ship's bearings, found its position in regard to her, and resolved to maintain it.

Of course we hate the monsters.

All seamen who have sailed in tropical waters hate and despise and curse the lovely brutes. Lovely? — Yes. Seen from above or from the side they are unsurpassed in their beauty. It is only from the front that the shark is ugly; but then it's as hideous as all hell's devils together — with its stupid, idiotic little pig eyes and its loathsome gape of a vastness almost contrary to nature, crammed with the sharp, serrate teeth which grow and grow and fall out and are continually renewed from within. All its life the shark endlessly produces new teeth, over and over again, in a few hours — as if the whole meaning of existence were to bring forth teeth, which in time will be spat out and sink to the bottom. Where it has been possible to explore the sea bed in shark-rich waters, the banks have proved to consist in great part of such worn-out sharks' teeth.

Nearly all of the larger species are man-eaters; the best-known are the striped tiger shark, the blue shark — and the great white shark, found chiefly in the waters south of Australia. I think this white man-eater the most awful creature that the powers have brought forth. With its huge head, its five-foot gape and the large, irregular teeth in its colossal steel jaws, it looks as if created by Satan himself as a portrait of Absolute Evil. Once, on board an American schooner in the southwest Pacific, I helped hoist such a devil out of the sea, and have often dreamed terrible dreams about its mug. With its small, dead, indescribably stupid eyes and its gigantic wide-open gape over the iron hook and steel cable, it looked like the summation of all life's cruel and cannibal forces. And the sharks are indeed quite literally cannibals: As soon as its fellows scent blood from a wounded shark, they will eat it alive.

Still: The shark must needs be included in creation that the world might be complete.

The shark is a very old race. Nature produced it early; in an age infinitely remote, thousands and thousands of years ago, the shark reached its perfection. It became a unity, a fulfilment of its function: tail fins, jaws, teeth, hunger.

In its perfection it's a very primitive fish; only the primitive is perfect. It has little central nervous system, almost no brain; its entire conscious life takes place in the spinal cord and gut.

Zoologically the sharks are classed as cartilaginous fishes, though the cartilage may be ossified. That shows how old the animal is. It has little sense of pain; strictly speaking it feels but one passion, yet that passion is eternal and constant. The shark is accursed from birth, and this curse is manifest in its anatomy. It has almost no alimentary canal, and digests and voids its food just as fast as it swallows it. Yet the food is but half-digested. As a result the shark's life consists of a single feeling — an eternal gnawing hunger; from birth to death the shark is driven by one unquenchable desire, by hunger. This eternal craving dwells in the shark's rudimentary, spiriform gut, driving it on a never-ending chase — here, in its entrails, dwells the shark's soul, and that soul is its hunger. The shark is the ocean's Ahasuerus: eternally seeking to still a craving which *can't* be stilled, it cleaves the endless tropical seas down the millennia.

It is the most evil of all the ocean spirits.

The wind was steadily abating. Before going below to the wardroom to eat, I entered the charthouse and took the barometer reading. All was well; it showed only good weather.

Meals on board the *Neptune* were a trial. I think this was due to the inhuman silence which always reigned while we partook of our food. It was the captain who occasioned our mute daily hours at table. So oppressive was the silence which he spread around him that none of us could bear to utter any but the most essential monosyllables.

Everything proceeded after a cruel and soul-destroying ritual, which was in turn linked to our placement around the table, in strict accordance with our social rank within the closed world known as S/V *Neptune*. At the head of the table sat the captain himself. I don't think I've said anything about his appearance, perhaps because it was rather ordinary. Above the bull neck sat his round, close-cropped blond head with its utterly impassive moon-face. At that time he must have been around fifty; he was about my own height, but seemed shorter because of his uncommonly stout build. That, in fact, was his sole personal feature: his huge, broad, heavy body — so stout-limbed that his jacket sleeves and trouser legs were very tight on him.

On the captain's right sat his wife, a dark-haired American with sharp features — not a beautiful face, but alive and attractive. I later learned that she had considerable talent for business and always went through both the steward's and the first mate's accounts. She also took care of the economic sides of their family life ashore — not merely the household affairs, but banks and brokers, stocks and investments as well. But economics was not her sole interest.

It *was* the sole interest of our pious first mate. That is, if you disregarded his passion for the terrible accounting to be made between his God and humanity on the looming Day of Judgment — or 'Last Day,' as he liked to call it. If I understood him aright, this Last Day would begin with the sea's giving up its dead — quite a sombre prospect, when you think how most men of our calling would look after so many years in brine. The most salient thing about the first mate's religiose ferocity was that he pictured both the Resurrection and the Judgment as literal, earthly, material events; when the hour came, we should all turn up with seaweed and mussels in our hair. The mate, whose earthly name was Jeremy Cox, was of Scottish descent, but born in the United States. Whether he was Mormon or Anglican I no longer recall, but I still see him clearly before me: everything about him was long and thin — figure, legs, fingers, face, lips, nose. His bony physiognomy was framed by long, dark hair and a beard. He bore an almost eerie resemblance to President Lincoln.

Like his captain, Jeremy Cox was a silent man. He sat on his superior's left, and prefaced each meal by folding his long, bony fingers and saying a muted grace. He was the only one who prayed before meals, but had we known what awaited us on that voyage, we might all have been more assiduous in our prayers.

Below Mr. Cox sat the third mate, the idiot Mr. Dickson.

The place below the missus was mine.

To serve the officers was in fact the task of the steward, but since he was bunk-ridden, it fell to our little dark-brown galley- and cabin boy. And the ritual was difficult, especially the first few days at sea, when we still had supplies of fresh meat and vegetables and fruit on board. For the waiter that meant more courses and harder work — in addition to the order of precedence: first the missus; then to the other side of the table, the first mate; then back to the missus's side, where the second mate — I — sat; and so to the other side again: the third mate. Finally: the head of the table, where the captain sat. His duty as ship's commander — to abandon ship last in the event of catastrophe — he had broadened by demanding to be served last as well. Everyone understood this, so he got the choicest morsels anyhow. All the courses followed this strange series of tacks: soup, meat, potatoes, gravy, vegetables, and the fresh fruit we had for dessert — they all went back and forth, back and forth.

For little Moses — the cabin boy — the job was indeed difficult, but as always he bravely did his best. Moses and Pat were about the same age, but a greater contrast would be hard to imagine; the ashen, sickly boy in my cabin, and the square-set, muscular Moses: dark as coffee, alert, intelligent, with nerves like hempen rope — plucky and full of fight. The black boy was berthed amidships; he shared the cook's cabin and slept in the upper bunk. I was grazed by the semblance of an idea.

Then something happened. The captain raised his heavy, perspiring face and looked at me.

'Mr. Jensen,' he said.

'Yes, sir?'

'How's the steward getting along?'

'Badly, sir.'

'What's that supposed to mean? His head must be cured by now?'

'It isn't a head, captain.'

'Then what is it, Mr. Jensen?'

'Probably a stomach ulcer.'

'What!' His face darkened: 'That's just dandy.'

'I'm sorry, sir.'

'How long will he be laid up?'

'I don't know.'

For a while he sat there, knife and fork in hand, but silent again. Then he spoke once more:

'And the carpenter? That devil's bastard?'

'He'll probably live. Unless something else happens.'

'Hm.'

'I'm not a doctor, captain.'

'What a hellish crew!' he roared suddenly: 'What a pack of hellhounds!'

No one said a word.

'And the other fellow, that damned Peruvian devil who tried to kill him? How's he getting along? Just say it, Mr. Jensen! Just tell me everything at once!'

'One eye is gone and his hand is broken.'

'So he's out of commission too? The cur! The blasted swine! God damn them all!'

For awhile there was only the sound of chewing and of silver against plates. Mr. Cox coughed a couple of times, a deep, grating, ghostly cough.

'Devil take me if I've ever seen the like of this crew,' the captain mumbled softly: 'In all my damn life.'

I think that only Moses was wholly unmoved by the outburst. Very calmly he brought the fruit around, in strict accordance with the ritual. It may have been so hard for him that he needed his whole brain and everything in it just to remember the order of rank and precedence. Then he went amidships with the serving dishes.

The captain shoved away his plate and stared at me again:

'And that blasted little orphanage kid, that bloody little slum rat from the privies of Soho? That damned rag-heap of a deck boy — you know who I mean, Mr. Jensen?'

'Yes, sir.'

'Has this new Prince of Wales thought of getting back to work?'

'He can't, sir.'

'And what's wrong with His Grace?'

'Nervous breakdown, captain.'

'*N-e-r-v-o-u-s*?!'

'Perhaps that isn't the right word, sir. But I fear he's going out of his mind. He lies there clinging to the bunk.'

'Where is he?'

'In my cabin.'

'In *yours*??'

'The sick bay is taken, sir.'

'Send him forward, mister.'

'I would very much rather not, sir.'

For a moment he just stared into space, as if he had heard something incomprehensible. Then he turned his impassive moonface to me again and wiped the sweat from his brow with his napkin.

'Mr. Jensen,' he said, 'I don't need to remind you that you didn't join this ship as a nursemaid.'

I couldn't help glancing at the third mate. He smiled. A triumphant smile of glee spread across his red, bloated, unintelligent face. It was impossible to say which it beamed forth more strongly — stupidity or spite. Had Moses not taken the gravy pitcher, I could have thrown it in his face.

'Sir,' I replied: 'Better the voyage continue with a ship's boy in possession of his reason than with a lunatic.'

He seemed to relent. In any case, his voice was calm and no longer unfriendly as he replied:

'Well, well, Mr. Jensen. It's you who have the role of medicine man on this ship. But what are we to do with him? He certainly can't stay in your cabin; he can't just loaf. Have you thought about that, mister?'

'Yes, sir.'

'And?'

'I have an idea.'

'Yes?' His voice was downright friendly now. Something must have happened in that round head of his. At that time I occasionally pondered whether the captain, that crude, money-grubbing monster, had a soul. Just then it looked as if he did indeed have something of the sort. His small eyes were clear and questioning.

'Pat will doubtless be equal to lighter work in a few days, and he has sailed as cabin boy before,' I said. 'I suggest that Pat and Moses change places — that Moses move forward and Pat get Moses's bunk with the cook. We'll switch their berths.'

He bowed his head and commenced eating his orange:

'Do as you like, mister.'

The door opened, and Moses came in to clear more of the dirty dishes from the table.

'Moses!' said the captain gently.

'Yes, sir!'

'You know, my boy, that the deck boy Pat, the one with the long blond hair, is very sick?'

'Yes, sir, he can hardly talk. I've been down to Mr. Jensen's cabin with soup for him. He talks like a little kid.'

'The second mate doesn't think he can go aloft any more.'

'He'd die of fright, sir.'

'If you two change jobs, then Pat can be in the galley and sleep with the cook, while you go forward. You'll get two more shillings a month.'

'Thank you, sir! Thank you very much, sir!'

Moses did his best to control himself, and he managed. But when he bowed, I could see how happy he was.

75

I stuck my orange in my jacket pocket, still dumbfounded at the captain's calling Moses 'my boy'. At the same time I sensed that *Sancta Vénere* was becalmed, merely rolling in the swells. The wind must have died down altogether. I sighed with relief; the suggestion about Pat had gone through much more easily than I had expected.

'Listen, Mr. Jensen, that damned bandit of a bastard from Peru must go back to work at once. At least he has one usable hand. He'll take the helm for a watch as soon as we get enough wind for steerage way.'

'Aye, aye, sir.'

'What's the scum's name?'

'Carlos, sir.'

'I wish the devil would take him, mister.'

'Yes, sir.'

'And I wish the devil would take the chips and the steward and that huge bloody thug of a mulatto. He's a troublemaker.'

'Well, sir. That would mean four men less on board.'

'What's the damned swine's name?'

'Arrowmith, sir. James Arrowsmith. Able.'

'Hm. From the look on his face you'd think the swine's name was Rockefeller.'

'He's a man with self-respect, sir.'

The captain looked at me. With his round head, his fat face, and his small grey-blue eyes, he was almost the very spit of a ship's pig I sailed with as a deck hand. Slowly his eyes grew bigger out of sheer astonishment:

'Self-respect?'

'Yes, sir. Self-esteem.'

'In the first place the cur is a nigger, in the second place he's a deck hand — and then he walks around with *self-esteem*! Mr. Jensen, Mr. Jensen! It's your word!'

'You can ask the third mate, captain, if James Arrowsmith doesn't have self-esteem,' I rejoined piously, with a friendly glance at Mr. Dickson. The shot hit home; he shone with active, primeval hate.

'Tell me one thing, second mate: Is there a single white man in the forecastle?'

'I believe that the sailmaker may have been white at one time. It's not easy to tell. Maybe the boatswain too.'

'That's all?'

'It's possible that the other deck boy is white, sir. But he's very sunburned.'

'Jesus!' he sighed: 'We're sailing with a forecastle full of niggers, Malays, redskins, bastards, and cannibals!'

As if on command we all raised our heads and stared at the first mate. Mr. Jeremy Cox had coughed — and the cough came as from a sepulchre. He had laid down his fruit knife, and now sat with open mouth, preparing to speak. The resemblance to good old Abe Lincoln was eerie, frightening. Cox looked as if he were about to present the defence budget to the Senate. He was as solemn as if he were about to count his money. Then he coughed his ghostly cough once again and took the floor; the syllables fell like silver dollars on a plate:

'There isn't,' he said menacingly; 'there isn't, God damn me, one Christian man before the mast. We sail with wild beasts on board; with brutes of strange colours and races, full of rebellion, malice, and self-inflicted diseases — syphilitic, mangy, clap-rotten whoremongers, sodomites and pederasts, murderers and cannibals — with heathens and aborigines! Wrath shall strike this spiritual deadhouse of a ship. We ought to go forward and baptize them all in the Holy Spirit's name. But, God damn me, it's too late for the hour of salvation!'

He looked around, then continued in an even more menacing tone:

'We sail with the whole world's sin and guilt on board. Chastisement is at hand. The Lord Jehovah is a jealous God, and the sword of vengeance sits loose in His scabbard.'

We all sat in numb silence.

'I know that the Lord is a jealous God,' I said; 'but, Mr. Cox, your religion also contains words about love and forgiveness.'

77

I cannot describe the scorn which I met in the first mate's deep, dark, burning eyes.

'Mr. Jensen,' he said, 'there is no forgiveness, no mercy, without prior retribution. Whom He loveth, He chastiseth. To love is to punish.'

Then he stood up — six foot six — and went out. His Holiness, First Mate Jeremy Cox, had spoken.

I felt depressed and out of sorts after the meal — not so much by what my colleagues-in-command had said as by my own reactions: my aversion to the captain and the first mate, my loathing for the third mate. No, I didn't hate them, you mustn't interpret it so. But the One who sees into the human heart, He knew — may the Lord have mercy on my sinful, wanton soul! — He knew that I bore no love for them either. I looked upon them without charity. And since each shall be judged by the standard of his own judging, so I myself, once the brine had closed over me, would be judged after my own animus — without love.

Further: these men, these three white officers of the world's greatest merchant fleet — they were my peers, my colleagues and brother officers; in a pinch we should have to trust each other like bedrock. The truth was that I didn't trust them — and the truth was that we had a very difficult crew. The truth is a terrible thing, and we should not take Her name in vain. So much have I understood.

And in this case the truth was that I regarded the third mate, who should have been my younger friend and brother and ally, my right hand in a grapple with the passion of men or sea — the truth was that I regarded him with loathing, mistrust, and contempt. He was an incompetent navigator, he was stupid — and he was brutal. Like so many brutal men, he wasn't courageous; he was no man of mettle. He had struck the Malay, who was considerably smaller than he — but he had not dared to strike James Arrowsmith. He was spiteful, coarse, and cowardly. That's how I looked upon him.

As to the first mate, I quite simply doubted his sanity.

Only with regard to the captain did I feel uncertain. Did he have a soul? Was anything going on beneath the close-cropped pig bristles on his round skull? Was he merely reserved, or was he making fools of us all?

With these three I was to sail *Sancta Vénere* from Manila, with a call at Rio, to Marseilles. My white brothers in a black, yellow, red, and brown world of long-haired folk with rings in their ears! We four had thirty human fates in our hands. On board the *Neptune* we were the British government. No, I didn't view my fellow-officers with love.

Engrossed in such thoughts, I walked over to my cabin, took the orange from my pocket, and gave it to Pat. As his thin white fingers closed around it, I again pondered my misrelation to my colleagues. Every truth, carried to its extreme, is lunacy. Is this the truth of madness or the madness of truth?

'Mister,' said Pat: 'Thanks a lot for the orange.'

'My boy,' I said; 'I have good news for you.'

'What, mister?'

'You're not going forward.'

The gaunt, homely face lit up:

'Am I to stay here with you, Mr. Jensen?'

'No,' I said: 'That's impossible.'

'I like you so much, mister. I want to stay here. Can't I stay with you?'

The orange rolled across the blanket. He half sat up in the bunk and put both arms around my neck:

'Mister Peder! Mister Peder! Take me along! Let me stay with you! I have nowhere to go.'

'You'll sleep amidships, with the cook. Moses will be deck boy and you'll be cabin boy.'

He clasped my neck even more tightly, and I noticed that he was crying.

'I'd rather die!' he whispered: 'I wish I'd fallen down from the skysail. I just want to stay with you.'

'No, Pat.'

'I want to be your son, mister — or do you have other children?'
'I have no children, Pat.'
'Mister,' he said softly; 'you're the nicest person I know. You're the only one in the whole world who's been nice to me.'
'You've been nice to me too, Pat.'
'But you have no other children, Mr. Jensen; so you can keep me. There's nobody who owns me.'
'It won't do, Pat.'
'Yes, I can stay with you. There's something called adopting, taking somebody as your own child. That way I could be with you all the time, in your own town — home with you.'
'But I don't have such a place, Pat. I don't have a house, and I don't have a home. I don't even have a bed or a dock. I have no place and no home to give you, Pat.'
'Don't you have anything, mister?'
'No — nothing, Pat.'
He paused; then slowly he let go of my neck, and played with his orange. He smiled:
'Then I'm richer than you, mister.'
'How's that?'
'You have nothing — and I have *you*.'
'You don't *have* me. People don't *have* each other.'
'Yes, you have me. And besides, you also have....'
'What?'
'You know yourself, Mr. Jensen.'
'I have my violin, some notebooks, and a few books. That's all I own. I told you: it's the sailor's lot.'
He seized my hand:
'I want to stay with you always!' And the tears began afresh: 'I'm so fond of you.'
'Pat,' I said, 'I'd like to have you as a son. But I *have* nothing, I *am* nothing — I can promise nothing. I have no home.'
'You're my father!'
'I can't promise anything, Pat.'
'Yes you can, mister, I have no one but you in the whole world!'

'Pat,' I said, 'we're both alone.'

He pressed my hand against his cheek and went on crying. God, all the pain of humanity was there, in one weeping child. And I thought: Why must I be this way? Why must all suffering go to my heart so? Why do I grow fond of all who have it bad?

'Mister,' he went on: 'You've been sailing for so many years, don't you have money so you can buy a house?'

'I have some money. It's in a bank.'

'The Bank of England?'

'No. Another bank.'

'Have you enough to buy a house?'

'I don't know. I doubt it.'

'But if you have?'

'I can't promise anything.'

'How long have you been sailing, Mr. Jensen?'

'Twenty years.'

'How old were you when you went to sea?'

'Thirteen.'

'What does your father do?'

'He was a sailor.'

'Is he dead?'

'He drank a great deal, and so one night when he was drunk, he fell in the water and drowned — in Amsterdam.'

'My father's in the workhouse.'

'Has he been there long?'

'Several years.'

'What did he do before that?'

'He worked in a shoe factory and made nineteen shillings a week.'

'How many children were you?'

'Five.'

'How did he land in prison?'

'He took an iron last and hit his boss on the head with it. So that he died.'

'So you didn't get those nineteen shillings any more?'

'No.'

'And then?'

'Then Mamma couldn't pay the rent for our room.'

'So it was the street?'

'Yes, Mr. Jensen.'

'How old were you then?'

'Nine, I think.'

He began on his orange. He was skinny and thoughtful, no longer crying. He peered over the fruit in the direction of my violin case.

'Hey, mister?'

'Yes?'

'Are you good at playing the violin?'

'Not particularly.'

'In London there are lots of people who can fiddle. Some of them play on the street.'

'Yes.'

'Will you play for me?'

'Some other time, Pat.'

'Have you been in London?'

'Yes.'

'When?'

'Twice, when I didn't have a berth.'

'London is a fine city.'

'Yes, maybe.'

'The Queen and the Lord Mayor live there, and they have big carriages with white horses.'

'That they do, all right.'

'Mister?'

'Yes?'

'Where do you come from?'

'From Hammerfest in Norway. The world's northernmost city.'

'Is Hammerfest like London?'

'No.'

'What's it like there?'

'Outside the city lies the Arctic Ocean, and further west is the North Atlantic. Sometimes the houses are lashed to the hillside with stays, since it blows rather hard up there.'

'Have you sailed on the Arctic Ocean?'

'As a boy.'

'What's the Arctic Ocean like?'

'When the weather is good, it's very lovely there. It's a fine ocean.'

'And the rest of the time?'

'Sometimes there's a storm. Once in a long while a hurricane. But we don't have cyclones or typhoons.'

'Is it long since you've been there, mister?'

'Fifteen years, I think.'

'Don't you live anywhere?'

'No.'

'So you live all over, mister.'

'Yes.'

'All over the world. Wherever there's salt water.'

'Yes, just about.'

He smiled:

'And now you're on the Pacific Ocean!'

'Yes.'

'With me!'

'With you.'

'Don't you ever want to live anywhere?'

'I don't think so. I have my sea chest and a berth on every ship.'

'And in your chest you have money?'

'Some, yes.'

'How much?'

'I don't know. It's a long time since I've counted it.'

'Don't you care about it?'

'Not any more. When I was sailing before the mast, I saved up my money to go ashore and take out my papers.'

'Is it in silver dollars?'

'Some of those too, I believe.'

'Don't you ever count them, mister?'

'Why should I count them, Pat? I have food and lodging on board.'

'Don't you want a house on land?'

'I don't like it on land.'

'You like it on the sea, Mr. Jensen?'

'Yes. I like to stand watch. I like to take the height of the sun. I like to see the stars at night. I like quiet. I like to be in my cabin and lie and read, or play my violin.'

'I wish I was your son, mister.'

On deck there was no wind, and I recognized the smell the instant I came up. The waist was covered with blood. Thick and heavy and dark it ran about between the forecastle, the galley, and the rail. The water alongside was likewise red with blood. The men were gathered on deck; among them I saw the huge back of the first mate, now manifest as one of them, and on the friendliest footing. To the starboard main yardarm, which jutted far out over the ship's side, was fastened a heavy block and tackle. The men on the bloody deck were seized with an almost manic excitement.

The shark-fishing had begun.

Amid the ecstatic, whooping men three maimed sharks wriggled and snapped. People waded barefoot in the blood. One, the sail-maker — a rather light-skinned man whom I hadn't much noticed before — was equipped with a huge shark knife, and was doing most of the butchering. Malay pearl-fishers use these knives when diving, as a defence against the sharks. To penetrate the rough, sandpapery skin one needs an instrument of uncommon quality. A shark knife is a good foot long, of specially hardened steel, and sharp as a razor. It is kept in a tallow-filled sheath to protect the blade against rust or other damage.

A shark is an unusually hardy beast, precisely because of its primitive physiology. But it bleeds heavily. Its flesh is suffused with uric acid, and is thus inedible to humans. Only in the Mediterranean lands is the meat used: they cut it into bits and pickle it in vinegar, pepper, and other sharp spices to mask the taste; then the shark meat is falsely sold as canned tuna, or *tonno* as the Italians call it. Of course it is only dagos who do this; honest, civilized people use only the shark's liver and fins. The latter, however, are a world-renowned delicacy; the Chinese in particular know how to make an excellent soup of them.

One by one the three snapping brutes on deck now tasted the shark knife.

First the tail fin was chopped off, and the dorsal fins severed with a few swift strokes. Lastly the belly was opened and the liver extracted. The blood poured almost black from the gaping wounds; the entrails spilled from the slit in the white belly. Then the monster was dumped back overboard.

It was down in the sea that the drama began in earnest.

The bloodred water seethed with sharks crazed by the scent of blood and the taste of meat. The sea was a bubbling witch-cauldron of white bellies, pink foam, and thrashing tail fins, of black bodies and white teeth. No famished Siberian wolf-pack could have evinced greater savagery. Where did these brutes come from? They had popped up as at the sound of a whistle; the smell of fresh blood brought them up from the depths, from the sea's farthest abysses.

One by one the mutilated devils were heaved overboard. Without tail fins they could no longer swim, but the blood streaming from their wounds summoned their hungry fellows, who came as to a festal board and tore huge mouthfuls from the thrashing, helpless bodies; they gulped down the loose entrails, turned like lightning and came back. The suppleness, pliancy, and strength of these selachian bodies, perfected so early in the morn of history — it was incomprehensible, as mysterious as the earth's childhood which produced them.

It was strangest, perhaps, to observe the disfigured monsters who were thrown overboard. Missing fins and slit bellies notwithstanding, they were more alive than ever. And they were just as crazed with hunger as the other demons, though the scent of blood and meat came from their own wounds and their own

85

entrails. You could see them gobbling pieces of flesh from their own tails, yes, even swallowing their own intestines, as they themselves were eaten by their brothers. It was incredible, the sight of a thus-crippled shark body curving into a ring of living steel to get hold of its own bloody tail-stump.

But the meal progressed rapidly. After a few minutes only the hungry beasts remained in the ever-reddening water, which they whipped into cascades and eddies.

On deck the next shark was being vivisected, maimed and slit amid a new torrent of dark blood. Then it went over the rail, and the repast began anew. From the last piscine devil the men carved out large pieces to fasten to their three shark hooks, to be thrown to the brutes after the last invalid had been devoured hide and cartilage and gut, spine and jaws and skull. A shark usually leans far over on its side or back when about to bite, but by no means always — as could readily be observed in this marine tableau of a cannibalistic hell — a picture which made both Bosch and Breughel pale.

As I stood gazing down into inferno, a huge triangular dorsal fin glided through the bloody foam. It was the hammerhead I had seen astern earlier in the day. Like a battleship it pressed forward, shoving the other bodies aside. Its goal — the last of the three butchered on deck — was just a wriggling lump of flesh now, but the hammerhead approached it, reclined so far that its whole white underside glittered in the sunshine, then opened its jaws and took the whole head in one gulp. The jet of arterial blood stood high in the air, and the other sharks pounced upon the corpse in a frenzy.

Wild yells sounded from the deck at the sight of the giant shark, and soon the hooks went overboard. Everyone hung over the rail, staring into the whipped-up sea. The hammerhead struck out from the ship's side and circled through the waves. Then it turned back.

It swam along our side, past the three baits, then glided stern-ward; but it was back in the bloody water among the other fish at once. It was swimming by smell alone, the small pig eyes saw nothing; it was, as it were, sniffing around in the dark. For a brief second it was so near one of the hooks that the bait trailed along its body. It must have noticed something, for it straightaway turned and came back. It took aim at the bait now, and all at once it rolled over and swallowed the meat, hook, and a couple of feet of the steel chain which had been used as a leader.

A roar came from the deck. The fish was fast.

In a swirl of red water it set out, and the hempen hawser was soon taut as a violin string. Then the shark went straight down, and they let out more line. As far as I could determine, the monster was twenty feet long or more. Never had I been so sickened as by the repulsive protrusions on the sides of that Satanic head.

The crew hauled away, and amid whines, wails, and tears from the block and tackle, Behemoth-Leviathan was drawn toward the water's bloody surface. Soon they had him alongside: big, cannibalistic, and wild — with his awful saw-toothed mouth agape. So the hook was not wholly painless. They dragged the head and half the upper body of this Satan in piscine form out of the water. They could do no more. There he hung, twenty feet of him, whipping the red brine into blossoms of rosy froth. The giant devil must have weighed a good two tons. His face dangled gyrating from the steel chain, the face of a malice and a hideosity without name or word. It was quite simply the deep's hell which hung there.

Little by little the sailors worked a noose over his tail fin, and with the aid of a creaking, howling block and tackle hove this manifestation of all the world's heathen, cannibal forces up from the sea, up into the free air, where its Herculean strength was broken. With a crash it landed on the deck planks, and a yell of glee came from the men's throats.

The dismembering of Caliban began forthwith.

The man with the shark knife could neither cut nor hack off the tail fin. At last another sailor with bloody feet and rolled-up trouser legs came over the deck with the carpenter's broadaxe, and they managed to chop it off. The snapping, gasping gape was more than a yard wide. The teeth were large, irregular, and crooked.

Otherwise all was shouting, passion, and blood. I stood quietly on the poop, looking on.

It occurred to me that the largest of all these monsters called sharks plies my own childhood waters in the North Atlantic and the Arctic Ocean: the Greenland shark, which grows up to thirty feet long, but which isn't a man-eater; a philanthropist of a giant shark, resembling the people who fish it — that pious, hard-drinking, brave, cheerful, and big-hearted race which inhabits the coast of Finmark.

As I thought about this, I felt an icy gust on my nape, as from a morgue. It was the tall, lean, Lincolnesque, cadaverous first mate. I got gooseflesh down my back.

Raising a long apocalyptic forefinger, he pointed toward the deck and the waves:

'Mr. Jensen,' he said; 'the devils from land meet the devils from the sea.'

'What's that you say, Mr. Cox?'

'The sharks are the incarnation of lost seamen's souls!'

'Mr. Cox, you're raving!'

'The souls which drown unsaved and unbaptized come back as sharks — gnawed by eternal hunger and desire.'

'The sea gives back its dead, you mean? In the form of sharks!'

'Yes!' he said: 'as blue sharks, hammerheads, tiger sharks, white sharks.'

'You frighten me, Mr. Cox!'

'Look at them!' he cried: 'Look at those bastards — yellow, brown, black — they are the devil's children on land, even as the sharks are in the sea.'

'Do you know what you're saying, mister?' I said. 'Do you know that that's blasphemous talk? You're blaspheming God and the meaning of existence!'

'When the sea has closed over this lewd, heathen, devil-ridden ship, you shall all return in the guise of sharks — dead seamen's souls!'

I stared at him, and knew that I was looking into the despairing eyes of a madman. Only the sea was mirrored in them.

'Look at them!' he shouted; 'look at the deck! The sharks have met their masters! They too are the devil's damned, unredeemed souls — accursed, deformed, red, yellow, black, and brown heathen creatures — Satan's progeny all — but the sea will revenge itself! Wait until the next typhoon!'

'When the sea gives up its dead, then the Last Day is at hand? Is that so, Mr. Cox?'

He considered.

'No,' he said; 'the first token that God's wrath draws nigh, as the Day of Judgment — yes, as the Last Day — that sign shall be manifest as a fall in the stock-quotations — in the prices on the London Exchange, the drop on the Exchange shall usher in the Day of Wrath!'

I felt queasy, sick, and despairing. The sails slatted deadly against the masts. There was nothing in the world but blood and doldrums. Then I heard a voice behind me:

'In half an hour we'll have a wind from the west-northwest.'

I turned and met the captain's small, stolid, incurious eyes. He was as heavy as a mountain and didn't even trouble to glance at the deck or at the bloodbath in the sea. He just looked vacantly up at the sky.

The soulless idiot of a captain was right; before sundown *Sancta Vénere* was ploughing at good speed through the greedy, bottomless swells of the Pacific. Again the wind sang in the rigging, the deck was washed and clean.

May God have mercy on our souls.

The Chinamen

Fifteen men on a dead man's chest,
Yo-ho-ho and a bottle of rum!

On the eighth day at sea the steward developed *mania potatorum.* When I looked in on him that morning, he seemed at first glance to be much improved. He was sitting up in bed with his knees drawn up under the blanket. It looked as if he were busy with some kind of work.

'How's it going, Mr. la Fontaine?' I said. 'Shall we soon see you up and about?'

'I'm hard at work already,' replied the Belgian, with a meaning nod at his knees: 'but there are things that don't tally in the account books.'

He cast a worried look at the woollen blanket. Then he shook his head.

'Well,' I said: 'small inaccuracies easily creep in.'

He looked at me. And I noted a certain cool contempt in his look.

'Small?' he said: '*Small?*'

'Well, no, then. It's not my department, steward.'

He lowered his voice.

'Tell me, mister: Do you think the cook steals?'

'Certainly not. The Marxist Ti-Pong is an honest man.'

Again he stared at the blanket over his drawn-up knees. He was clearly engaged in some inquiry which caused him much puzzlement and worry.

'I can't possibly have ordered so much pepper,' he said.

'Pepper?'

'Yes, black pepper. Here it is: Two hundred eleven tons of black pepper!'

'Two hundred eleven tons?'

'Yes, have you ever heard the like, mister! Two hundred and eleven tons of pepper!'

'No,' I said; 'I've never heard of anything like that in my life!'

'If it had even concerned the cargo,' he mused; 'but here we're talking about supplies!'

'Hm,' I said. An eerie feeling of dark dread stole over me.

'It must be the cook,' he went on in a logical tone: 'Only a Chinaman can find a use for so much pepper!'

'Mr. la Fontaine, that's preposterous!'

'That's as much as you know, mister. Preposterous!!! In '86 I sailed with a Chinaman who stole spices; he was cook on the schooner *Janus* out of Liverpool. He stole nutmeg.'

'I mean it's unthinkable that we can have laid in....'

'Nothing is unthinkable! Everything, everything is possible — nothing is unthinkable — a seaman should know that, especially when, like you, he sails as an officer!'

'We can't possibly have....'

'Now listen, mister! Let's keep to the point, to the naked facts. If one Chinaman steals nutmeg, then another Chinaman can steal pepper.'

'That's not what I mean.'

'Why can't he steal pepper? Tell me that, mister! Give me a logical answer: Can he or can he not?'

Now the steward's obstinacy was irritating me beyond measure, and I yelled back in order to stop this talk which was making the world idiotic and life meaningless:

'We're not sailing with two hundred and eleven tons of pepper as supplies!'

He smiled scornfully, full of superior knowledge — as at a child.

'Well,' he said condescendingly, 'if you won't take my word for it, mister, you can see for yourself.'

With both hands, after first sticking an invisible copy-pencil behind his ear, he lifted an invisible ledger from his knees and held it out to me:

'Perhaps this will convince you, sir.'

I took the record; I was in no condition to reply.

'Well? You're silent. You've seen for yourself. You will see, too, that in the blank column I've added my own comments. What do you say?'

'I'm speechless, steward.'

'You see, you see!' He held out his hands: 'May I have it back?'

I handed him the 'book,' and he rearranged it across his knees. Next he took the copy-pencil from behind his ear and wrote a few words at the bottom of the page. Then he leafed over and wrote on. When I showed signs of going, he turned to me, breaking off his work.

'Just a moment, mister! Unfortunately there's more here. For example, we have the linen and all the starch! Have you ever in your life heard of so much starch, mister? Just tell me if you've ever seen anything like it before!'

'How much starch do we have?'

He opened his mouth and stared at me thoughtfully, then consulted the ledger.

'To be quite exact, sir: We have eleven hundred forty-three and a half pounds of starch.'

'Hm,' I said; 'that's incredible.'

'Incredible but true. Do you want to see for yourself? — You don't?'

'I rely on you completely, Mr. la Fontaine.'

'Thank you, mister. And I haven't yet mentioned the linen. I assure you that we have so much linen on board that if we unfolded it, we could walk on linen from Manila to Cape Horn.'

'You don't say!'

'We could stroll from the Philippines to Tierra del Fuego just on tablecloths, napkins, towels, sheets, and pillow cases!'

He went back to the ledger, reading on alertly and with interest, now and then making use of the pencil. He underlined a few words or a figure here and there, and occasionally added a marginal note. I put my hand on the latch. He turned:

'No, mister, don't go! You've no idea how much funny stuff there is in this book. And by the way, tell me: What shall we do with the starch?'

'We can dump it, steward.'

'But then the whole sea will get stiff. No, no!'

'Then we'll have to keep it on board.'

Again he consulted the book and shook his head doubtfully:

'And then, in the midst of all this: one and three-quarters pounds of dried prunes! We'll never get to Marseilles on a pound and three-quarters of prunes!'

'We can lay in some at Rio, steward.'

'Yes, that's true. But even to get that far, a pound and three-quarters is terribly little. A terribly small supply of prunes!'

'We'll have to do without.'

'*You* can say that! It's easy for *you*, you're not responsible for the ship's provisions. I know of stewards who've been lynched.'

'Lynched?'

'Yes. Lynched. For less than that.'

'That won't happen here.'

'That's what *you* say!'

He resumed work on the accounts. And in hope of disappearing unnoticed, I turned to the door again; la Fontaine's society was beginning to get on my nerves. I was stopped by a loud shriek.

'Aha!' he cried, in a voice at once triumphant and bitter: 'Didn't I know it?'

Like a conquering Roman Caesar he raised his head and stared at me, self-righteous and sovereign:

'Didn't I know it?'

'What did you know?'

'Don't pretend that you don't understand!'

'I have no idea what you knew.'

'The insect powder, of course.'

'What insect powder?'

'I ordered four hundred pounds of insect powder.'

'Four hundred pounds?'

'Yes, of course.'

'So?'

'It's disappeared. The whole order is gone.'

'Oh?'

'It's been erased. He has stolen the insect powder and erased it from the ledger.'

'Who?'

'Tai-Foon.'

'Who the hell is Tai-Foon?'

'The cook, of course.'

'His name isn't Tai-Foon.'

'He deserves to be named that. The lemon-yellow Satan.'

'Now listen, steward: Why should he remove the insect powder?'

'You ought to know that; after all, you're a mate on board this latrine of a ship.'

'I *don't* know it.'

'Well, why do people steal insect powder in the first place? Think about it logically and clearly, mister. It's a logical question which warrants a logical answer. Why do people steal insect powder? To use it? No. — *To keep us from using it.* Understand?'

'No. There are no insects on board the *Neptune*.'

'Insects! Use your reason, man!'

'What were you going to sprinkle four hundred pounds of insect powder on?'

He sighed at my hopeless stupidity, then said in a calm, friendly tone:

'On the Chinamen, of course.'

'The Chinamen? But we've only a couple on board.'

'The ship is crawling with them.'

There are one or two in the forecastle, and then the cook here amidships.'

'Tai-Foon, yes — the devil.'

'Now the cook doesn't deserve such a stormy name, Mr. la Fontaine. He's a calm and balanced man.'

'Calm? Yes. — Balanced? You don't know him, man.'

'I signed on in Manila.'

'You see? You signed on. But I've sailed with him for two years. *Why* did you sign on, mister? I'm just asking: Why?'

'Because the previous second mate had left the ship.'

He laughed, a cutting, scornful laugh:

'Left the ship? — Yes, you can call it that! Left the ship! — 'Left!' One can put it that way!'

The steward slammed shut the imaginary ledger; I could almost hear the bang. Then he laid it on the bed, between himself and the planking.

'I'll tell you how he 'left the ship,' all right! Yes, we dropped him into the China Sea — into the Yellow Sea! We dumped him, mister. We quite simply dumped your entire predecessor.'

'Do they usually do that with second mates on board this ship?' I said.

He considered seriously:

'Not with all of them. It depends on you.'

'Hm.'

'Have you seen his huge Malay shark knife?'

'Yes.'

'That's what he uses.'

'It's very sharp.'

'Yes, extremely. He cut him up with his clothes on. His guts spurted out like a pig's. And Jacco — the near-sighted swine of a sailmaker — sewed him in from his crown to the soles of his feet — and then, yes, then it was only a matter of dumping him.'

'What does the captain say to this? The cook should at least have his pay docked for that sort of thing.'

The steward shook his head wearily, almost in despair.

'He wasn't docked — not so much as a penny,' he said: 'He and the captain are in league.'

He was silent a moment; then he went on, in deep sorrow:

'And now they've stolen the insect powder! With the whole ship full of Chinamen!'

'What Chinamen, steward?'

'All of them. It's crawling with them, thousands.'

'I've only seen two or three.'

'It's the little ones. The little tiny ones. Just look at the floor, mister!'

I looked at the floor.

'See how many there are! The whole floor is covered with them. I even have a couple of dozen under the blanket. As I said, They're enormously small.'

'I don't see any little Chinamen, steward.'

'They're all over, man. They're sitting everywhere, from the keelson to the skysail yard, from the bowsprit to the taffrail. Thick as little — tiny little rats. They're no bigger than mice. But you must have seen them, man!'

'I haven't seen them, Mr. la Fontaine.'

'I wouldn't have mentioned the Chinamen to you if they weren't there. They sit and ride on the yards all over the rigging. Thick as sparrows. — And now I don't have any insect powder.'

'Would you like a cup of soup, steward?'

'Oh, yes!' he replied bitterly: 'Soup! Go ahead, poison me. Now old Tai-Foon is out there making soup of my insect powder. Oh, Lord!'

In despair he clapped his hands over his eyes. After sitting thus for a while, he said softly:

'Send Moses in, mister — he can help me turn out and get dressed.'

I went, and sent Pat to him. Almost at once a piercing scream issued from the cabin:

'Lord Jesus! He's changed colour! Moses has changed colour! Get out! Out with you! And don't step on the Chinamen — they revenge themselves, boy!'

When I went aft, I was in no doubt of the diagnosis. I opened the journal, found the hour, and wrote in: 'At 10:25 the steward Jacques la Fontaine, after six days of stomach pains, fasting, and abstinence from alcohol, had an attack of *mania potatorum*.'

Soundlessly, without my noting it, the captain had entered the charthouse. He placed himself silently beside me and looked down at the log, where my writing was not yet dry. Without a word he set his thick forefinger under the word 'potatorum' and turned his face to me. The small, indifferent eyes looked at me questioningly.

'*Potatorum*,' I said, 'comes from the Latin verb *potare*, meaning 'to drink.' *Mania*, of course, simply means madness or insane excitement — in other words, rage or delirium. He's got the jimjams, sir.'

'Ordinary delirium?'

'Yes, sir. Delirium tremens.'

He looked at me with a kind of unbudging, impassive contempt:

'May I ask, Mr. Jensen, why you have availed yourself of this Latin monkey's word, which reminds one only of potatoes, instead of the ordinary term *delirium tremens*?'

'Yes, sir. Firstly because the *tremens* is lacking; he's not shaking at all. Secondly, sir, for reasons of discretion.'

'What? Discretion! With regard to that filthy Belgian alcoholic wreck of an ex-human being? Really, Mr. Jensen, one must hear a great deal before one's ears fall off! Discretion! He's been on this ship for two years, and hasn't been sober for so long as five minutes. Had he not been white, and such a damned able steward, I'd have thrown him overboard with my own hands. Discretion!'

He looked at me as if trying to decide who should be drowned first — I or la Fontaine.

'Excuse me, sir,' I said, 'but the ship's journal is a public document, admissible in court, and it can fall into alien, inappropriate hands. Should la Fontaine recover, and abstain from alcohol in the future, he will again be an excellent steward, and then it concerns no one that he's had an alcoholic delirium on board the *Neptune*.'

'Hm. What's happening with him now?'

'He's counting Chinamen, sir.'

'Chinamen?'

'Yes, sir. Chinamen. They are very yellow and enormously small, sir.'

'Enormously small?'

'Yes, sir. And frightfully numerous. Thousands.'

'Hm. Why Chinamen in particular?'

'You would almost have to ask Mr. la Fontaine himself, captain.'

'They could just as well be Malays?'

'Undoubtedly, sir.'

'Then we must forget about him as steward?'

'Absolutely, sir.'

'How long, Mr. Jensen?'

'For several weeks to come.'

'Have you met with this kind of thing before, mister?'

'Yes, sir. Twice previously. Once on the ship *Erna* out of Arendal. The captain — old Marinius Hansen — had a full-blown case of delirium tremens in the fall of '93, down in the Persian Gulf. It lasted for weeks, but he got over it splendidly. It broke out just inside the sound, off Abu Musa, with the result that we lay over long past schedule in Abadan. The other time it was an Australian steward who got the jimjams. He barricaded himself in the anchor-cable bin, captain, and claimed that two of the deck hands wanted to eat him — they were from the Fiji Islands and had filed teeth. Finally he died. He also had a monkey which blew overboard, sir. The steward claimed that the crew had eaten it.'

'He died — of delirium?'

'Of heart failure. People with D.T. are often so violently active around the clock over several weeks, that the heart can't stand the strain.'

'Hm. But old Marinius Hansen, who didn't die; what form did his delirium take?'

'Well; you see, sir, Captain Hansen had a farm just outside Arendal — not a big farm, but a very nice little homestead, which he was most interested in cultivating.'

'Yes — and?'

'Captain Hansen walked about the deck hoeing potatoes for three weeks, sir. Just north of Abu Musa he ordered all hands out into the potato field to hoe. But of course it didn't work.'

'So the captain hoed alone?'

'Alone, sir.'

Here the conversation halted as a corpse-white, deathly scared, barefoot Pat entered on the run.

'Excuse me, sir!' he gasped: 'The steward wants to kill the cook! He's taken his big shark knife, and is calling Ti-Pong 'Mr. Tai-Foon', and Ti-Pong is sitting on the floor crying!'

The captain didn't react visibly. Or so it seemed to me. But something must have happened inside him, for he sauntered out onto the poop and looked toward the galley.

'The shark knife?' he said to Pat.

'Yes, sir. The big shark knife.'

Then that huge, hippopotamian figure crossed to the ladder, to go down to the main deck. At the door to the galley a couple of men stood peering in. They seemed agitated.

'Excuse me, captain,' I said; 'but to go to the galley — isn't that a bit rash? The shark knife....'

He didn't reply, didn't even trouble to look at me. He climbed slowly down the ladder and walked toward the galley. Clearly the man lacked even the imagination to be afraid. He was a tower of massive, phlegmatic obtuseness. The men at the galley door looked by turns at him and into the deckhouse.

Then something happened. The two sailors screamed and fled. And out of the galley came la Fontaine. He was stark naked as from his mother's womb, and the shark knife was in his hand. Gingerly, almost fearfully, he laid it on the deck. Then, with the utmost caution, he walked over to the ratlines, at each step looking before him with the care of a tightrope walker.

The captain turned to me, his round face painted with astonishment.

'Mr. Jensen,' he said, 'why is he walking in such a remarkable manner?'

'So as not to step on the little Chinamen, sir,' I replied.

He nodded, as if it were all a matter of course. Now he had patently lost all interest in the episode, and climbed to the poop again.

Nearly all the crew stood clustered on the deck or forecastle, following the naked steward's progress up the ratlines. When he had reached the crosstrees, he sat down and stayed there. The poor cook — now more white than yellow — appeared in the doorway, and with narrowed eyes gazed up along the mainmast. Then he bent and picked up the shark knife from the deck, looked around in terror, and went in again. His whole form seemed to shine with the resolve: never again to sail over the same keel with white men.

One of the sailors, a slim, lithe Cuban with an uncommonly noble and appealing exterior, swung himself up into the ratlines; in a few seconds he had reached la Fontaine. They conversed for a time, then the sailor came down again. The steward remained motionless on the crosstrees.

'Hallo!' I called to the Cuban: 'What does he say?'

'He doesn't want to come down, sir. And he talks about some Chinamen who have eaten up his pepper and done something with some insect powder. He's very disturbed.'

The captain cast a surly look at the crosstrees.

'I'll have to speak to my wife about it,' he said. 'She has sailed as steward before. For all of me he can sit there till doomsday.'

Thus it happened that she took over la Fontaine's duties.

The Men

Give me that man that is not passion's slave....
— *Hamlet*

A short time later there was again fighting among the hands. And this time it was more serious than the affair between the carpenter and the ordinary Carlos, for more men were mixed up in it. On the whole it seems to have involved groups, or groupings of pugnacious men, athwart of race and nationality.

In general it amazed me that there was so little cohesion, so little solidarity in the forecastle. There was incessant hostility and bickering, eternal factional battles — between group and group, man and man, between races and colours.

Today it's easy to see that this lack of unified thinking, of cohesion and solidarity — all the passions, the splits and the power struggles, all the internal strife in the forecastle — was the sole reason why we aft were able to stay in power, in command of the ship, for as long as we did.

For when all was said and done, we were only four officers — soon no more than three — against the forecastle's almost twenty men. Yet for a long while we remained masters of the situation.

It began during the first mate's watch. But I heard the shouts, the tramping, and the din, and hurried up to the poop. The two combatants were the Cuban with the thin, learned face and the slender hands, and the rather blond man who had dismembered the live sharks with the aid of the cook's shark knife. He didn't have that cruel murder weapon now, but it soon transpired that he had another knife. Both men were in their forties and in good fighting trim. Of the Cuban I knew only that he was a good seaman, that his first name was Juan, and that he bore the historic name of Cortez as a surname. His opponent was the ship's sailmaker, and I had earlier formed the impression that he was white. However, that proved not to be the case; he was called Davis and was a half-caste, with a white Australian for a father. He was a burly fellow, rather square-set, and certainly a good deal stronger than Cortez. Nonetheless the slight, nimble Cuban appeared to have the upper hand: when I arrived on the poop, Davis was bleeding hideously from the eyebrow. He kept trying to get at the other with long, whistling swings — which either ended in the air about Cortez's head or were parried by one of his arms.

Cortez tried chiefly to avoid the heavy punches; when he hit back, it was with direct, fast, well-aimed jabs. With light dancing movements he kept beyond the other's reach, striking only when he was sure of his mark. He got him on the mouth, the jaw, the bridge of the nose, the eyes. Davis grew ever more senseless with rage, till it seemed that fury would blind him. Each time he struck out at Cortez, his own besmeared face was rammed by a new blow. You could hear the soft thuds clearly as the Cuban's knuckles met that bloody lump of flesh.

Then all at once the sailmaker stopped dead, thrust his right hand in his pocket, and brought something out. He held the thing before him at face-level, and I heard a faint metallic click. Something thin and shiny glittered in the sun, and with the clasp-knife in his hand he flew at his opponent. From the sailors massed as onlookers came a loud cry.

If, during the first phase of the battle, the fleet Juan Cortez had seemed to descend from agile Spanish bullfighters, now — once the long, thin knife-blade had entered the scene — he grew nimbler still. With bare fists he defended his life against the loathsome blade of the assassin. Swift and supple as a deer he eluded Davis's attack, and despite the weapon landed two or three more blows on his face.

Then disaster: the sailmaker caught hold of him and struck. A short, sharp cry came from the other, and all at once the left side of Cortez's shirt was dyed red. He tore himself loose and with his hand to his side sprang away, several paces off. Davis was still mad with fury, but now he acted faster and more consciously. Again he caught hold of the Cuban and raised his hand for a new thrust. At that instant there was a loud, savage yell, and swift as a shadow one of the crew jumped into the fight and seized his right wrist with both hands. It was the Malay — the sailor who, with the huge mulatto James Arrowsmith, had asked the third mate's leave to fetch Pat down from the skysail yard. Both fell headlong and rolled away down the deck. Then the sailmaker dropped the knife, which landed beyond reach of them both.

But in the same moment two men sprang on the Malay, and Juan Cortez pounced like a tiger on the knife. It went in a high arc over the rail and vanished into the sea. Then he planted his foot soundly in the face of the knife-wielder Davis. He was knocked down almost at once by one of the two who had attacked the Malay. Yet another two hurled themselves into the fray, and in a second almost the whole lee side of the main deck was a throng of fighting, shouting, cursing human bodies.

In truth it all happened so lightning-fast that the events themselves took less time than the minutes needed to recount them.

I looked at the first mate, who was now no longer to be distinguished from Abraham Lincoln. He was altogether unmoved by the bloody battle, and observed it with utter calm.

'Mr. Cox,' I said, 'this is your watch.'

For a second he fixed his dark eyes on me, full of pity and contempt. Then he returned his gaze to the throng of humanity on the deck.

'Beasts from the abyss!' he replied: 'Mr. Jensen, all these are things which come to pass of necessity and after the divine law. They shall kill and devour one another like sharks. Blood and murder is their lot. All shall be made manifest on the Last Day.'

'When the prices fall on the London Exchange?' I replied, almost palsied with rage at his scarcely seamanlike attitude.

He turned his high, thin, black-haired and black-bearded head to me, with the same expression of boundless moral disdain. He was a man sure of his case.

'First the sea shall have its dead,' he declared.

'To hell with the sea and to hell with the dead, Mr. Cox! It's the *living* I'm thinking of. I won't see the crew massacred!'

With deep, unyielding contempt he repled:

'You don't believe in God, Mr. Jensen. That is the whole of it. You yourself are one with these children of the abyss. You ought to die with them.'

'I believe in God, Mr. Cox — but possibly not the same god that you believe in.'

Down on the deck still more men had joined the fray. Now it was simply a chaos of all against all. Juan Cortez slumped against the hatch, his hands pressed to the wound in his side. The sailmaker had been struck on the back of the head with a plank, and lay hunched on the deck.

Later I found out why the two had flown at each other: it was partly a political, partly a practical disagreement. They were sitting side by side in the mess, and Cortez was a follower of the Russian Krapotkin, while Davis held with the German Karl Marx. They had been having a heated political discussion; then the tray of meat came their way. The Cuban sat first, and helped himself to a large piece of pure and boneless meat.

'I saw that piece first!' said Davis.

105

'It's mine!' replied Cortez.

Davis stuck his knife in the other's piece of meat and transferred it to his own plate. Juan took it back.

The fight had begun inside the forecastle and continued on deck. It had become a battle without aim or sense, an orgy of violence which made life sick and nasty and death meaningless.

'Mister,' I said; 'you are my superior. But this is your watch, and if you don't do your duty and stop the bloodbath, if you don't go down on deck, I shall enter every one of the idiotic words you've said into the log.'

He didn't even look at me.

'*You* may go down and stop the bloodshed among those human sewer rats,' he replied indifferently. Then he crossed the poop, cast a glance at the compass, and entered the charthouse.

I had no choice. I was obliged to descend the poop-ladder and intervene in the hell evolving below. And I didn't feel courageous. My heart was pounding, my feet were leaden with fright.

'Lay forward!' I shouted, once I stood on the deck. It had not the slightest force. I repeated the order time after time, but no one heeded it. It was a swarm, a hurricane, of the most sickening thing I know: uncontrolled human passion.

Then I noticed that someone stood motionless beside me. I turned and saw James Arrowsmith; he bent his head and spoke into my ear:

'Mr. Jensen, go back up to the poop.'

'What's that you say?' I replied, astonished.

'Go up to the poop, sir.'

He looked at me earnestly, gravely.

'Are you giving me orders, Mr. Arrowsmith? Really, this is going too far!'

'No,' he said, 'it's not going too far. You must go back up to the poop, mister. At once.'

'Have you gone mad, Arrowsmith? You can't give me orders!'

'It's not an order, Mr. Jensen.'

There dwelt an enormous will in him, and I felt the strength of it. It was like a physical pressure which emanated from him, making me weak and uncertain.

'What is it, then?'

'It's a piece of advice,' he said firmly: 'Good advice. You mustn't stay here on deck.

'It isn't because I like you, mister. It's because your life is in danger here. Go back up to the poop.'

'In danger?'

'Yes. Your life is in danger.'

He regarded me again with the same grave, penetrating look.

'I don't believe it,' I said.

He lowered his head and looked me in the eyes.

'You don't know what's happening on board this ship,' he said.

For a moment I felt as if dread would overwhelm me, so strong was the power, the unbendable will, which beamed from that huge figure.

'*What's* happening?' I said.

'You'll find out soon enough,' he replied.

For a moment we stood looking at each other.

Then I turned and went aft, up to the poop.

History

Seele des Menschen, wie gleichst du dem Wasser,
Schicksal des Menschen, wie gleichst du dem Wind.
— Goethe

If ever, in my old age, I become too weak to sail, if ever I'm left with
only the joys of mind and spirit — then I'll buy me a house and plant
a tree and write a book about the history of freedom.

It won't be a learned book, for I'm not a learned man. But it will
be an honest book, a true book. In a sense I've begun on this *History
of Freedom* already, as I try to record what befell *Neptune* and her
crew in 1899-1900.

To explain my meaning, I must first tell something about
myself; I shall be forced to deliver up my inmost, certainly my
deepest, and perhaps my only secret to the reader's mercy.

I'm quite an ordinary man, a bit taller than the average European, well-built — but no athlete, no giant. It is within that I'm
furnished so differently; my brain as it were lacks walls, floor, and
ceiling. The stars shine straight through this abode of reasonable,
ordered, normal thoughts. The sea, the trades, the monsoons — they
all come driving through this brain which is mine and no one else's.

I must explain more fully. As a child I grew up under the northern lights, just as in adulthood I have sailed for long years under the Southern Cross. I cannot say that I received the gift of 'second sight' in my cradle; nor have I been markedly sensitive or ecstatic, or known transcendental states of feeling or bodiless raptures.

No. Within me all has been balanced, aware — on the plane of *thought*. All has been fully conscious. Where the stars were concerned, the northern lights, the sea, the reindeer, the whales, the fish, the storm — the whole world of my childhood — I never *felt* the spirits, I *saw* them; for all that lives is of spirit. Many years passed before I understood that my brain was built differently from others' in this respect. It wasn't better, but different. This has been with me all my life — and thus it's not a matter of feelings, presentiments, or 'faith;' it's a matter, for me, of experience.

I sail all the seas of the globe. I have a few books, some worn notebooks, my navigator's papers. I have nothing else. But I'm *never* lonely, never forsaken. I need only the sight — only the thought of the ocean, the earth, the sky, to sense the spirits' unbounded closeness — closer than any friend or kinsman, warmer than any beloved. As I said: it's not a feeling, a dream — not ecstasy. It's a prodigious *awareness*, a vast clarity and calm. Infinite sobriety.

It is thus an intellective experience — not of thin, abstract thoughts, but of living thought, of spirit.

Of course as a sailor and navigator I have much to do with the sea and with the heavens. But I don't think in terms of a globe sailing through space, nor of dead, empty planets ruled by laws of mathematics and mechanics. For me the planets, earth, the stars are held in their cosmic places by an immense, conjunctive, creative, all-sustaining spiritual force.

I sense the same all-buoyant spiritual power within myself, in my inmost consciousness, in my all-embracing, living inspiration — my deepest, half-conscious *I*. The same infinite cosmic soul which dwells in the Milky Way and upholds it, is also my own, central *self*

— the inmost reality which causes me to *be*; it is my and the stars' existence.

In every person, in the lowest, the most brutal, most vulgar, I meet the same — suppressed, unconscious, abused — yet living spirit. In every animal and plant; in the wind, the sea, the mountains — this power resides in all things, from the tiniest straw to the Milky Way's unnumbered stars, from the atom's core to the ocean deeps and the infinitude of space.

No, I'm not lonely.

Always I'm enveloped by, swathed in this living spirit. It involves an abnormal *wakefulness*, a waking to absolute clarity. I see with my eyes this all-pervading, all-sustaining force in everything around me — in the flying fish, the gulls, each leaf on a tree, in the tidal ebb and flow, in the moon's complicated path as she embraces the water and sucks it to herself — and what I see is spirit, for it is the very force of life — the *élan vital*. It is the life-spirit, life itself, which forms my encompassment and my company.

Today a mathematician or an astronomer can calculate with the greatest exactness Mercury's position in the zodiac on the fourth of April in the year 2013. We know the earth's path and Saturn's position of two centuries ago; we know the mathematical laws and physical forces, and can express them in formulae, numbers, and graphs, we compute the wind's force in feet per second and the speed of the ocean waves in knots; but all our symbols and numerical relations, our log-tables and decimals — they are not the *thing*, not the living, all-sustaining spirit, not the spirit which upholds the cosmos. Our numbers and the relations between them are merely our translation of the reality, of the bird's flight, the starlight, the wind's force. They are reality's mighty, living, cosmic language rendered into that language of numbers, symbols, and formulae which our brains normally understand and speak.

We translate and interpret that reality by hieroglyphics and signs and numerical relations just as we capture, fix, and define the song of the spheres — music — as notes and symbols on a score. But none will claim that the page with its clefs, sharps, and flats is itself the music; for music is neither physically measurable air-waves nor ink on a lined paper, but living essence, the sprits' song, the discourse of the spheres.

Much as a musician hears music by reading a score, so — more or less — do I see the life-spirits face to face in the waves' foam, in the leaping fish, in the cloud drifting through the atmosphere — but also in a log-table, in the stars, or in a dandelion. That's what I mean by saying that my brain is differently constructed, differently built, from most people's — that it lacks walls, floor, and ceiling.

It took me many years to understand that what I saw in this way, I was alone in. Only as an adult did I learn not to mention it, to keep it to myself to avoid ridicule.

But I'm not always in this state of abnormal wakefulness and calm and lucidity. There are times at which my brain closes up — when my skull forms a solid barrier, so watertight that not even spirits or thoughts can penetrate the armour. Those are times of dejection, meaninglessness, confusion, darkness. For me, who am used to a cosmos where everything coheres, in which all, all has a clear and golden *meaning*, these times of perdition and meaninglessness weigh very heavy; they fill me with all the despair of hopelessness, with the hopelessness of despair.

Yes, I know these states of eclipse, but they are exceptions, caused by weakness and exhaustion, when thought has lost its power and the body its resilience; a century ago — in the still-mystical medicine of the seventeen hundreds — they would have ascribed the spirit's eclipse, its melancholy and impotence, to poisoned humours and rotten vapours permeating the nerves and brain. But for me such periods of despair are always followed by a new awakening, a deep renewal.

What most characterizes this state of awareness and lucidity is the experience of the *meaning of all things* — from the greatest cosmic relations and events to the very smallest. The world-soul, the life-spirit, pervades and sustains everything, from the furthest galaxy

111

to a snail and a blade of grass: the total, absolute creation; it is thus literally true that one sparrow shall not fall to the ground....This sense of the absolute meaning of all things is what restores my balance and my clarity after times of confusion and darkness. For meaninglessness is hell.

What's decisive is the meaning which fills human life — both the life of humankind: History — and the life of the individual: Fate.

History, world history, has its meaning, its goal; and humanity will reach that goal — but with the dreadful, the terrible adjunct that the road thither will be infinitely longer and far, far bloodier than we can bear to imagine. For me that goal — as most will agree, not least those furthest from my own experience of the purely spiritual nature of the cosmos — that goal is for men to share this planet in brotherhood, to divide the earth's riches among us in justice and in freedom.

This — to share the globe in peace and freedom and justice — this is humanity's meeting with itself.

But yet the road thither is a road of freedom, of choice; to choose one thing is to relinquish another, choice means loneliness — and freedom also means freedom for evil. Man's liberation must be man's own work. The road to that goal — of inhabiting the earth in brotherhood and justice — is one which we ourselves must walk; the gods can't walk it for us, for then it were not a road of freedom. And our way shall lead past abysses and into the depths, through deserts and over battlefields, through ruins and prison camps, with millions fleeing and hungry and homeless; our way shall lead to Evil's delusions, delusion's evils — and this road shall lead us to our meeting with ourselves.

This is History, it is freedom's road — and we walk this road in freedom, whether we desire freedom or no. The way will be filled with false guides, false leaders of men, seducers and false prophets — and we are free to choose the evil redeemers, to do them homage and to follow them, just as they are free to mislead us.

But this dark, bloody road of freedom, it is the road to humanity's meeting with itself.

The same all-buoyant, omnipresent spiritual power on which are borne the suns of the Milky Way and our own little solar system; which pervades each mussel in the deep and fills each sparrow with pulsating life; which fills the shark with unrest, hunger, and desire, and has given the lamb a timid and peaceable soul — this same spiritual force which drives the volcano to erupt and looses the cyclone, this force dwells also in the human interior. It fills the mind with dreams and visions, lets the Ninth Symphony arise in Beethoven's trembling heart and manic brain, it nourishes us with clear, pregnant images and thoughts — and it dwells in our very deepest, hidden, inmost *I* — in that mysterious, unknown spiritual midpoint — the immortal within us. In the typhoon's windless centre.

The single human life has a road as well; the same road as humanity's. It is the individual's meeting with himself — with his inmost spiritual *I* — with the cyclone's still interior within him.

And like the meteorological cyclone, this soundless inner storm centre too has a 'cyclone's eye' — that miraculous opening skyward, through which the stars become visible. With awesome power the low pressure blows the dense black storm-clouds aside to make a vast hole in the cloud cover, a landfall upward to fixed suns and known planets.

If Goethe spoke truly in the quotation which prefaces this chapter (and Goethe was a remarkably wise man) — if the human soul is indeed like water and human fate like the wind, this yields great vistas on human life.

The entire stanza goes:

Seele des Menschen, wie gleichst du dem Wasser!
Vom Himmel kommst du,
Zum Himmel steigst du,
Und wieder nieder zur Erde musst du!

Ewig wechselnd.
Seele des Menschen, wie gleichst du dem Wasser!
Schicksal des Menschen, wie gleichst du dem Wind!

Which means: 'Soul of man, how like unto water! / From heaven thou comest, / To heaven thou mountest, / And then again down to earth must thou go! / Ever changing. / Soul of man, how like unto water! / Fate of man, how like unto wind!'

That the immortal in man shifts its residence between heaven and earth is a thought older than Goethe; in the Gospel too the great rabbi asks his disciple: 'Who do men say that I am?' — and the disciple replies: 'That thou art Elijah.' And on this star which we inhabit there are hundreds of millions who share this thought — albeit of skin colours other than our own white: they are yellow, black, brown, and olive, and they dwell on other continents.

To me — the seaman on an eternal voyage, with all the round globe for a home — this is not strange, and I don't attach much weight to the differences between people; I don't despise the souls in those races which today are deprived of their lands, and who eat the crumbs which fall from the white man's table.

And to me these are not thoughts which I've puzzled out on the afterdeck under the stars during quiet watches, or read myself into during free hours in my cabin. They are simply things which I've seen. Unshakable experience. Thus the world is for me.

But now don't think me a dreamer, a visionary remote from life, unfit for earth and reality and the everyday. Not so: I read a log-table or a nautical almanac just as attentively, ply my earthly craft just as faithfully and responsibly, as any man who ever set foot on a deck.

But there are many men on the sea whose thoughts are their own.

The Rope (I)

There cometh a ship from the farthest sea . . .

Our poor, peaceable, mild-mannered cook was in fact known as 'Tai-Foon' from that day forward.

The steward la Fontaine had christened him, and the delirious, cyclonic name clung to him, just as the Belgian's own condition entrenched itself: his delirium became permanent, and in the ensuing weeks moved through all phases and variations. He had begun to converse in French with his little Chinamen, and seemed to have accepted them as a necessary and natural part of his existence. Worse were the traditional rats, snakes, and spiders which now likewise appeared, plaguing him till he crouched in a corner and howled with fright. Then again he would bury himself in invisible records and imaginary accounts; or quarrel loudly with ship-chandlers and clerks — whom he regarded without exception as criminals and cheats and embezzlers, and addressed in the tone the scoundrels rightly deserved. Yet he wholly changed his attitude toward 'Tai-Foon;' he not only ceased to suspect and threaten him, but developed such trust that the cook gradually became his true solace and support. Never again did he mention pepper or insect powder.

By and large he spoke French with poor Tai-Foon, who understood not a word — and Flemish with the ship-chandlers. He spoke English with me and Malay with the crew. He ate nothing, and never slept at night. La Fontaine was always active. And he mostly went around stark naked. There was only the captain's wife to take offence, and she had spent so much time at sea that it would have taken more than a nudist steward to impress her.

This singular person, whose chief interest was the banking and stock-market columns of the newspapers — along with the exchange rates — proved a thoroughly excellent steward; she kept track of everything, made a precise inventory of provisions and equipment, and patched, repaired, washed, and ironed the linen — something which la Fontaine, for obvious reasons, had sadly neglected of late. And she worked splendidly with our poor old philosopher Tai-Foon. I see that I've written 'old', but he was by no means far advanced in years; he must have been fifty-one at that time, and ran about lightly and nimbly in his pyjamas and paper slippers. Still, there was something endlessly ancient about his parchment-like yellow face and his narrow black eyes. It must have been his refined race, or even his exalted and ennobled culture, whose age one sensed. In any case, there was a superior calm and stoicism about him; the Belgian's menacing ballet with the shark knife he seemed to have wholly forgotten — or perhaps he had accepted it as a basically peaceful outgrowth of European forms of intercourse. Whoever knows a little about the British conduct in China will indeed scarcely wonder at his attitude. His free time Tai-Foon spent for the most part reading, very often in a shady place on deck — and he carried with him a fine library of Chinese and English literature. It was strange to find him engrossed in the German political and social philosopher Karl Marx, the pupil of Hegel.

Have I mentioned that he was an outstanding cook? Tai-Foon was an artist, both in the production of refined delicacies (to which, by the bye, we were not often treated on the *Neptune*) and in making bad, cheap, and extremely scant foodstuffs edible for the men in the forecastle. That the crew's miserable rations first passed through his hands must have been one reason why the hate pervading the ship didn't blaze up sooner. The fact is that the provisioning on my beloved *Sancta Vénere* was quite simply scandalous; the rations were considerably smaller than permitted, and their quality indescribable. This was because, as I've mentioned, both the captain and First Mate Cox were shareholders in the shipping firm and were thus interested in the lowest possible food costs. And if Captain Anderson had put up so long with the chronically drunk la Fontaine, it was not at all because the latter was an efficient steward, and even less because he was white. In economic respects Anderson was just as colour-blind as his fellow shareholder and first mate. La Fontaine sailed with *Neptune* because he was to an unusual degree a 'company man': he could be bribed from above to squeeze the money spent for food down to a level which would have made the captain of a slaver die of shame. What was bought in to be served to the forecastle was in truth scarcely fit for dog food. Only that virtuoso and master of a thousand arts, the revolutionary and mild-mannered Tai-Foon, kept the galley above water in a moral sense.

He seemed to enjoy having the captain's wife as steward, and whenever they talked about soups, sauces, and stews, something obviously happened to them both. Tai-Foon's expressionless mouth smiled, and her strange, pleasant face no longer bore the stamp of a passion for sums and columns of figures; the family's pathological greed and avarice left her and she grew beautiful as she and Tai-Foon bent over a pot together or sniffed at a pan of gravy. Of course the intelligent yellow wizard had an aim in all that he did; and the missus's newborn interest in the kitchen's joys brought a liberalization of the budget. Naturally this bounty applied only to us aft. We ate caviar, *foie gras*, and bamboo shoots.

The crew got the same half-rotten pig's fodder as before, and only Tai-Foon's arts with pungent sauces and soul-stirring condiments induced them to swallow it.

This new situation in the galley even affected la Fontaine's occupational interest, and one day he came aft to 'inspect the provisions,' as he put it. He was in buff as usual, and Mrs. Anderson, standing on the poop with her two children, didn't bat an eye at the sight. The Malay Huang — the sailor who had once wanted to fetch Pat down from the skysail, and had later wrested the clasp-knife from the sailmaker's hand when he wanted to kill Juan Cortez — was at the helm, and if possible troubled himself even less about the naked Belgian.

La Fontaine came into the charthouse and looked around contentedly.

'M-hm, mister!' he said with satisfaction: 'Here we have it all.'

'What?' I asked.

'The provisions. I just wanted to inspect them.'

He scrutinized the charthouse from floor to ceiling with the same contentment as before. Then he took pencil and paper from the table, seated himself in the saloon, and noted down all that he saw around him. Slowly and mumblingly he listed the provisions exactly, and only presently did I realize that he thought he was in the galley stores — and that he actually *saw* every single thing he thought of: spoiled potatoes, green soap, rotten cabbage; all the dog food, the putrid meat and rancid salt pork, intended for the forecastle; the liquor which, with his bribes from the officers, he had laid in for himself; kerosene for the lamps, wicks, wood alcohol, canned fruit for the officers' mess, canned milk for the captain's children, tobacco, butter in cans, matches, hard tack, flour sacks with mites and maggots, sewing materials and mouldy vegetables — he saw it all, everything, stored and stacked around him in that tiny room on the poop deck. Not a thing was missing.

Thus several days passed, with lovely weather and a steady wind. *Sancta Vénere* sailed like a dream, and the whole seemed to confound all evil portents and forebodings.

Even our half-dead Javanese carpenter, van Harden, was better. He was taking food, and had begun to talk a little — in a mixture of

Malay, Dutch, and English; then one day he came staggering out on deck. With the bandage like a turban round his head he looked like the ghost of a murdered Hindu.

Shivers ran down my spine as I saw him met his foe and adversary, the ordinary Carlos, who still had his arm in a sling and a patch on his left eye. But nothing happened. Both were doubtless too battered to resume hostilities. But they were biding their time. With slant looks they scowled at each other like panthers. Their carnivore blood seethed within them.

Carlos's eye was decidedly better, but it still squinted toward the bridge of his nose. Van Harden's right thumb must have lamed or destroyed some of the muscles which converge the two fields of vision. In any case, he saw double if he used both eyes, so I had to let him keep the dark sea-rover's patch. It became him very well. The bite on his cheek I had cleaned and sterilized daily, and the inflammation had subsided, though the bloodred scar had a sinister look.

After the latest free-for-all on deck I had a number of extra jobs, but they were by and large minor. Even the knife-thrust in Juan Cortez's side wasn't serious. The long, thin blade had not pierced the muscles or the peritoneum; the thrust had entered the skin just over the hip, passed along the side muscles and out through the skin at the back. I put a couple of stitches over each opening, disinfected and plastered the wounds, and left the rest to God and nature — both of whom seemed to be doing their duty.

Pat, of course, was a problem in himself.

I don't know if there exists such a thing as 'ship's psychiatry;' but if so, Pat was my first patient. And I do know that there are wounds and hurts to the human heart which can't be sewn up, can't be repaired with needles and catgut and sterilized clamps, aseptic compresses and plaster. The hours on the mainmast head had not merely held Pat in irreparable terror of death; they had loosed all the appalling terror of life which he had amassed during his wretched fourteen years. And besides being the embodiment of universal dread and loneliness and despair, a sort of deputy Crucified One for us all, and hence an objective problem for metaphysics and psychiatric philosophy; he had also become a personal, a private problem for me — my unwillingly adopted problem child. In a sense he bore the guilt of all, but at the same time he was one living, personal human child, bearing his own life's frightful burdens.

The trouble was that he mercilessly insisted on being my 'son'.

That didn't suit me. My life was my own. It didn't belong to others; it had its own course, its own path, its own traverse. I was bound to no one, nor wished to be. I must be independent, and none should depend on me. My life was a coherent sequence of new decks, new cabins, new, brief sojourns on land between new voyages, new ships, new crews. Haven't I said that I should never marry, never leave a sorrowing widow and breadless children?

Physically Pat was much improved since moving in amidships with old Tai-Foon. It was obvious that he was on the officers' diet and not on the crew's slops; he ate as much as an undernourished fourteen-year-old can wolf down; he also received some of the milk intended for the captain's children Mary and Bobby, as well as fruit, chocolate, and canned, genuine butter.

There can be no doubt that Tai-Foon's sun-dried old heart had its weaknesses and soft spots. At bottom his philosophic, calloused heathen soul bore a deeper likeness to the great Galilean rabbi than all the flourishing missionaries who, in the name of the London Exchange, were flooding his Chinese homeland — the Middle Kingdom — with their European spiritual pollution. Tai-Foon's pious heathen heart housed many gods and many thoughts — and it also had room for Pat from Soho. Then, too, our cook was an expert on social conditions in London's East End, and had a clear idea of the cabin boy's background.

In short: Pat was gaining weight. He looked good.

Still: Food didn't help. He grew rounder-cheeked and visibly stronger. But it was neither Arrowsmith, who had saved his life, nor

Tai-Foon, who fed him, that Pat named as his father. It was I, for I had consoled and tended him.

The dread and homelessness survived the bloated, underfed London belly; it lay deeper than the lack of proper proteins, fruit, and fat. The earthly nourishment from Tai-foon did make good the material deficits in the small, half-famished body; but the mental distance between the highly intellectualized, middle-aged man and the primitive European street urchin, who in fact couldn't read his own tongue, was far too great. And Pat was no mere fourteen-year-old; in much he was no more developed than a child of seven.

Arrowsmith he feared because of the mulatto's great, self-confident will and enormous physical strength.

For the orphaned, terrified, godforsaken Pat only I remained; and so, despite all the goodness and kindness which he received from old Tai-Foon, it was I whom he adopted as 'father.' He showed me his devotion in all conceivable ways; were I standing watch, Pat would suddenly pop up with sweet, strong, hot tea; were I lying below and reading, he might come to ask if I wanted something from the galley. He would have much preferred to sleep in my cabin, even if it had meant lying on the floor.

He did fine waiting at table, though not nearly so well as the intelligent and grown-up Moses had done. It was painful to watch him serve the red-faced idiot of a third mate, but Pat did it bravely and politely.

Thus passed the next few days after the big fight.

Sancta Vénere sailed like an angel, and day after day we averaged from thirteen to fifteen knots.

Only one thing happened which I still recall, and it was on the same day that la Fontaine sat in the house on the poop listing the provisions stored there.

The Malay sailor Huang stood at the helm, and all at once he shouted to me.

'Mister! Mr. Jensen, sir!'

I went out onto the poopdeck.

'Yes?'

'There's something adrift off the starboard bow, sir.'

I glimpsed a dot, and went back into the charthouse for the binocular glass.

'Lord!' I said; 'it can't be true!'

'Yes, mister,' replied Huang; 'it's a man.'

I went over to the companionway and called down.

'Captain! I must ask you to come up, sir.'

He was on deck at once. I handed him the glass and pointed in the direction of what I had seen. He stood awhile with the glass to his eyes. Then he turned to me.

'There are two of them,' he said; 'remarkable.'

He addressed a word to the helmsman, who swung the wheel around, and then:

'We'll lower the second starboard boat, mister.'

The ship lay to.

When we had the boat down, I took four men: the Malay Huang, the Chinese Lee, the Arab Ahmed, and the coal-black Congolese André Legrand — all able-bodied. From both temperament and principle I shun the customary yelling and roaring used by most coxswains to induce the oarsmen to row. They really don't row any faster under the obligatory cascade of oaths and curses from the mate. I merely informed them that the two people drifting in the swells might yet be alive, and that every second could be vital. The sailors rowed like demons, and my back was almost broken by the jerk of the boat each time they dipped their blades into the water and pulled.

In four or five minutes we had reached the castaways. They were a young man and a young woman. Both were wearing life jackets; both were dead. The sharks hadn't touched them. To drown while afloat in a life preserver takes a long time, and must be a horrible death. The man's beard and hair were blond, the young woman was dark-haired. They must have been dead for three or four days, and the pallor of their faces was frightening.

122

If the two had kept so near one another, it was because they were linked by a line several fathoms long. That may well have been the last thing they did, to knot the rope fast to both their life belts. Thus they kept company and didn't drift asunder.

André Legrand and Lee took the bodies up into the lifeboat, and very quietly we rowed back to the *Neptune*. No one spoke. It was as if the meeting with the two young dead, and the sight of the tie which bound them, had made quite a strong impression on the whole rather calloused band of young seamen which, despite all, we were. Not least did the rope which kept them joined in death have this moving effect.

We heaved the boat up along the ship's side and laid the bodies on the hatch. Everyone gathered to see them. I noticed someone beside me, and looked up. It was the big, athletic mulatto James Arrowsmith; he stood perfectly motionless, as if cast in bronze, and stared at them. Never in my life shall I forget the expression on his face. It was one of absolute stillness and inwardness. An immobility, a bitterness, of which I've never seen the like. One would have thought that the young dead woman with the wet, dark hair was his own beloved.

The mates too came down to the main deck, and for once Dickson behaved like a human being. He kept his mouth shut. The first mate, Jeremy Cox, stood right next to the dead. The look framed by his long hair and beard was one of mingled scorn and triumph. For him the two lovers were clearly but an image of the evanescence and vanity of all things. He shone with a deep disdain for all human destiny, all human love.

'Well, mister,' I said to that smug, Lincolnesque person: 'The sea gives back its dead?' Slowly he turned his bony face to me:

'Mr. Jensen,' he replied: 'Wait till the next hurricane!'

After this menacing, insinuative reply he turned and went back up to the poop. Contrary to his wont he glanced at the compass.

Even the captain came down to the deck to look at them. He wasted no time, and the blue pig's-eyes lacked any trace of interest.

'Is the sails here?' he said loudly.

'Yes,' replied Davis.

'Get them sewn up as soon as possible, so that we can give them a decent burial.'

'Aye, aye, sir.'

The captain looked more closely at the bodies, then turned to me.

'Funny, Mr. Jensen!' he said: 'The sharks haven't bothered with them. Funny! But such things happen. I once found a Dutchman who had been swimming for two days in the Indian Ocean without the sharks' touching him, though the sea was so full of the monsters that you could have walked to Singapore on their backs. He developed a bad case of nerves afterward.'

Captain Anderson turned and went aft. I noticed that he was wearing slippers.

The next moment I felt someone holding my hand. I looked down; Pat was beside me. He looked at the dead, biting his lower lip. He was white about the mouth and nostrils.

'Hey, mister,' he said; 'why did they tie themselves together?'

'Probably so that they wouldn't be parted even if they died.'

He didn't answer, but went on holding my hand.

'Pat,' I said, 'this is my watch. Will you come aft with tea in a little while?

'Aye, aye, mister .'

After dinner they were both sewn up in the same canvas, with large lumps of coal at their feet. And when the captain had read the service over them, they were sent overboard. Neither had any identification.

Book Two

The Ascension of Jeremiah

> Je suis sain d'esprit, je suis St. Esprit.
> — Van Gogh

Sancta Vénere sailed like an angel.

Off our bow one morning we saw a column of smoke on the horizon, as from a burning ship. In a couple of hours we could descry that it came, not from a sailing vessel, but from a steam 'ship' — one of those slow, ridiculous craft whose sole task should be that of tugging real ships in and out of the harbours, but which today are allowed to pollute the seas: heavy, lumpy, and smelling just as terrible as they look. By dinnertime we had overtaken the flatiron, which was Dutch; and true to tradition Stavros, the Greek deck boy, went to the bulwarks and waved a broom as we passed it, to remind those on board that the Dutch government is said to have declared that Holland would sweep all other nations off the seas. As we sailed to leeward of the filthy thing, we received in reply a smarting cloud of coal vapour, like the stink of a locomotive. It groaned on through the long, clear swells as if it were suffering from a combination of heart disease and asthma.

A couple of hours later the iron box had almost disappeared.

It may be that I'm conservative — like most seafolk; but anyhow it's a consolation that these things will never compare with sailing ships for speed and size.

I stood at the taffrail, watching the steamer disappear, as I thought with concern about my 'foster son.'

Pat was truly the most ignorant human being I had ever met. A Tierra del Fuegan, an Australoid, a Bushman is at least versed in the myths and legends of his tribe, knows about the moon and the stars; he knows that there's something above all this, he's mindful of the spirits of earth and sea and of his fathers. He can worship them, pray, fish, hunt. Our ordinary seaman Lilly, a Fiji Islander with teeth filed to points, was at twenty-one a real sage. He could stand at the helm, tie every possible knot, and knew the name of every detail of ship, rigging, and tackle. He had his forebears' religion, had eaten human flesh and was tattooed all over, could 'cuss out' our sixteen-year-old Greek deck boy Stavros in English, and climbed like a god in the rigging. He also had the temperament of a tiger and could stand on one leg for hours at a time. The name Lilly he by no means owed to any beautiful or feminine traits — he was as ugly as the most frightful of Australian aborigines; he had probably picked the name himself because he liked its sound. Lilly was a promising seaman in every respect, and he was murderous and good at languages and knew much about the spirits.

Only poor Pat from London — a hub of white culture — knew absolutely nothing. Could do nothing. Was nothing. His ignorance was fabulous; he had no tribal history, no myths, no religion. I doubt that he had been christened. Pat spoke his own Cockney like a pig, and of course didn't know one letter of the alphabet. He knew nothing of the spirits of sea or moon or wind. He couldn't even pray.

I was about to say that he was a *tabula rasa*. But *that* he was not. Pat possessed a ghastly wisdom of hunger, filth, homelessness, malnutrition, crime, terror, vice, violence, disease, imprisonment, and madness. And this knowledge of life's snake-pits was joined with innocence, common sense, and naïveté. He was privy to the blackest mysteries and ignorant of all else, but his capacity for devotion was matchless.

The one with whom I could best talk about this was the old Chinaman, Tai-Foon.

As I stood thus at the taffrail, I remarked that someone was beside me. It was the captain; once again it struck me how strange it was that that mountain of flesh should move in such total silence. He turned his face to me, and the small pig's-eyes were, if possible, even more phlegmatic than usual; they expressed not even lack of interest, only emptiness.

'Mr. Jensen,' he said, 'I've known the first mate for years, and I can't imagine what's come over that gloomy, silent man. Now he talks like a waterfall all day long.'

'I've observed the same thing, sir. At the beginning he didn't say a word; he seemed uncommonly melancholic — perhaps the most taciturn person I've ever met. But after some days at sea, Mr. Cox began to talk. It's also remarkable *what* he says, sir.'

'Right, mister. Most remarkable.'

'He would gladly see us all drowned, sir.'

Captain Anderson was silent awhile, then he said:

'He has intimated the same in regard to me. He wished me a watery grave, down with the Beast of the Abyss.'

'Really, sir?'

'It's not often a captain is privileged to hear such a thing from his first mate.'

'No, sir. Very seldom indeed.'

He paused, then went on:

'Today he has struck work.'

'Beg pardon, sir?'

'First Mate Cox refuses to do ship's work, Mr. Jensen.'

The captain had ended our thoughtful conversation, and stood for a few seconds with open mouth. He looked like the corpse of an idiot. Then he disappeared noiselessly. What the captain had just confided was no news to me.

Not for several days had Jeremy Cox stooped to commerce with earthly things. He didn't so much as peek at the compass, cast not a glance at chart or positions, didn't touch an instrument, didn't open the log. Whether we were doing two knots or twelve was no concern of his. Canvas, tackle, helm, rigging were mere earthly phantasms. Nor did he sleep. He was a prophet, an archangel, with no need of rest. The only thing he did was to talk. He talked around the clock, spewed forth his Old Testament threats and curses, in a voice of thunder wished us down to the sharks, one and all.

He bathed us in vitriol, grilled us in hell, and made soup of us in Gehenna. And he did it with glee; Wrath — the Great Wrath — was come, the Last Day would be spewed forth from the sea, and Behemoth and Leviathan would possess our lost souls and unclean bodies.

What had happened, I suppose, was that the Biblical solace with which, through many silent years of black melancholy and despair, he had filled his desperate and darkened soul — that this had broken through his muteness with volcanic force. Hopelessness and taciturnity were transformed into fire. In any case there wasn't much light.

He often conversed with the steward, la Fontaine; the latter — who had not the least interest in things spiritual, and whose unhappy, lonely life had for years consisted solely of liquor — not only listened to him, but confirmed that you were surrounded by devils of earth and sea wherever you went on the *Neptune*. He doubtless saw before and around him, with the intense iconographic force of his delirium, all that Jeremiah Cox mentioned — just as clearly as the rest of us saw masts and rigging, or as he himself had seen the provisions in the charthouse. It was dumbfounding to see the deliriant and the maniac strolling the main deck together — pictures twain of man's boundless confusion over his own state.

But the first mate still took his meals with the officers aft, and was then calmer — though the threats and innuendoes continued.

Then one day it happened.

From my cabin I heard an enormous to-do on deck. I ran up to the poop and looked down. The whole crew was gathered on the main deck in a big circle, yelling and shrieking with laughter or with horror. In the centre of the ring were the steward and the first mate, now both of them naked.

Mr. Cox was dancing.

It was a sight which hell itself could not have invented. Imagine Abraham Lincoln's head on a white-skinned body as shaggy as a giant wolf's. The black beard passed unbroken into the hair on his chest and belly. He was indescribably gaunt and sinewy, and the pale skin against the hair of his body made him resemble a grotesque woodcut in black and white. He was dancing with bowed knees and stooped back, and at each step he stamped fiercely on the deck with his big, naked feet.

As he danced he cried in a strange, singsong tone:

'Even as King David bared himself like a woman and danced before the temple of the Lord, so do I dance for you, Baal-worshippers and heathens!

'In thanksgiving to the Lord of Hosts do I dance like David through the holy streets of Jerusalem; for you, for my people, for the tribe of Judah which is fallen into idolatry, I dance!'

Now and then he would right his back and stretch his white arms toward the sky as the steps of the dance continued:

'Even as King David do I dance for the Lord of Sabaoth!'

One or two of the spectators began to clap in time to the mate's dancing, and were soon followed by more. It greatly excited him, and he quickened the tempo.

'Generation of vipers!' he roared: 'Children of the Abyss and of the Deep! Soon shall the crabs and fishes eat out your eyes from the hollows of your heads! The great Satan of the Sea and the sharks, your brethren, shall digest you — the molluscs and the mussels suck on you — ah, ye sons of Beelzebub!'

Then all at once he stopped, raised his right hand heavenward and clenched the left one menacingly at the seamen:

'Ye have mocked a man of God, a holy man whom He sent unto you, even as He sent Jonah to Nineveh! But I, I! — shall not be swallowed up by the whale!'

The menacing attitude became triumph, and again he began to dance, this time a quiet, stately measure — almost like a sort of triumphal polonaise.

'And the Lord shall take up His servant alive unto heaven, in a chariot of fire, in a fiery chariot will He take him!'

Then the steward joined in the shouting. La Fontaine had a far more powerful voice than one would expect, and he cried in the language of his childhood, in French. The effect was so surprising that even Mr. Cox froze for a moment.

'I see it! I see it!' shrieked the Belgian: 'The chariot of fire is coming on the clouds!'

Hardly any understood the words, but they all grasped his meaning, for he pointed at the sky as he yelled. The two joined hands, and now the dance became wild, ecstatic. The crew appeared to find the scene no longer comic, but frightening. At all events, it was a rather sombre circle which witnessed the outbreak of these Neptunian powers of hallucination and madness.

And for many of the crew there was no distinction between lunacy and contact with the divine. Medicine men, wizards, nocturnal orgies and wild ritual dances, devils and demon possession — these had been natural parts of their childhood lives. It was almost solely the whites who had no link with the supernatural.

Yet now, strangely enough, it was precisely two white men who were touched — if not by the supernatural, then at least by the subnatural, by the lowest spirits in Neptune's kingdom.

The first mate let go of la Fontaine.

'Behold, I am taken up alive into the band of the saved, unto the Hosts, unto the angels, archangels, powers, thrones, seraphim, and cherubim; while ye shall rot in the brine!'

With his arms flapping like a giant bird's he now began to go in circles on the deck, repeating:

'I am taken up alive unto the Kingdom of Heaven!'

'He is taken up alive!' cried the steward, this time in English. I still see those two before me, pictures of despairing mankind's total break with reality — our answer to our mysterious, incomprehensible circumstances. Each in his pristine, eccentric loneliness had had no more to lose than his reason, and now it was accomplished.

'To the Kingdom of Heaven on the Last Day!' cried the mate, and stopped dead. Then he did something which only a seaman can do: he grabbed the ratlines with one hand and swung himself, light as a monkey, up onto the bulwarks. There he stood, six feet six, naked, white, and hairy.

'For your sins!' he cried.

He let go of the ratlines, stretched his arms heavenward, and shrieked with all the force of his lungs — a long yell of pain. Then he flew into the air.

The foam was whipped up by two tail fins; a dorsal fin cut through the surface. A white, long-stretched belly glinted.

At dinnertime the trembling Pat set the table for four.

The Captain

Neptune, then, is no longer home and world for thirty souls — only for twenty-nine.

The captain never mentioned the incident; it was I who entered it into the log. In fact, he never again touched on the subject of Jeremy Cox. Of course they had known each other for years, were co-owners of the vessel, had the same interest in bank and stock-exchange dealings; perhaps there was something in Captain Anderson's unknown interior which forbade him to speak of the other — something having to do with feelings.

It was indeed remarkable that this should happen just to the first mate. But then one can likewise ask: who else in the world should it have happened to? I thought of him a good deal after the mishap; for all his avarice, for all his forlorn confusion, the originally silent and sombre Cox was a man of soul.

I took a great deal of care with Pat; first I taught him to read and write. It went so easily that I was soon convinced that the boy had a good mind, if only it received the nurture to develop. As a one-time schoolmaster I enjoyed this simple teaching in my off-watch hours. Pat was a boundlessly grateful pupil, and I augmented his 'schooling' with elementary arithmetic and with facts I remembered from world history and geography. But above all I told him (and this he liked best of all) myths and legends — of Odysseus, Samothrace, Jonah in the belly of the whale, the Flying Dutchman, and much else. The episode of the first mate had of course left a strong impression, and his weak nerves were in need of other influences. Indeed for mathematics and geography we had fine equipment on board, and Pat's unused brain proved ever more receptive. It did him good.

It also did me good.

It gave my thoughts healthier trains and better occupations than they were otherwise inclined to at the time.

For me Mr. Cox's death had had something frightening about it, and even the baroque circumstances in which it took place had no comic or liberating effect.

My perennial dread of the sea was markedly stronger than usual, and now it pressed all the way up to the surface of my consciousness. I felt the terror throughout my waking hours. We were in the midst of the typhoon season.

On top of this, something was going on in the forecastle, something mysterious and opaque; no one aft knew what it was. But situations and incidents arose so often that none could fail to sense that something was afoot.

The captain had lapsed into his old taciturnity, and was more reserved than ever. But his look had changed; it was more watchful, and he was on deck far oftener than had earlier been his wont. He sometimes walked the whole ship, even to the forecastle deck, and it wasn't for the sake of the prospect over the blue tropical sea. He was observing the men. Something had happened to him. But he never said a word.

The atmosphere forward was so tense and so laden as to leave no doubt that the men's threatening, hate-filled air was indeed the expression of something concrete. Several fist fights occurred, but left no serious injuries. My needles and forceps were allowed to rest in peace. Most frightening was the silence. To tell the truth, I was so afraid that I needed all my strength of will to venture amidships or forward. Just to go to Tai-Foon's galley was enough for me. Still,

135

I went now and then to borrow some of his English sociological literature.

What was actually taking place in the forecastle was a power struggle, between two or perhaps three groups. But I didn't know that then.

One day an incident arose between the third mate Mr. Dickson and his old adversary, the Malay Huang. The mate used the occasion for revenge, and knocked the Malay down. I did not witness this part of the spectacle; when I arrived a quarrel was in full swing between Dickson and the big mulatto James Arrowsmith.

'This is one of many things you'll regret before long, mister,' said Arrowsmith.

The third mate replied with a cascade of oaths.

'You damned son of a whore, you filthy nigger, I'll teach you discipline, I'll show you who's in charge here, you rotten brown bastard. I'll make your nigger blood flow....'

Those were the first words I heard.

'I am of royal blood,' replied Arrowsmith; 'which is more than you are, you louse of a third mate.'

'Are you calling me a louse?' shrieked Dickson.

'I'm not *calling* you a louse; you *are* a louse.'

The officer seized a rope-end from the hatch coamings and struck Arrowsmith hard across the face. With one blow the mulatto knocked him to the deck, where he lay senseless.

The rest took place almost before I knew what was happening. Suddenly the captain stood before Arrowsmith, and it seemed that he merely raised his hand; the other crashed backward and rolled a couple of times over the planks. In disbelief he got to his knees and sent the captain a stare of ineffable astonishment and hate.

'I know you, Captain Anderson,' he muttered: 'You're the biggest, bloodiest swine that ever sailed a ship! And I'm not the only one on board who knows you and your murders. But you'll get what you deserve, you Satan!'

He was upon Anderson at once, and was again knocked to the deck. He took longer to rise this time, but attacked once more; all the lower part of his face was bloodied. What happened next, I should never have thought possible: the captain seized him by the hips, by the belt at both sides; lifted the giant into the air above his head — and dashed him full force to the deck.

Arrowsmith lay there.

The third mate had got to his feet, and staggered aft. I helped him up the ladder to the poop. The captain slowly followed.

On the poop he turned to Dickson.

'You are the biggest idiot I've ever sailed with,' he said; 'I wish *you* had gone overboard instead of the first mate.'

'Well, sir,' he replied.

Then the captain addressed us both:

'From now on none of the officers goes on deck unarmed. Understand?'

'Aye, aye, sir.'

From that day forward we always went with firearms on us.

The Dutchman

Who can sail without the wind....

'Are you fond of Mozart?'

It was Mrs. Anderson, our new acting steward, who addressed me as I stood on the poop surveying our floating world of sail, rigging, and deck planks.

'Of course, madam. Who isn't fond of Mozart?'

'I heard you playing him last night.'

'Lord, the caterwauling I do on the violin, you can't call that 'playing.' Did I disturb you?'

'Quite the contrary, Mr. Jensen. It was lovely to hear music again. The way we live, there's never occasion for that.'

'You're really fond of music?'

'Especially Mozart. I console myself with him.'

'Do *you* need consolation, madam?'

'We all need consolation, mister.'

She stood silent for a moment, thinking about it. Then she turned her face to me, open, questioning:

'But perhaps you don't, mister?'

'There's so much to console oneself with,' I replied: 'I like to stand at the helm; I like the sea, though I'm afraid of it; I have my music, I have books — a few, at least; I like to sail as second mate, and I love the stars. Besides, I know that nothing is meaningless, all is a great journey toward an end.'

'I envy you, Mr. Jensen,' she replied slowly: 'But tell me one thing: Why do you sail as second mate? After all, you've commanded ships yourself?'

'I had my first command at twenty-seven — six years ago. But I've since discovered that I'm happiest in my present berth.'

She thought it over.

'I hope you'll continue to play a bit during your free watches,' she said.

'If it disturbs no one, of course I'll play now and then.'

'I miss music greatly when I'm at sea. But this is one of our last voyages. Soon the children must go to school and get a proper education, and then we'll settle down in New York. The city has a good music life. My husband doesn't need to sail any more. We have more than enough for our wants.'

'Then you can seek solace in the concert halls, madam; that will be quite another thing from my wretched fiddling.'

She was silent for a bit, then she smiled:

'Each seeks consolation in his own way. La Fontaine had his liquor and the first mate had his Bible and his prophets of doom ....Some console themselves with a great dream.'

'And some with reality,' I added.

She stood for a time looking out over the sea.

'It will soon be dinnertime, Mr. Jensen,' she said abruptly: 'Tai-Foon has made something to console us with.'

'Who was the Flying Dutchman?'

Pat had come down to my cabin with tea. He set down the teapot and the cups and regarded me with alert, curious eyes.

'He's one of the ocean's evil spirits, Pat. The Flying Dutchman is homelessness and unrest. He bodes misfortune to all who see him. In a sense he's every seaman's fate. Why do you ask, Pat?'

'The steward said he'd seen him.'

'Oh.'

'Mister, can't you tell about the Dutchman.'

'You see, it's bad luck to talk about him too. If you speak of him, you risk seeing him, and the sight of his ship of death brings storm and shipwreck and mishap. Old seamen never mention him. Some have seen him two or three times and survived the shipwrecks. It's not a good idea to tell about him, Pat.'

'Yes, but mister! Where does he sail?'

'In all the oceans. He's been seen in the North Sea and in the North Atlantic too, but he mostly keeps to the waters around the Cape of Good Hope. There's often rough weather in those parts.'

'Like around Cape Horn?'

It struck me how fast Pat had changed of late; he was much more alert, caught up in the things around him — though of course he was still unstable and easily frightened.

'No,' I said; 'it's not so stormy as off Cape Horn, but it can be very bad there too. There are many sou'westers, and if you're coming from the Orient, it's often hard or almost impossible to round the Cape. With the ships they had back then, there were certainly times when they couldn't, or they'd tack in the head wind for weeks without leaving the spot.'

'Back then?' said Pat: 'I thought he was sailing today.'

'He sails today too.'

'But why did you say 'back then,' Mr. Jensen?'

'Because the Dutchman became the Flying Dutchman a long time ago. He's been sailing for four hundred years now.'

'Four hundred years!'

'And he'll go on sailing as long as there's a sea, as long as there's brine to sail in.'

'That means forever, then.'

'Not forever, but a long time,' I replied.

'And he's sailed for four hundred years already. Why's that, mister?'

'Because it's four hundred years since it happened.'

'Since what happened?' he persisted.

'He cursed God,' I said.

Pat stared at me, deeply shocked.

'He cursed God?'

'Yes.'

'Why did he do that?'

'Well, you see, the Dutchman was a very rich captain who owned the ship he sailed. He had made many voyages to the Orient, sold goods there and bought valuables in India — gold and precious stones and fine cloth and carpets. Spices were also immensely rare and costly in those days, and back home in Holland he sold them at a huge profit. All his life he had been sailing and trading, and had amassed a great fortune.'

'So he had no reason to curse God?'

'No.'

'What was his name?'

'Vanderdecken.'

'But why did he do it?'

Pat was one big question-mark now.

'Why did he do it, mister?'

'Well, you see: Vanderdecken had again been to India or China, and had his ship filled with valuables. She was laden with spices and with treasures — several hundred tons. Enough to make everyone on board rich. His ship had cannons to defend herself against pirates and the Portuguese, for there was a war with Portugal.'

'Were they attacked?'

'No.'

'What happened, then?'

'Vanderdecken had such great treasures on board that he knew this would be his last voyage. He didn't need to sail any more, he had enough wealth to settle down peacefully on shore and eat, drink, and be merry. At home he had a wife and a son, and he didn't need to work any more.'

'And still he cursed God?'

'Yes.'

'I don't understand, mister.'

'The ship was coming from the Orient, and when they came to round the Cape of Good Hope, things went the way they do at Cape Horn; you know that ships can tack against the sou'westers for weeks on end. There are ships which have plied against the storm for six or seven weeks, until the crew hadn't the strength to go aloft any more. Until all the men were exhausted.

'South of Africa Vanderdecken hit a storm from the southwest, and he couldn't get past the Cape. This was four hundred years ago, Pat.'

'Yes?'

'Vanderdecken was a hard man and a stubborn man, and he feared neither God nor the saints. For nine weeks the ship fought the wind off the Cape of Good Hope, and the captain cursed and blasphemed and swore. The sails blew out of their bolt ropes, but he bent new sails, and he swore that he wouldn't give up though he should stay there tacking till the Last Day, till the hour of Judgment. And when Vanderdecken had made up his mind, no one could budge him. He was not old, so he was a strong man, used to having his way. He drank his beer, sang foul songs, and said to hell with everything. One of the masts went overboard, but Vanderdecken didn't give in.

'The storm rose to a hurricane.

'The crew was exhausted, and begged him to fall off and seek a haven till the storm subsided. But the captain refused; he cursed and swore that neither God nor the devil nor any storm at sea should cow him. When the crew tried to talk him over, he killed the first mate. He knocked him down and threw him overboard. Then he went up to the afterdeck and swore by the Holy Cross which his wife wore around her neck that he should conquer the storm and heaven and hell, even if he must tack south of the Cape for all eternity. Meanwhile the hurricane grew, and the sea was a hell of foam and breakers and darkness and flashing lightning. All the spars went overboard, and the lifeboats were pounded to matchwood. And amid it all Vanderdecken drank his brandy and sang his ungodly songs.'

'Was he mad, mister?' Pat broke in.

'In a way he certainly was. We all have attacks of madness now and then — and in Vanderdecken it expressed itself like that.'

'Go on!'

'Vanderdecken placed himself on the afterdeck with a pistol in hand to intimidate the crew, and there he began to mock and curse God and the Saviour. He cried: "Jesus — Satan! God in hell! The devil take you! To hell with God! I curse Thee, God! I curse Thee! I curse Thy Son, and I curse the Virgin Mary! I damn you all to Satan and to Hell!" '

'But mister, why did he curse them?'

Pat had drawn up his legs under him and sat far inside the bunk, leaning against the bulkhead.

'Because he thought God had sent the hurricane to keep him from getting home to Holland with his treasures and his riches.'

'Then what happened?'

'The crew came again and begged him to fall off. "Captain," they said: "We must turn, we must come about. If you keep trying to round the Cape, we are lost. We shall surely founder, and we have no priest on board to absolve us of our sins."

'But the captain only laughed and sang his terrible songs, songs which blasphemed God and life. And he drank beer and brandy and smoked his pipe just as calmly as if he'd been sitting in the inn back home in Holland. "To hell with God!" he cried; "I curse both Him and His Son, and God's mother too! To hell with everything!"

'Then the sky split open with a great crash, and the lightning lit up the night, so that they could see the waves and the foam-crested breakers high above the ship — and down from the sky came a huge figure and alighted on the afterdeck. Everyone on board was numb with terror, but Vanderdecken calmly went on smoking his pipe.

' "Captain, thou art a stubborn man," said the figure.

' "And thou art a scoundrel!' shrieked the captain: "Who the devil wants a peaceful voyage! Not I! I want nothing from thee, so begone ere I blow off thy head!"

'The figure — who was Almighty God himself — didn't reply.

'Vanderdecken cocked his pistol and fired, but instead of hitting the mark, the bullet pierced his own hand. Then he tried with his other hand to strike God in the face, but his arm was palsied and without strength. In his impotence he could only use all the worst oaths he knew, which was no small number — and curse God again and again.

'Then the figure spoke to him:

' "Henceforth thou thyself art accursed, doomed to sail till the Last Day without anchorage or haven. Glowing iron shall be thy meat, and gall thy drink. Of all the crew only the cabin boy shall remain to thee, and horns shall grow on his brow, and he shall have fangs and claws like a tiger and a hide which is rougher than a shark's."

'The captain laughed loudly.

' "Always shalt thou watch, and never sleep. And thou shalt be a curse to all seamen, since it pleases thee to torment them. For thou shalt be the ocean's evil spirit. Thou shalt ply up across all latitudes without peace or rest, and thy ship shall bring ill to all who see it! And thou shalt neither live nor die."

' "Amen!" shouted the captain, and roared with laugher.

' "And on Doomsday thou shalt belong to Satan."

' "Hurrah for Satan!" yelled Vanderdecken.

'At that very instant the figure and all the crew disappeared, and the captain was alone with the cabin boy, who had already grown horns and fangs and claws like a devil.

'Since then the Flying Dutchman has ploughed all the seas, but mostly the waters around the Cape of Good Hope. He brings bad luck, shipwreck, and death to every ship he meets, runs them onto submarine reefs, and chases them into the surf by rocky coasts. He makes the provisions mouldy and the wine sour. And little by little he has gathered a new crew: the ghosts of all the criminals, pirates, and murderers who have died unsaved at sea — the ocean's lost souls.

'For four hundred years he has sailed thus, and he'll go on sailing till Judgment Day.'

Pat sat still, with his knees drawn up under his chin.

'The steward has seen him,' he said.

'I don't believe it,' I said: 'After all, he also saw the fiery chariot coming on the clouds to get the first mate.'

'Mr. la Fontaine *has* seen the Dutchman,' he repeated, and thought for a long time. Then he looked up:

'Is there more about him, mister?'

'Yes, there's a legend that if Vanderdecken's son can find his father and go aboard the ghost ship with the crucifix which his mother wore around her neck and which the captain swore by, and if Vanderdecken can kiss the cross and pray for peace and forgiveness, then he'll be released and can finally die.'

'Do you think his son has found him?'

'I'm afraid he's still sailing.'

'Yes, but he *could* have found him, mister.'

'Then at least the steward couldn't have seen him!'

'No, that's true.'

Pat leaned his head against the bulkhead and closed his eyes. He was thinking. He sat thus for a time, then he smiled — a long, contented smile with his lips compressed — and opened his eyes once more:

'Mister?'

'Yes?'

'At bottom you're a Flying Dutchman,' he said softly: 'Because you always and forever plough all oceans and latitudes, and wander the world with no home and no peace.'

I was rather taken aback by Pat's train of thought.

'There's something in that, all right,' I replied.

145

'You live on all the seas,' he went on; 'without anchorage or haven, like you told in the story. Are you doomed to sail till the Last Day?'

'It may look like it.'

'Have you cursed God, mister?'

'I daresay.'

'Why did you do that, mister?'

'Because there's so much wrong in the world.'

Pat paused, thinking it over very seriously; then he said, slowly and gropingly:

'But now you aren't mad at him any more?'

'No,' I replied; 'now I've forgiven God.'

'That's good,' he went on, with a contented smile; 'then I won't have to be a cabin boy and grow horns, and claws and fangs like a tiger and skin like a shark.'

'It's a good thing for both of us that we're not sailing with that unlucky ship.'

'Happily we're sailing with *Neptune*.'

'Yes, at least this isn't a ghost ship. You can take hold of *Neptune* and feel her; she's a solid craft.'

'Mister? Is the Dutchman a real ghost?'

'He can't be, because he can't die.'

'But if he's not a ghost, then what is he?'

'A sort of half-ghost, neither dead nor alive. A kind of spirit, and evil spirit.'

'But his crew — they're ghosts, mister?'

'Yes, they're the shades of dead murderers and scoundrels.'

Pat sat for awhile in thought.

'Do you think there are spirits or ghosts on board the *Neptune*, mister?'

'No, I don't think so.'

'Yes, but the first mate, Mr. Cox — don't you think his ghost could appear?'

'No, certainly not. He harmed no one, so he won't walk again.'

'Hey?' Pat looked very thoughtful: 'I feel sorry for the cabin boy who must sail with the Dutchman till the Last Day, looking so awful. But he hadn't done any wrong.'

'No.'

'Then why was he punished too?'

'I don't know, Pat. But it often happens that the innocent must suffer evil.'

'That's not fair!'

'No, there's much injustice in the world. That was why I cursed God back then.'

'Will it be like that always?'

'No, one day all will be different.'

Pat rose, picked up the teapot and cup, and betook himself up to his kindly superior, Tai-Foon, to do his work and earn his bread.

My patients were making progress.

Both Carlos and the carpenter improved amazingly fast, once the process of recovery had begun. To be sure, the big wound on Van Harden's forehead had left a frightful scar; but it had healed without complications, and so I removed the stitches and the dressing and left the rest to the sun and the air and all of nature's miraculously curative powers. He still suffered a bit from headaches and dizziness, but these effects of the violent concussion waned steadily. The sole permanent damage was the loss of the two lovely carnivore teeth.

The ordinary Carlos too had had the stitches and the bandage removed from the bite wound in his cheek. The scar was red and cruel, but had healed well. Even the ill-used, squinting left eye seemed to be righting itself, but I let him keep the black leather patch because he still saw double, although to a lesser degree than before. His left hand was less swollen now, but he continued to carry it in a sling.

It was eerie to see the two tigers in proximity on deck, but they were as yet too weak for anything to happen.

147

Even la Fontaine gradually improved somewhat. Granted that he still both saw and heard things which weren't entirely of this world, but he was decidedly calmer. And he had begun to eat a little.

The sailmaker, the Australian half-caste Pete Davis, was weak from the blow to his head, but not actually sick; and the knife-thrust he had dealt Cortez had left only a flesh wound, which healed splendidly.

On one of these days the Congolese able Legrand was at the helm during my watch. I sent him forward and myself took the wheel, to savour yet another blissful hour sailing *Sancta Vénere*. Always I knew the same joy at feeling her in my hands; my love for her was the same as on the first day.

As I stood transported and happy, feeling the faint quivering in her hull, I became aware of someone standing beside me. It was the captain; as usual he had come without a sound in those white, well-chalked canvas shoes of his. For a time he stood silent and unmoving.

'Herr Jensen,' he said softly: 'It's funny; I regard you as a reasonable man, and yet you take this attitude.'

Something about his voice touched me strangely, and only after some seconds did I realize that he had spoken Norwegian. Those were the first words between us in our mother tongue. It amazed me, too, to hear the soft dialect from the very southernmost strip of coast.

'What attitude do you mean, Captain?' I replied in Norwegian.

'That you won't move into the first mate's cabin, which is both larger and lighter than the one you have now.'

I kept my gaze fixed on the rigging and waited before replying: 'I've settled into my own cabin and feel very happy there.'

'And you still won't take over as first mate?'

'I signed on as second mate and wish to go on that way.'

He was silent awhile, but remained standing beside me: 'I don't understand you,' he said softly: 'I don't understand you at all.'

'I know from experience that I'm happiest as second mate, Captain.'

'But this is a promotion, Jensen.'

'I'm aware of that.'

He shook his head, mulling it over.

'Now listen, mister: It means significantly higher pay.'

'I realize that, captain.'

'After all, you've not only sailed as first mate but have skippered vessels yourself. Why don't you want a promotion?'

'Because I know that it entails duties and responsibilities which I'm not comfortable with. As first mate I should be doing a great deal of business work, I should have to familiarize myself with the accounts and take charge of the cargo. Those are things I'm not suited for, captain.'

'Why on earth aren't you suited for them? Surely you have more than enough sense in your head to manage these "business affairs", as you call them.'

'Of course I managed them when I had to, but it destroys something inside me, it disturbs me and upsets my equilibrium.'

He regarded me with half-closed eyes, as if he were observing a strange, unknown species of animal.

'Doesn't it matter at all that you would earn much more as first mate or ship's commander?'

'No,' I said; 'it doesn't. I earn more than enough now. I don't need more money.'

'This is the first time in my life that I've met someone who doesn't need more money. I can scarcely believe it.'

He looked up into the rigging and again shook his head in disbelief:

'Can you explain it to me, mister?'

'I don't know,' I said; 'but I'm a seaman, I like making voyages. I have food and lodging on board. I have no need for more money than what I have. I even have money left over.'

'You're an odd one,' he mused: 'Money left over!'

He tacked back and forth on the poop, then returned to me, stopped, and looked me in the face.

'But listen now, Jensen: One day you'll settle down, get yourself a place on land. You need money like everyone else. No one can have enough.'

'Captain Anderson,' I replied, 'I won't settle down, I don't want to be on land. I'm free; I'm dependent on no one, and no one is dependent on me.'

'Are you really so naïve?' he said, and smiled.

'Naïve?'

'Yes, do you really know so little about people?'

'What do you mean, captain?'

'You say that no one is dependent on you?'

'Yes?'

'And what have you in mind to do with Pat? Throw him overboard?'

'Pat isn't my son. I haven't adopted him.'

He looked at me again, penetratingly, searchingly.

'Yes,' he said; 'you *have* adopted him. Whether you like it or not. The boy is wholly dependent on you. You've acquired a child, mister. It would be kinder to throw him into the sea than to leave him on his own.'

I didn't reply. He went on:

'Do you really think that you can help someone without taking the consequences? Helpfulness commits you, mister. Philanthropy is a costly pleasure.'

'Anyhow, I don't wish to sail as first mate,' I said; 'even if it pays more. I don't need money.'

He looked up from the compass to the rigging. Then he went on:

'It's strange to hear you say that. I've spent my whole life amassing money. That was my way of seeking independence. Ever since I earned my first shillings I've saved, collected.'

'When did you go to sea?'

150

'When I was thirteen. In 1864.'

'And you've been sailing all that time?'

'Of late I've occasionally stayed on shore to arrange my bank affairs, look after my stocks, and invest my money. But otherwise I've sailed. I took out my papers early. At sixteen I went seal-hunting; it was a hard business back then, but it paid better than sailing as an apprentice. I did nothing but work and save money; and that's all I've ever done. That has been my way of seeking independence. We have our illusions, mister.'

'About independence?'

'That too. Don't you understand, mister, that if you help someone, you're binding yourself? You're caught in the net.'

'So the moral is: never help anyone?'

'Yes.'

'You became an officer very early?'

'In '74 I had my first command. I was twenty-three years old. Since then I've sailed only as skipper. And I'll doubtless go on that way. I've put most of my income into shipping stock. That too I daresay I'll go on with. I distribute it among different firms; that's the safest thing. Of course I could form my own company, but to stake all on one keel is too risky. I have shares in about twenty firms in all. Anyhow, it's my wife who looks after most of the financial matters. We've been into oil, too.'

'Does it pay?'

'Yes.'

'Do you find excitement in speculation?'

'No. It's the money which interests me, not the game. I'm not an adventurer, I'm not a gambler. I'm interested solely in profit. Had you been first mate, you would have known that I also carry cargo on my own account. I have an agreement to sell it in Rio; then I'll buy other goods which I'll dispose of in Europe. There'll be several thousand dollars in extra income just from this one voyage.'

He paused before going on:

'I can't conceive of your not being interested in money, mister.'

151

'It's a passion I don't have.'

'Hm. Funny.'

'You have a considerable fortune now, captain?'

'Yes. At first I thought that I'd retire when I'd laid up a million dollars. I'm almost there now, but it's hardly likely that I'll go ashore. I'm not yet fifty, and if my wife looks after the business affairs at home, I can still make a great deal from sailing — in my own way.'

He raised his head abruptly and looked at me:

'As co-owner of the ship I have an agreement that I may carry a quantum of goods on my own account. There's no hugger-mugger about it; I'm simply a kind of wholesaler.'

He fell silent, and the round, expressionless face closed up after this orgy of confidences and talk.

'Excuse me, captain,' I said; 'I had a question.'

'Yes?'

'It concerns the encounter with Arrowsmith .'

'Oh? — Well?'

He regarded me with alert, watchful eyes, full of distrust.

'The man is enormously strong, and you were finished with him in an instant. I didn't know you had such colossal physical strength.'

'Oh! Was *that* what you wondered about!' he laughed: 'I've always had that. I was born with it, but I've worked at it too. I could have killed Arrowsmith on the spot — and Lord knows whether I shouldn't have. In the old days I'd amuse myself by going aloft and hanging by one finger from the end of the skysail yard. When I did it as a young boy, my father — he was the captain — stood on the poop and vomited at the sight.

'I was generally rather wild and unruly, and it was my father who sent me sealing to straighten me out. In those days there was a custom, a tradition in fact, that the first thing a green hand got when he came aboard was a thrashing — a *real* thrashing, there were some pretty rough men on board. I was sixteen years old, and when

152

it came time for my thrashing, things turned out quite otherwise from what they expected. I licked the whole crew. After that I was left in peace.'

He stood still, smiling at the memory. Then with a nod he went into the charthouse, and thence down to his private cabin.

I remained at the helm until the watch changed.

What the captain had said about Pat and helpfulness had upset me. Was it indeed true that helping someone commits you to continued help? Was independence indeed an illusion, so that to meddle in another's fate binds us fast in mutual dependence? Was it so that our every act toward others enmeshes us further in an invisible web of fate?

If it were true, and one refused to take the consequences of one's acts toward others, then all such actions — even the best — would be capricious toying with human fates. In short: You can't give part of yourself; you must give all. And expect nothing in return.

The thought of what would become of Pat if I left him on his own in Marseilles was painful. And the conclusion of it all was this: One can't conceive of an individual save in relation to others. It was odd, too, that the one who had set me thinking along these lines was the captain — himself doomed by his quenchless greed for money to plough all the seas forever, never satisfied.

When the watch changed I went down to the main deck to see Tai-Foon, who was standing over the stove as usual. I was astonished to note that he had the shark knife in his belt. He turned his face to me, calm and grave, with those black, fathomless eyes.

After exchanging some neutral words, I pulled myself together and asked straight out:

'I heard that the captain is carrying cargo on his own account. Do you know what these goods consist of?'

'Cargo?' he said, and smiled: 'Cargo?'

'Yes?'

'He may be carrying cargo as well,' Tai-Foon replied thoughtfully; 'but the main thing is that he's bought up a large lot of pearls.

153

He buys pearls in the Orient and sells them in Europe. He's been in the buying business for years.'

It both surprised and didn't surprise me. In a sense it was quite natural. It would be hard to imagine him trading in copra or sugar.

'Had he lived earlier, Mr. Jensen, he would have sailed as a slave trader. But perhaps it comes to the same thing; the Malay pearl fishers live in misery, and the buyers pile up fortunes. In reality it's based on slavery.'

'Do you know how much he has with him?' I asked.

'No,' he said; 'I know only that their worth is very considerable.'

Pat was standing beside us, listening.

'Has he amassed great riches?' he asked, wide-eyed.

'Quite a lot,' I replied.

'Will he sail till the Last Day?' Pat went on.

That was one of the few times I heard Tai-Foon laugh aloud.

'It depends on what you mean by the Last Day,' he said.

'What's going on in the forecastle?' I asked.

Tai-Foon raised his head and turned to face me fully. He looked me in the eyes.

'That I have absolutely no opinion about,' he said emphatically. Then he bent over his pots. The audience was over.

I asked Pat to bring tea and went aft, down to my cabin. On the way I caught sight of James Arrowsmith leaning against the bulwarks, looking out over the sea. His tall, handsome form appeared perfectly calm and relaxed. He had the air of a man utterly at one with himself.

Which I certainly was not.

Down in my cabin I sat on the edge of my bunk, smoking. What engrossed me was the thought the captain had started me on: A person exists only in relation to others; there is no true independence. One's every act toward another — help included — brings obligations and creates fate. One is caught in the net.

154

The Beginning

Seid umschlungen, Millionen!

Again there had been unrest in the forecastle. This time serious. It's impossible to date it exactly; both the time and the positions are unclear. When the pearls and all the rest returned to Poseidon, the ship's journal went the same way — back to the deep whence all has come. With the aid of the log book the whole could have been precisely reconstructed, but the log no longer exists.

The affair began with a fight between the sixteen-year-old Greek deck boy, Stavros, and one of the apprentices — a young criminal of nineteen from the American South, who had gone to sea upon his release from prison a year earlier. Prison had scarcely improved him; it had merely hardened and coarsened him. At that time I knew little about the men in the forecastle; it is one of the sea's unbreakable laws that the barrier between command and crew must never be transgressed. The abyss between masters and slaves is unbridgeable.

Stavros, the Greek, was the ship's beauty. Oddly enough he was blond, but with dark-brown eyes and eyebrows. In a sense it was a brutal, almost evil beauty. With his halo of long golden curls he resembled a sick angel — a depraved cherub from the waterfront districts of Shanghai.

The lad from Dixie, Julian, was bigger, but lean and loose-jointed; his face bore the clear signs of his stay in prison and the brutalization it had entailed. The two boys staged an exhibit of barbarity and vile tricks of which I'd never — in all my twenty years at sea — seen the like. Stavros, despite his youth, was probably the stronger; but Julian had his experience from the 'reformatory,' and knew the more refined tricks. The battle seemed decided when he got his left forearm across the other's throat from behind, gripped his own left wrist with his right hand, and pulled with all his might. Stavros raised both legs into the air, and his face turned almost dark-blue. He couldn't make a sound. Then a sudden violent spasm went through his body, and the next moment his arms and legs hung lifeless and limp.

Almost at once the other apprentice — Taddeo, a boy of eighteen from Brazil — attacked Julian. His fist caught him hard on the cheek; Julian let go of Stavros and staggered backward. Taddeo pressed the attack and got both hands around the other's throat. Stavros lay awhile on the deck, senseless and unmoving; then he began to writhe convulsively: the blood had again reached his brain, he was conscious, but had no control over his body. The Southerner and jailbird Julian countered the hold on his throat with a knee driven into the groin of Taddeo, who loosed his grip and, doubling up in pain, was met by a forceful and well-aimed kick in the face. At once Julian was knocked down by the Chinese sailor Lee — a tall, muscular fellow, in every way the antithesis of Tai-Foon: primitive, brutal, and stupid.

His learned countryman stood at the galley door and looked on impassively. The ordinary, the cannibal Lilly from New Guinea, was balanced on one leg, leaning against the bulwarks. The other foot rested against his knee, so that the leg went out almost at right angles to his body. With his coal-black skin, the tattoos, the flat nose, and the fiercely beetling brow under his curly hair, he looked like a spirit from the nether world, an idol from the earth's childhood. He was utterly motionless.

As Lee felled Julian, he himself was rammed by a running butt from the Arab sailor Ahmed — like most seafaring Arabs a highly intelligent, capable seaman. Lee stayed on his feet but staggered backward, his face streaming with blood. Ahmed pressed the attack with another butt, and Lee fell to the deck. What happened further is impossible to recount; in a few seconds the starboard side of the main deck was a jumble of bodies and arms and legs. Nearly all the crew was involved in the fray, and it was plain that there were two parties; but you couldn't say who was siding with whom. All was just blood, shrieking, and movement. Stavros lay apart, still convulsed, vainly trying to rise to his knees.

A corpse-pale Pat came running up the ladder to the poop, where I stood beside the third mate, who had a large-calibre Colt in his hand. The other two children in the forecastle — our dear Moses and the cabin boy Elias, yet another black American — were likewise scared witless.

At the helm stood Juan Cortez — slender, elegant, and refined, with the two gold circlets on the ring-finger of his left hand. With utter nonchalance he kept his gaze fixed on the rigging and the ship as close to the wind as possible.

Of the adults I can only say with certainty that Arrowsmith, Tai-Foon, and Lilly were not involved in the fight. It now had a desperate ferocity which far surpassed that of the earlier skirmishes — even the fight between the Peruvian Carlos and the carpenter. (For obvious reasons these two as well were passive onlookers.)

Had I known then that this hate and this murderous passion would one day be rallied and ordered and directed at us aft, I don't know what I should have done.

The sailmaker, the Australian half-caste, was the first to draw a knife. He was quickly followed by the Congolese André Legrand — a tall, slender man in his mid-thirties, able seaman. In a moment several more had knives in their hands, and it made the battle quieter, more expectant and sinister, craftier. The fight took on a different rhythm; it became a kind of crazy pantomime, no longer rightly a hand-to-hand struggle. Distance, dread, and forethought had come into it. I remember Lee — the Chinaman — bleeding heavily from a gash which rose from his belt-line to the centre of his chest. And Julian, the reform-school boy, was bleeding from a stab in the shoulder.

Beyond these, four more had joined in the fighting. There was the able seaman Edgar Danson — white, a British subject, but born in one of the colonies. He was about thirty. A cut in his right forearm was bleeding copiously; the hand holding the knife was drenched with blood. Yet another able was involved: a French Canadian in his mid-twenties, Pierre Tronchet by name — a slim, dark-haired man who, like Julian from the South, had rather lately been released from prison. His handsome face had a strangely gloomy and forlorn aspect — an air of 'to hell with everything,' which is why I see him vividly still. The boy was not unattractive, and his always furrowed brow and pinched mouth betrayed continual suffering. He had gone to sea very early, from rather wretched family circumstances — the French-speaking are the poor in Canada — and during a stay in Mont Real had been arrested for some crime of violence.

In addition two ordinaries took part — both about twenty years old, both Malays. Like all Malays, they were born of the ocean and were excellent seamen; they were well acquainted with the spirits, both of air and of sea, and had communed with the souls of the dead. They were the only two whose names I don't remember. Both were small of stature — not strong, but with tiger's blood in their veins — and had yellowish skin and long, blue-black hair. In reality they did the work of ables, and it was a delight to watch them go aloft, light and sure as cats up on the skysail or the top. Both were good helmsmen, attentive and alert. They too used knives in the fight — which grew into a full-scale war, a war so chaotic that you couldn't see who was on what side. Both the third mate and I were frightened; I could see that he was afraid, and I understood his terror. His face was no longer red, but white. For the first time I felt sympathy for him. And he wasn't just stupid; he was full of terror, of terror and desolation and hopelessness. With white knuckles he clutched the Colt in his hand. I discovered that I was doing the same. No power on earth could have made me go down to that deck as it was then, chaotic and bloody. But it was my duty; it was my watch. Yet I dared not go, for fear of their fists and their knives. As I watched, Tronchet was stabbed in the belly just below the ribs. He collapsed and crept away on all fours like a beast.

Soundlessly a white figure slid past me and down the ladder to the main deck. The white shoes were immaculately chalked, and the man was utterly calm as he walked up to the combatants.

'Throw down your knives!' he said loudly.

It had no effect. It was as if they neither saw nor heard him. Indeed they may not have. Because of his slow, soundless, catlike way of moving that heavy body, it was possible.

The first to notice him was the sailmaker Davis; he turned to him, knife in hand. The captain scarcely moved; the blade of his hand caught the other across the throat. Davis fell writhing to the deck, and it later turned out that his larynx was injured. He could never again speak normally.

Almost instantly three men fell upon Captain Anderson; two of them — I can no longer say who — attacked him from the front, and the sailor Lee got both arms around his neck from behind. The scuffle couldn't have lasted half a minute. The captain took one of his assailants by the hair and bent his head downward, at the same time driving his knee up into his face. Once that man was down, he felled the other — again with the blade of his hand, this time over the ear. Then he seized the tall, muscular Lee; gripping his knee with one hand, and his arm, just below the armpit, with the other, he picked him up and carried him off to the bulwarks.

'Captain!' I yelled with all my might: 'For God's sake!'

It was as if Anderson woke up; he dropped the man to the deck, where he lay, palsied with terror. He had been right by the ship's side. It was clear that the captain had regained his self-command; in his light, soundless way he took a few steps back and drew the revolver from his side pocket. In a low, controlled voice he said:

'The first one who moves will be shot.'

The fight was over. They all stood motionless, and the captain backed toward the poop and up the ladder. His water-blue, red-rimmed pig's-eyes were devoid of expression. The third mate and I stood with revolvers in hand. On the main deck a total silence now reigned. Mrs. Anderson stood leaning against the door to the charthouse.

Her husband walked to the railing on the poop.

'Come closer!' he called: 'Come here!'

Slowly, grudgingly, the hands came aft. They stopped.

'Never in my life,' he went on, 'have I put out to sea with such a hellish band of pigs as you. You're sewer rats from the world's filthiest ports. But damme, I'll teach you who's in command on this ship. Before I'm through with you, you'll be eating out of my hand, all of you. You're a bunch of cowardly, rotten cadavers — imbecile swine, a pile of garbage which doesn't even *look* human. Before this voyage is over I'll have taught you law and order. I have maritime law on my side; I have the right to shoot. If the three idiots who jumped me are still alive, it's due purely to compassion on my part. I'd have been fully within my rights to kill all three of you. This is open mutiny, and I should have thrown the whole dungheap overboard. I'm telling you once and for all: Anyone who refuses ship's work or disobeys orders will be shot. This is my last warning, you filthy rabble of morons and criminals. Anyone who defies me will be shot or struck dead. On board this vessel *I* am the British government!'

For a moment there was utter silence.

'Do you understand?' he shouted.

No one answered.

'Do you understand?'

When no one answered still, he went on:

'If you don't understand, you'll see.'

Then there sounded a loud, clear voice:

'You murdering bastard! If you think you'll finish this voyage alive, you're mistaken!'

All turned toward Arrowsmith. Anderson pocketed his revolver, so that both of his hands were free. Slowly he descended the ladder to the main deck, and made for the mulatto. Arrowsmith stood still for a moment, but once the captain was a few yards away he sprang backward, caught hold of the ratlines, and swung himself up. In a few seconds he was on the crosstrees. The other stopped on the deck, threw back his round, close-cropped head, and looked up into the rigging. Then he shouted:

'When I catch you, you damned filthy nigger, I'll break your neck with my own hands. That's a promise.'

Calmly he returned to the afterdeck, hands in the pockets of his jacket, his back to the crew. No one stirred.

Only when the captain was on the poop for the second time did I notice that his white uniform jacket was red with blood, on the right side of the breast. Somewhat later I put three stitches into the cut, and for the first time received an impression of the man's physique. Under a thin layer of fat covering that enormous torso was a musculature of which I've never in my life seen the like. His upper arms were as thick as my thighs, and I — as I've said — am a well-built man.

After that we seldom ate together in the wardroom; around the clock there were always two officers on the afterdeck. The only one — aside from the helmsmen — who moved both amidships and aft was Pat, when he waited table or visited me.

Thus several days passed.

The World

I was in prison, and ye came unto me.

During my last few days in Manila there was a French ship in port. And I went aboard to ask for newspapers or magazines from Europe. There was also a Norwegian bark, and two English vessels — a ship and a brigantine.

On each I drank a glass with the officers, but it was only on board the Frenchman that I found any reading matter of interest: Two numbers of *La république révolutionnaire*. With the English sociological journals I borrowed from Tai-Foon, they gave me a deal to think about.

I've never liked Manila; I still don't. Yet the city has its redeeming features, first because in places it's very lovely architecturally. All of the old town — the part south of the river, within the original city walls — was built by the Spaniards in the 1600's, and thus has a strict, noble Renaissance style. I've often had great pleasure from wandering through the streets with no other aim than to look at old houses. There's much music in those buildings.

But the districts around the harbour, which the sailors frequent, were — as in most port cities — richly supplied with grog-shops and bordellos. Here it was that I caught sight of *Sancta Vénere* and fell in love, a good while before I signed on. Meanwhile I lodged in an inexpensive boardinghouse, and spent my time poking about the bookshops, looking at many books and buying a very few.

Yet as I lay in my berth on my off-watches south of the equator and read, it was chiefly Tai-Foon's journals which engrossed me. They were like meeting London again. First the tight rows of disconsolate houses one meets when arriving by train from the port city of Tilbury — those forlorn, greyish-yellow two-story houses. As far as the eye can see these dwellings are just alike, with roofs almost flat and fronting on something which tries to resemble a garden — without a trace of grass or trees, filled only with needy children, rubbish, offal, and clothes hanging out to dry.

Then there was Whitechapel Road with its raw, damp, stinkingly bitter anthracite fog and its drizzling mixture of rain and dust. Just as depressing was the memory of the hopeless, grey, and grimy factory and dockhands who filled the district — a numberless human mass, as dreary as the fog and the coal-vapour, stamped by their lifelong environment, doomed never to escape from this prison-camp of want and meaninglessness.

This was Pat's background and world, where he had starved his way through the first fourteen years of his godforsaken life: the precincts of the East End.

I saw before me the poorhouse next to the People's Palace — grey, closed and locked like a prison; the gas jets in the pubs and shop windows, and all the carts along the gutter with mussels, crabs, and fried fish, or warm potatoes. I remembered the countless alleys and byways in blackest Whitechapel, with houses all alike, the crowding darkness only at rare intervals dimly lit by a gas lamp. I remembered the stink of cheap, rancid fat from frying pans in the dirty grub-shops along the larger streets; the famished, ragged children; the hate-filled, bitter oaths of drunken men. You can walk for hours in this maze of filth and darkness and misery — from Cable Street through Stepney to the Mile End Bridge — without catching a glimpse of hope. Except possibly the sight of the poor

Jewish old-clothes dealers and their unquenchable vitality. Saddest of all, perhaps, were the dwellings — for the most part without lights or curtains, built as speculation in poverty. Or the children, with their ash-grey skin, gaunt faces, and swollen bellies; the figures for child mortality here in this vast slum are more than twice as high as in the rest of London.

And this giant city is the hub of the whole world's trade; more wealth is concentrated here than anywhere else on the globe.

This East-End slum, which has more inhabitants than all three Scandinavian capitals — Copenhagen, Christiania and Stockholm — has perhaps marked its daughters especially. They look different from other women.

I remembered too the colossal throng of grey-pale prostitutes, crippled both in soul and in body. In this jungle of a modern metropolis the flower-sellers rank just above the whores — so primitive, so wild that they form a race apart in the midst of this human sewer. Though shabby and wretched, they nearly always wear large ornaments of brass, and their faces are not of the usual ashen Whitechapel colour. They have brownish skin and seem like a gypsy breed. They're always on the street, from early morn till late at night, in the hope of earning their six or seven shillings a week. None of them can read or write. They have — studies have shown — no religion, no form of marriage; they leave their parents at twelve or thirteen and often have children themselves when they're fifteen or sixteen years old. Most of their meagre earnings go to pay for a wretched lodging. All of them live below the starvation line.

The same is true of the many thousand factory girls, a class ranking beside, or a scarcely visible notch above, the flower-sellers — in fact yet another race of wild children and famished youth in the metropolis; once again a world of want, crime, and hunger. Outside the factories they live a sort of life of uncivilized 'freedom,' like their sisters the flower-girls — and charitable institutions, 'homes,' or philanthropic societies which have tried to tame or civilize them have been bitterly disappointed. At the slightest call for discipline they go their way, having no conception of morals, law, or religion.

The whole East End yields a picture of starving children and ill-used women, of men slaving most of each twenty-four hours for a wage of sixteen or seventeen shillings a week; of alcoholism, cruelty, homelessness, despair.

Scientific studies of the conditions, begun in recent years, have merely confirmed this. From Tai-Foon's journals I still recall a few figures: Over a hundred thousand people in East London live in constant hunger; they are slowly starving to death. Twice as many suffer from chronic malnutrition and periodic hunger, but have roofs over their heads. Something under four hundred thousand are, according to the studies, 'common labourers' who live right at the starvation line — usually with a family income of less than a pound a week, on the brink of misery.

The leap from the beggar or the unemployed to the common underpaid worker is not great, but there is an abyss between them. The jobless and the poorest of the poor are always in pursuit of work, and thus depress wages for everyone in a feeble-minded competition. It becomes a war of all against all.

I remember the sight of the ragged proletariat gathered each day at the dock-gates to fight for occasional jobs which could bring a day's wage of a couple of shillings. There were always more men than jobs. Those who didn't get work had to go home empty-handed, to weeping wives and starving children.

From Tai-Foon I also borrowed a six-hundred-page treatise on *Living and Labour Conditions in East London*, an outstanding and pioneering work in descriptive sociology. It analyzes the economic circumstances and way of life of nine hundred thousand East End inhabitants. More than a third of this jungle population suffer from daily hunger and want. Among the workers, the harbour- and dockhands are the most wretched of the wretched: the dregs of the Empire's white population. Once you have begun occasional work on the docks, all hope is gone. Your family will live on, at best, twelve shillings a week — which means slow starvation, filth, and endless despair.

I recall a strike with attendant mass demonstrations earlier in the 'nineties. More than fifty thousand men of the slum proletariat took part in the marches. By the heavy prison- or fortress-like gates to the West India Docks and the East India Docks at the end of Commercial Road, the famished people streamed forth. They marched in ordered ranks, ten abreast; it was an earnest, resolute demonstration, and gave the newspapers something to write about. Of all the banners and symbols borne by the tattered, for the most part gaunt, exhausted figures, I recall most clearly an oblong bundle of rags on a pole with the inscription 'the dockhand's little child.' Like a standard it rode at the very head of the procession, borne by a white-haired old man with a humped back. Someone else carried a round of black bread on a pole — under the text 'The dockhand's breakfast.' On another pole the same black bread plus a herring: 'The dockhand's dinner.' In this hell of hopelessness they were trying to collect money for a strike fund. Many of the strikers hadn't had a square meal in days. Among the black coal-whippers and the crookbacked beasts of burden also marched an occasional underfed factory girl. For a whole week the demonstrators kept going on empty stomachs. Scabs from all over the country, unmindful of what a crime they were committing, were sent home again with tickets paid for out of the strike fund's treasury. Wives of slightly better-paid workmen stood along the pavements, doling out food to the strikers.

But the dock companies didn't give in. At last the strike collapsed, and the slaves went to their work on the same terms as before, compelled by their hunger. The only way forward must be the total general strike which would paralyse society and bring it to its knees. But the solidarity was lacking.

The French magazines revived an image of the poor man's Paris, which I've also seen for myself: a misery just as terrible as in London — and under the motto 'liberty, equality, fraternity,' words

166

which stand over the entrance to every public building, and which are a blasphemy against the truth. The City of Light, gleaming Paris, casts a night-black shadow over the abyss and its breadless people. They are many; more than half a million receive a wretched sum in aid from the municipal charities — from four up to twenty francs a month; and this half-million consists only of unsupported children, indigent lunatics, and others known to be unfit for work due to serious illness. It is estimated that twenty thousand abandoned waifs continually wander the streets; in 1890 alone, thirty-five thousand minors were arrested for beggary, theft, or prostitution.

Paris remains a whole world of poorhouses, charity hospitals, prisons, and asylums — yet there are not enough for the city's vast numbers of the starving. A typical institution is the 'almshouse' — a home for the destitute aged which doubles as orphanage and insane asylum.

The articles covered all this in detail. The degradation of poverty, the workhouses, public executions and their bloodthirsty audience. Most who view the guillotinings are poor or breadless — prostitutes, pimps, felons, beggars — the lees and dregs of the city. Trueborn children of their society. They themselves will be next under the blade.

How many needy, starving people live in Paris scarcely anyone knows, despite the thousands and thousands employed by the charities' hundreds of offices throughout the city. As an old joke has it, the charities function satisfactorily for all but the poor.

To this very day French workers pay taxes on their windows; taxes on air, light, and sun. And you see it in their children, small fellow-citizens with pale, old, tired faces — poverty's children, they don't shout, they don't make noise. They've lost their freshness and their childhood inside that lone dark room where people cook, eat, and live in the shadow — and where the whole family sleeps in one and the same bed.

If you walk through the streets of the workers' quarter, you see the tired, prostrated working folk sitting on the stoops before the houses; and if you glance into the *bistros*, you find drunken women and men reeling about in a fog of filth and alcohol. From the windows above, wet work shirts hang in the close air of the street; centuries of misery, mishap, and injustice are lodged in this poverty — a burnt-out, bitter poverty, special to Paris, corroded by crime, madness, alcoholism, and prostitution, by violence and hunger.

Straight through the workers' quarter behind the Place des Vosges cuts the Rue de Rivoli, like a river of gold and wealth. The street was built by Napoleon III to quell popular uprisings; it was so laid out that it could be hit by cannon from the Tuileries. Thus the emperor had the poor under control, and poverty could continue to serve its purpose — as a precondition for wealth. It's remarkable that hunger is so rife in a city which is famed for having the world's best cuisine.

For one of the magazines a journalist had been allowed to partake of a banquet attended monthly by the biggest restaurateurs in Paris. It is regarded as the best dinner of our time. Sixteen gentlemen in white tie and tails met at the Restaurant de Paris. I shall never forget the menu.

An unbreakable law of these repasts is that absolute silence must be kept during the meal. Most of the party had had their bellies massaged before arriving. All were glum and melancholy. They went to the table without a word, almost in suffering — as if they had undertaken a great and heroic, painful task. The journalist described the company's aspect; all were restaurateurs and were marked by a sallow, wizened plumpness. They called the waiters by their forenames, but preferred to express their wishes by a subdued pantomime of dull winy glances, scarcely perceptible nods, and well-nigh invisible hand movements.

This being a winter dinner, it was introduced by oysters on the shell and a glass or two of warm wine. In deathly silence they slurped down the animals, and were next served soup: turtle and

168

then crawfish. A Spanish white wine was drunk with the soups. Then followed two fish courses, first trout, then carp — with a sauce of mussels and shrimp. With the fish they drank not white wine, but a light, young red. After that, a semi-dry white Bordeaux.

Now their digestive organs were limbered up, and the meal could begin.

There followed two preliminary courses: first tenderloin with a truffle sauce, then chicken — both charcoal-broiled, of course, for men of the profession can taste at once whether gas has been used. These were accompanied by a Médoc wine.

Now the roast veal was brought to the table, and the dinner was in full swing. After the roast came the great wines, heavy Burgundies of famed vintages and *châteaux*, accompanied by asparagus and fresh *petits pois* from Algeria. Then they took a glass of wine with ices and fruit.

There followed an intermission, with cigarettes and soft conversation in the adjoining room. It was the general opinion that the dinner was not going to be an outstanding one; and with no great expectations, but with an air of pained melancholy, the company returned to the table.

Now followed roast fowl, enhanced by a noble white wine. After the fowl came *foie gras*, and then the banquet's climax: a salad, about which the journalist in question claims that a book could be written — one mystery being that it was composed of vegetables not to be had at that season.

Once the salad had been eaten, there was lobster — and after the lobster a hot pudding as an *entremets*. Thereafter a choice of thirty different cheeses; then fruit — among other things, strawberries at a franc apiece — followed by pastries, coffee, liqueur.

Over the Havana cigars they began to talk, and the exchange turned thoughtfully on great and especially outstanding dinners, along with each one's favourite dish.

The poor journalist, stuffed half to death, thought that the repast was now over. But no! When the clock struck twelve, the company rose and marched over to the Grand Hôtel, down to the enormous kitchen, and ranged themselves along a huge, white-scoured wooden table. Here they were attended by the cooks themselves with heavy, filling soups, smoked ham and cold ox-tongue, etc., along with hearty peasant's fare. All was consumed and washed down with big glasses of Holland gin. It smelled wholesomely of simple food; and after the dinner — he wrote — it was like a return to nature. Now the company woke up, they talked eagerly, and the men with the wizened yellow faces, the stooped backs, and the flabby stomachs laughed loudly and told improper stories.

At the end the journalist wrote as follows: When he got home and opened his window, he saw, across the rear courtyard, a lighted pane. Behind it a young girl sat over her sewing. She had been there when he left for the dinner, and would doubtless remain over her work the whole night. He related that when he saw this poor, industrious creature in the lamplight, he became aware of a faint sense of shame. But this very thing had been discussed during the midnight snack — and all had agreed that this was the most refined feeling with which one could retire after every single man had partaken of food and drink whose cost that seamstress would have lived on for three or four months.

Another of the magazines told of a meeting with France's great anarchist, the 'Red Virgin,' Louise Michel. She is described as rather commanding, somewhat priestlike of aspect; but the strength of her being is tempered by two blue eyes which shine with love of her neighbour, with that love of humanity which is anarchism's basis and starting-point — the hope of uniting socialism with freedom. She shone with love, peace, and tenderness, and none who didn't know her would have suspected that she was Europe's most notorious woman street-fighter, insurgent, and arsonist — sentenced to life at hard labour for her part in the murder of Generals Thomas and Lecomte in the March days of the Commune in 1871; released after some years, and sentenced anew to eight years for leading the

170

band of starving women who in 1883 looted the bakery shops on the Boulevard St. Germain — and once again released because of her outstanding good works in the prison, that boundless love of humanity which had defined her life.

The writer accompanies the Red Virgin to a back street in the slums, and down a dark alley to the anarchists' meeting-place, where several hundred poor women and men filled the hall. She spoke to them as a believer would have proclaimed the gospel, gently, earnestly — for more than an hour. Then she turned to the evening's prime task: to 'baptize' a child in the Revolution's name. A worker wearing the common French smock rose and brought her his small eight-year-old daughter, clad in a white dress, with roses on her shoulders and in her hair. After first releasing her from her Christian baptism, the Red Virgin solemnly dedicated the child's life to the Revolution, for a society of freedom and equality. Louise Michel blessed the girl by laying a hand on her head. As the gathering broke into rejoicing, the Red Virgin departed — for a new meeting.

What the gentle, humanitarian old lady had said to the journalist was roughly as follows: There has been no progress in France in the past hundred years. Every movement has created a new supreme authority, and to the people it's all the same whether he be called king, emperor, or president. If we wish to create a new order, we must execute a whole generation of men. We must build scaffolds in every public square. One for civil servants, one for priests, bishops, and noblemen. One for generals and colonels, for all the officers of the army. And a giant, automatic scaffold for those pillars of society, the prosperous bourgeoisie. All of it, all the old society of injustice, must be levelled to the ground. It will be a baptism of fire, blood, and beheadings. Every trace must be expunged.

I understand her.

Some of the magazines also had news of the Boer War in South Africa, where the English and the Dutch were slaughtering each other and shutting each other in concentration camps. Just then, in

1899, things were still going badly for the British in Africa; they lost battle after battle. The Spanish-American War had just concluded in the Americans' favour. The whole world was in turmoil — between nation and nation, class and class, man and man.

These days Pat often came down to see me during my scant free time. He told of his life as an orphaned beggar-boy in London, and I told him all the Bible stories — about Abraham, Joseph, Moses and Aaron, David and Jonathan and Goliath. And he swallowed it all as dry earth sucks up rain.

Otherwise I spent most of my time on the afterdeck, standing watch with Captain Anderson or the third mate. The whole situation was loathsome; we all three carried revolvers in our jacket pockets, and the crew just barely obeyed orders — slowly, listlessly, and grudgingly.

In the forecastle a mustering was taking place. Gradually Arrowsmith was bending them to his will. He was not only physically but mentally the superior. Of the forecastle I had my own impression; it was narrow, dark, and dirty — a world of filth, poverty, ignorance, and hate. But this hatred of all for all was being marshalled and directed against us aft.

And aft there was a division; only bitter need and the dread of mutiny held us together. My loathing for Third Mate Dickson grew, and one afternoon it exploded. From the afterdeck I heard shrieks and blows, and when I came out of the charthouse I saw the mate thrashing Pat. He was gripping him with the left hand and striking him with the right across the face and ears. Pat was screaming.

Dickson was both bigger and stronger than I, but I hit him full force on the jaw, and he fell to the deck without a sound. Pat clung weeping to my outflung hand, and noiselessly as always the captain appeared beside me. He said not a word. The third mate turned heavily on the deck and tried to rise, but came no further than to his hands and knees.

Huang was at the helm and witnessed the scene without batting an eye.

The captain's small, water-blue eyes looked at the third mate and at me. Then he shook his head and returned to the charthouse. Dickson's reason for maltreating Pat was that the boy was supposed to have answered him rudely. I didn't believe it; I only knew that the mate hated him after the episode on the skysail. Besides, I was too outraged to think clearly.

That same evening the captain came over and placed himself at my side. For the second time he spoke Norwegian.

'Jensen,' he said; 'Twice you've heard Arrowsmith call me a murderer. Is that correct?'

'Yes, sir.'

'So that you won't misunderstand, I must explain that I've twice had to put down a mutiny. It all happened out of necessity, and I had the law on my side. On each occasion the case went to the maritime court, which merely confirmed that I had acted fully within my rights.'

'Yes, sir.'

'I only did what was necessary. Two men were shot, and the third died from a blow I dealt him.'

'I understand, Captain.'

'I just wanted you to know. To avoid misunderstandings.'

He turned quietly and went down to the wardroom.

The Boatswain

For thou art the one who shall have all,
And nothing give in return.
— The Mother's Song

The worsening of relations between crew and command distressed me greatly and placed me in a real dilemma, in a plight which yielded no way out. My sympathies were decidedly with the crew. I liked neither Captain Anderson nor the third mate, but felt drawn to men like the Cuban Cortez, Huang, and Arrowsmith. The men in the cramped forecastle were both underpaid and underfed, doomed to lifelong servitude on ship after ship, always with miserable pay and wretched food, in a dark and overcrowded lodging, in filth and poverty, with no diversions on shore save liquor and brothels. Earlier, from the age of thirteen until I was twenty-three, I myself had sailed in the forecastle, and I knew the conditions. Granted that the crew seemed rough, brutal, and primitive, but what and who had made them that way? Yes, my sympathies were with them.

On the other hand, I had signed on aft. I was an officer; I had accepted the system. My place was among the rulers, and I enjoyed great freedom, had my own cabin, ate abundantly and well, and earned more than I needed. In a real conflict I should be duty bound to stand on the masters' side against the slaves.

Three-fourths of the crew could neither read nor write; they were illiterates. But the captain and the third mate were at least as coarsened, as brutal, although they knew better.

I myself had my freedom, I could indulge in the luxury of having books, I could play my Mozart when I felt the need. In any larger port I could draw what I required from my savings, from the excess money laid up during my years as an officer. God knows that as second mate I wasn't one of the mighty of this world; but I was established on their side, I belonged to the system — I ate bread at the table of the great, not the crumbs which fell from it. I had no economic or social ambitions, but I knew the rules of the game and got along very well within this sick society where might makes right. What I really prized was my individual freedom, my independence, and my own way of thinking: my experience of the music, the ocean, the stars — and of the spiritual forces which pervaded and sustained the world.

Naturally at this time too I had my love for *Sancta Vénere*, Holy Venus — or, if you will, for Psyche, Neptune's higher octave. And never a day went by but I stood a few hours at the helm and sailed her — still with the same feeling of bliss and love. The quivering, the fine vibration from rigging and hull, went straight through me and caused my own heart to tremble. The relation between *Sancta Vénere* and me was mutual and perfect, without conflict, without strife. There was peace between us. And freedom.

Of course I'd been long enough on land to know earthly love, and it had always ended in a battle, in each wanting to be the stronger, the superior in the relation. It is commonly called 'the battle of the sexes,' but I don't know if that is the right term. In truth it's a question of a power struggle, of a battle not to lose oneself, to maintain one's sovereignty — one's property rights. Only the very strong can live with no fear of losing their autonomy. Still, this is the precondition for loving: not to want power — not to want to *own* someone.

There can be talk of love only when one gives up one's self-assertion, when one lays down arms and capitulates fully. When one no longer defends oneself. Love is the absolute yielding, the total surrender — unconditionally. It knows no reservations, no defence. Love creates no need to be the strongest; it knows no lust for power, no personality struggle. Love is pure devotion, absolute self-surrender. Only one who is strong enough not to fear losing his personality can love. To love, one must be able to forsake oneself, to make the other free. And it is this which we're not strong enough to do.

My love for *Sancta Vénere* was not of this world. Therefore we had no problems, no power struggle. Neither desired power over the other. It was an ideal love relation. She was weaker than I, and I was weaker than she. We were both freely subordinate.

And we sailed on the Pacific, over the volcanic Lemurian continent which, like Atlantis, had sunk into the sea — but with this difference, that the volcanoes had caused fire to rain from the sky before the continent sank. A culture was smothered by ash, fire, and lava. And parts of the ancient mainland lay as much as thirty-six thousand feet beneath the surface. Was this continent, Lemuria, the same as what the Bible calls Sodom and Gomorrah, destroyed by fire which rained from heaven? Just as Plato's myth of the sunken Atlantis is the same as what the Bible calls the Flood? Who knows? Who fathoms the earth's childhood?

The Pacific's floor is dramatic; crags of lava tower to break the surface, while chasms and deeps lie many miles below.

Was Lemuria truly a culture burnt out and drowned, older than that of the Incas or the Aztecs, undone by its lust after the angels? No one knows what the depths of the sea or the past conceal. Were there not even ten righteous in Sodom? The Bible tells in the legend of Sodom and Gomorrah that only Lot and his wife and daughters were to be saved, and only on condition that they not look back as

176

they fled the city before the rain of fire set in. But Lot's wife turned to look, and became a pillar of salt. Is this the problem of conservatism — that he who looks back, who clings to the past, will perforce turn to a pillar of salt — be petrified, calcified, become a mineral — never more to grow, be renewed, and develop? That he who cannot free himself, tear himself loose, from a used-up, dying past will himself become a living corpse, a frozen pillar of salt? But the daughters conceived children by their drunken father.

Sometimes I thought of the Pacific's strange aboriginals — the Australoids, the people of New Guinea, all the ocean realm's cannibals scattered over its isles and island groups. Primitive as Tierra del Fuegans, lacking even that crumb of abstractive power which one needs in order to learn to read and write, but filled with experience of nature, the sea, and the spirits of the dead. Were they the heirs, the scattered remnants, of the folk on sunken Lemuria? I thought of our own Lilly from New Guinea, with his pointed teeth — raised in a society whose people were still honest enough to eat not only their slain enemies, but also each other, their friends and relatives; our own ordinary Lilly, illiterate of course, but a good seaman and a great philosopher with a deep knowledge of the spirits. Just before *Neptune* sailed from Manila there was a story making the rounds in the bars and hotels: The natives of the Fiji Islands had just eaten a missionary, they had baked him and roasted him whole in a big stone oven. He was roasted by all the rules of the art; fat and good and correctly seasoned this servant of God was, too. In short: Everything promised a successful feast. Yet during the party people were displeased with the meal. In particular the tribe was indignant because the missionary had had such hard skin on his feet. It turned out that the cook had baked and served him with his boots on. He had been chewed and swallowed with soles and uppers and shoelaces. Afterward — when the scandal had come to light — the cook himself had been roasted and eaten.

177

The story was often told or alluded to in the seamen's clubs, and always with a certain merriment. Well, that's the way life is. A trifle cannibalistic.

Another story was also fresh and current at that time. It came from a tribe in the Australian outback, by way of a half-caste who had been present during the feast; only by fleeing through the virgin forest that same night had he escaped ending up on the menu himself.

In this Australian tribe one of the women — after much too short a pregnancy — had given birth to a dead foetus with hair all over its body. If my poor medical knowledge is correct, we all pass through a stage of foetal development in which we're as hairy as little apes. Thus the woman had miscarried while the child was in the hairy phase, and the Australoids had scant acquaintance with this gynaecologic possibility.

The tribe's elders and wise men then held a council on the phenomenon. After lengthy discussions and explanations they concluded that the woman could not have conceived the changeling by her husband or by any other male of the tribe. What, then, was more obvious than to surmise that the child's father must be a kangaroo? A big, hairy buck.

The woman in childbed, however, most emphatically denied having had intimacies with any kangaroo whatever; and to speed the inquiry and get the matter cleared up, they laid her beside the campfire. From the fire the sages now pulled forth heated, glowing stones which they applied to the woman's stomach, breast, and thighs. Having been roasted medium in this fashion, she at last confessed the truth: The child's father *was* a kangaroo. The old men were right, as always.

She was then mercifully clubbed on the head by her husband and laid on the fire, along with her hairy progeny. Now, the cuisine of the Australian bush is less exquisite than that of the Fijis or New Guinea, and mother and foetus were fried rather superficially — merely singed on the outside, as it were — and then consumed unseasoned in a half-raw state. During the first part of the feast the poor half-caste from Hawaii lay on his belly at the forest edge, puking with dread and despair. Then he stole off into the jungle and ran like a madman for six days and nights. Half-dead with hunger and exhaustion he was found on a highway near a missionary station, where he was then put to bed and fed instead of being grilled and served.

Indeed I often thought back then that we live on a strange planet. I think I've mentioned that in this year — in '99 — the Spaniards and the Americans had just done murdering each other by the thousands, and the English and the Dutch were still slaughtering each other with a will in South Africa. Is the occasional consumption of a missionary, a mother-in-law, or one's wife really so much more despicable than systematic mutual extermination with Gatling guns and modern automatic firearms?

Each bird sings with the beak it has.

But life's cannibal forces are everywhere the same. Of course I mention anthropophagy only because in the end it plays a role in the story of the bark *Neptune* and her crew's fate. In and of itself it scarcely matters whether one eats turkey or people. We must live on something.

But at that time, when we three officers were always on the afterdeck with revolvers in our jacket pockets, I thought mostly of what was happening on board from day to day.

After I'd struck the third mate, our relation changed. He no longer hated me; he feared me. In a strange, sick way he seemed *glad* that I had hit him. It was as if he had found his place in society; he understood that he was my subordinate. He had grown more polite, and replied when I greeted or spoke to him. Inferior natures always have this in common: They conceive of goodness as stupidity, friendliness as weakness, and honesty as idiocy. When he was thrashing Pat and I intervened as I did, I had at last spoken to him for once in a language he understood.

More serious, however, was my own discovery that I had liked hitting him. I had actually enjoyed knocking the man to the deck. Had he not stayed down, I should gladly have hit him some more. When I pondered the matter more closely, I realized that nothing would have pleased me more than to knock him down again and again; to beat that stupid, healthy pink face into one dark-red bloody lump. We have sides to ourselves which it's no fun getting to know. One can play one's Mozart — badly, to be sure — and read one's Hegel — perhaps with more understanding; but behind it all, at the bottom of everything, there appears another face: The brutish face of the ruffian and murderer which we probably all — that is, in any case *I myself* — bear innermost in our hearts. It was scarcely pretty and scarcely cheering to see this murderer's face in the glass. Especially disheartening was the fact that I first saw this man inside me so late — when I was fully thirty-three years old. Naturally I'd been in fights and scuffles before, as a youth, and of necessity had learned to defend myself. But it was only now — or rather *then*, on board the *Neptune* — that I'd first felt this desire to kill, to murder. It was an experience which scared and shook me to the depths of my soul.

And what made the situation even more confusing was that I had hit Dickson because of Pat — Pat, who had become a burden to me, who had robbed me of my freedom and independence, the only thing on earth which I didn't want to lose. Because of the helpless Pat, whom I only desired to be rid of. Pat, whom I should prefer to leave in the first available port. Pat, who only brought me more and more duties and responsibilities, and who could give me nothing whatever in return. I couldn't so much as rejoice in a son of my own. He wasn't even my own flesh and blood.

After the episode with the third mate, Pat was more dependent on me than ever. It was a state inextricably bound to something invisible. I don't know what it was. But I was no longer just an older friend whom he trusted blindly. I wasn't even a fictive adoptive father. I had become all things at once: his father and his mother, his friend and elder brother, his teacher, his doctor, his protector — I had even become economically responsible for him and his life. And I was his pastor, storyteller, and comforter. Else he would go under.

At the same time a change took place in Pat himself. He no longer showed me the same gentle devotion as before. To him all was now a matter of course. If I hadn't adopted him, he at all events had adopted me. He demanded and expected of me, quite simply, everything. The child's total trust and fathomless egotism knew no bounds. And slowly the horrific truth dawned on me with all its implications: Once you've taken someone under your wing, it's no use giving *something*, you must give *all*. You must give absolutely *everything*, and you shall have *nothing* left.

The only thing I owned — my independence — Pat had taken from me. To abandon him was tantamount to murder. He couldn't get along in the world. Indeed I could never think seriously of killing Mr. Dickson, but there were moments when I felt that I could throw Pat overboard some dark night in cold blood, just to be rid of this unwanted child with all his claims on me, all the things to which he had now become entitled.

And, strangest of all: It was that brutal murderer and money-grubber, Captain Anderson, who had brought the situation home to me. What the devil was it that dwelt in the man?

He didn't even drink alcohol, not in the smallest quantities. The third mate always drank beer with his meals, and on his free watches as well — though by now he was much too frightened to get drunk. He was afraid of Arrowsmith, afraid of the crew, afraid of the captain, and afraid of me. Toward Pat he behaved in an almost fatherly fashion. Mrs. Anderson was fond of a glass of wine with her dinner, and I sometimes joined her. I've never liked beer or spirits. The only one who never touched a glass was Anderson himself. I suppose he was much too preoccupied with his pearls and his stocks to care about anything else. He was probably a teetotaller and drank nothing but the blood of the oppressed.

181

Between Mrs. Anderson and me there had arisen a certain intimacy — almost wordless, to be sure. Still, we would chat now and then about music, or sometimes about the children's rearing and education, since I had once been a teacher. One day she told me a story about her husband, from the time when he was a schoolboy of twelve in a little town on the south Norwegian coast. It showed that in his way he had had a kind of grim humour.

At school the boy had committed some sort of crime, and was sentenced by the teachers to be birched. The execution was to take place with his hind parts bared in front of the other pupils, and to make it sufficiently humiliating it was decided that he himself should go out to the town woods and cut the long, supple birch branches — which he then was to bind together, in full view of all, into the sturdy rod to be used for his punishment.

Well, the future Captain Anderson went up into the woods, but he did not cut a selection of suitably flexible branches. Instead he chopped down a whole birch tree, and being at that time already as strong as a grown man, he dragged the tree through the town streets and into the schoolyard. There he declared cheerfully that whichever of the teachers had strength enough to lift the tree would also get to thrash him. No other should be allowed to do it. It was thus a case of open rebellion. The end of it was that his father — who must have been a reasonable man — took him out of school, and presently sent him to sea as a deck boy. Later, when he proved to be much too unruly, he was then signed on as a green hand on a sealer — with the consequence which I've already related: at sixteen he licked the whole crew.

I remember, too, a dream I had at that time — if it really was a dream. In any case, through the whole remarkable experience I was fully aware that my body was lying asleep down in my cabin. Myself — or my soul, or whatever it was — had come loose and freed itself entirely from the two hundred pounds of sleeping flesh which lay in the bunk; and free and weightless this soul moved about the world at will, among lands and cities and people, but also on board the ship. It was surprising yet natural to find that I wasn't walking, but could fly — or more exactly, float. I repeat and emphasize that during the whole dream I was fully conscious and awake, and entirely clear about the fact that Second Mate Jensen's earthly and visible person lay sound asleep in his own familiar cabin as I drifted about. To this day I even recall that I was sleeping on my stomach. Several times my soul returned to my body, which then awoke in the small, dark room. But I needed only to close my eyes, with my face buried in the pillow, and the day grew bright around me, and once again I could move freely through bulkheads and closed doors. Two or three yards below me lay the deck in a kind of sunshine which cast no shadows — and up from the sea came the god Neptune and planted himself against the bulwarks.

It's difficult to describe him, for he was unlike the familiar mythic image of the sea's divinity and lord. Above all he was more personal, more concrete. A bit shorter than one would think, and at the same time more individualized. He was by no means so athletic as I had expected, nor were his hair and beard so luxuriant and billowing. He had a lot of seaweed and shells and mussels hanging on him, and his skin was young and firm and brown. Around the shoulders, chest, and waist he was rather slender, but his eyes were very large and blue, and they were full of sea and sky; they were — if I may use the expression — oceanic. He was the *realest* thing I've seen. I was still floating a good way above the deck and yet knew very well that I was in bed and asleep below. Then all at once, as I looked at his modest physique and his rather sparse, red-blond beard — then all at once I felt that it wasn't this now-visible Neptune who mattered — but the awful, appalling, all-dominant spiritual force which beamed from him, more violent than any hurricane, any cyclone. The naked, slender, wet man before me was quite simply a *god*, filled with a fathomless supernatural power. And at the next moment I was overwhelmed by one sensation, stronger perhaps than any other feeling I've tasted, stronger than the deepest mortal terror I knew; it was the vast, indescribable experience of my own *stupidity.*

Of stupidity and shame.

Then I floated straight through the wall of the poop, through the locked door to my own cabin — at that point we officers all slept with doors locked and revolvers in our bunks — and below me I saw, in a full, clear light, my own sleeping body. I entered that body and awoke in inky, pitch black darkness. Each time I closed my eyes in weariness, the same thing happened: All became bright around me, and I left my body and moved freely through space.

When I was roused for the next watch, I felt as sick as if I were dying. It was some time before I could stand on my feet; I was weak as an old man, qualmish and dizzy; my hands shook so much that getting into my trousers and socks was an unbearable strain. I had to hang on to bulkheads and door frames as I staggered half-dressed over to the sick bay and poured myself a big glass of cognac on an empty stomach. It was only after I had swallowed the nausea from the liquor and come up into the fresh night air on the afterdeck, that I slowly regained control over my body. With the revolver in my jacket pocket I took over the watch. One of the ordinaries — a twenty-year-old Malay, whose name I no longer recall — stood at the helm.

When I stop to think of it: Those two young Malays, both ordinary seamen, are the only ones of *Neptune*'s whole original thirty — not hands, but people — whose names I don't recollect. Malay names are difficult to remember. I no longer know who was who.

When I awoke, up on the afterdeck, I took a few turns on the poop, checked the position in the charthouse, then went over to the helmsman and peered into the binnacle. The lit compass dial showed that he had her a couple of points too low in a southeasterly direction.

'Good evening,' I said.

He didn't answer. Just looked at me with those narrow black eyes, still and hateful. I looked up at the half-invisible sails, which were hauled too close. I felt the direction of the wind exactly.

'Three points to windward,' I said.

'Up three points, *tuan*,' he replied, and laid the ship higher.

All the Oriental's deep contempt for the master race lay in his voice. I felt like hitting him, but at the same time I was aware that my one accursed duty was to get this vessel across the Pacific and around Cape Horn without real incident. If we couldn't reach Marseilles, it was at least possible to make Rio. In Rio we could exchange half the crew. We could get a new first mate, change third mates, and sail on up to North Africa and into the Mediterranean. My coming discharge in Marseilles I saw as the happiest moment of my life. I had never experienced a mutiny, and I didn't see why I should be involved in anything so loathsome on just this occasion. Dividing the time equally, we three officers had sixteen hours' watch these days. Sleep and meals came out of the eight off-watch hours. There were always two of us on the bridge, always with those damned guns in our right jacket pockets. And if that thin, wretched little Pat hadn't often come aft to bring me strong, sweet tea, I should doubtless have fallen asleep standing on the afterdeck. Over a stretch of several weeks, four hours' sleep a day isn't very much.

We were well south of the equator now, and had had almost incredible luck with the weather. A couple of times we had run into a full gale, but nothing more. What landsmen call a 'storm' is seldom more than a fresh gale: An occasional tree blows down, an occasional roof rises up and goes off on the wind. It's hard to walk upright on the street and you can't breathe against the wind. A storm is something else entirely.

The first time I experienced a full storm at sea, I was fifteen years old; and all that could be called porcelain or dishes was smashed by the time we fought our way out of the chaos in which we lay on the floor. As we came about — this was in the North

Atlantic off the west coast of Norway — to seek an emergency port, one huge breaker stove in all the oaken doors on the weather side. The whole ship was half-submerged, and we floated about among sea chests, doused lamps, clothes and movables and foreign human bodies. Two hours later we were in smooth waters. That was the first time I knew what it was to be literally so afraid that my urine ran out and mixed with the brine that my pants were wet with anyhow. The only difference being that the sea-water was cold and the piss warm.

However, a storm of this kind is but a moderate breeze compared to a real hurricane or cyclone or typhoon in tropical waters. On land they would call a real storm a 'tornado' or something of the sort. Trees go aloft, boats are cast ashore, a few houses are blown up into the woods. It's no worse than that. Of course you can't walk upright in such a wind. That is a storm.

A hurricane is altogether different. Beyond that we have the 'cyclone' or 'typhoon.' Before I sailed with *Neptune* I'd seen lifeboats blown — not beaten by the waves, but *blown* by the wind out of their davits, straight across the deck, and off to leeward, as if they had been huge gulls. And where the sea has struck I've also seen the davits — iron rods thick as my own arms — twisted along the deck like corkscrews, or as if they were made of soft butter, squeezed out over the breakfast toast.

That is the beginning of a typhoon.

I recall one time in the North Atlantic — en route from Mont Real to Hull — when the whole poop and the deckhouse were swept overboard by a single wave, and we came through it alive. Is it any wonder that all but the skipper and me (I was first mate) were drunk for three days after we anchored?

But this is a mere joke compared to a tropical typhoon.

Many writers have tried to describe what a cyclone is. The truth is that it can't be described; it's like nature gone mad. Strangely enough, a tropical typhoon doesn't last for so many hours, and I know of people — captains — who have sailed vessels of no more than five or six hundred tons straight through the storm centre. But if you reflect that ocean waves have been measured with heights of one hundred thirty feet and speeds of eighty knots, you can imagine what may easily befall a vessel if the helmsman and the navigators don't know what they're about. Every cubic yard of that devil-ridden brine weighs almost a ton, and moves faster than an express train.

But none of this happened to *Neptune* during the first period; we sailed almost constantly under a full spread of canvas, with a lovely fresh breeze blowing week after week — and generally averaged from fourteen to sixteen knots. Except for tacking, which could be manoeuvred from the deck, there was little for the hands to do. They chipped off rust and painted. The crew still obeyed orders, but sluggishly and unwillingly. However, we kept *Sancta Vénere* trim and white-painted and beautiful.

Once I had patched up the knife wound in Captain Anderson's shoulder, I naturally had a good deal of medicine-man's work after the big fight. There were wounds from knives and blows, but — oddly enough — no really dangerous injuries. No one had to be put in the sick bay. Even Tronchet with the stab in his belly and Davis with his injured larynx got along fine.

My old patients continued to progress. To be sure, the steward la Fontaine still saw thousands of tiny little Chinamen and talked aloud to himself and the late first mate Mr. Cox while strolling the deck; he was nonetheless calmer, and never again climbed naked up the rigging out of terror or to make speeches in French. He had definitely reconciled himself to the little Chinamen and no longer feared them. The Peruvian Carlos's eye was better and he squinted much less. I had removed the leather patch, though he still saw double, so that the eye would adjust and come back into alignment. At the helm he still had to close his left eye to see the compass clearly, but he was improving daily. He was also regaining control of the fingers of his left hand. But he was just as curt and just as hostile as before, at any rate toward me.

187

Yet strangely enough he had made up with his former deadly foe, the carpenter van Harden from Java. Like the bite in Carlos's cheek, the wound below the Javanese's hairline had healed splendidly, and the aftereffects of the blow to his head were wearing off; he no longer staggered when he walked, and I had taken off the bandage long since. The sole permanent damage from the fight was that two of his lovely white fangs were gone forever. Now and then the two of them would stroll the deck conversing. Lord only knows in what language they regaled each other — whether Malay, Spanish, or a kind of English; but in any case they did talk.

At the same time — in the midst of all this — I had a certain pleasure from the captain's children. The elder, the girl Mary, was six — almost old enough for school. There was a great deal that I could teach her, and much that she could teach me. She was a brunette, and with the medium-dark hair went two big dark-brown eyes. What she demanded of me was stories, from the sea and from my own childhood.

She would say to me:

'Tell about when you were little!'

And so I would tell, stories from Finnmark and the Arctic Ocean; tales of what had happened up there, in my own family and when I myself was a child. She sat listening, her dark eyes large and still, and demanded more and more. Best of all she liked me to tell the same stories again, and she wanted me to tell them word for word in the same way, over and over. Mary liked very much to hear about the times I first went fishing in the Arctic Ocean, or about going up into the mountains among the Lapps and living in their tents or their turf huts. And she always wanted to hear again about my biggest fresh-water fishing trip, when I had caught almost forty trout in one night, far in on the Finnmark plain, and the biggest problem had been how to carry all the fish — nearly fifty pounds in all — down to the village. Mary sat there with big brown eyes, seeing before her all that I told her.

'Tell that again!' she said.

She especially liked a story about the first time I had been in a shipwreck and had spent almost three hours in the icy water before another fishing boat picked us up. All my nails were destroyed and fell from my fingertips. But new nails grew in. I also told her how it felt to hang on one of the yards to reef the sail when it was below zero in a fresh gale and my fingers went numb and the wind blew straight through my body. And then the dirty, dark, ice-cold forecastle afterward.

With her little brother Bobby, who was only four, it was different. He was a little round lump — but with utterly blond hair and dark-brown eyes. Bobby just wanted to sit on my lap or my arm. He was too little to demand stories. He just wanted to be safe and snug. There was certainly something these children didn't get from their parents. I don't know just what it was they were missing, but perhaps it was something called love. Lord knows.

One thing which bothered me was the memory of how their father, during the fight, had picked up the sailor Lee and carried him off to the bulwarks, but at my shout had come to his senses and dropped the man to the deck instead of throwing him overboard. It was clear to me that Captain Anderson had been deranged, not responsible, when he wished to kill the man. Had he accomplished it, Lee would have been the fourth human being he had killed. This time as well Anderson would have had the 'right,' the law, on his side — that law which is created to protect the strong against the weak, to maintain the masters' power over the slaves, to constrain the oppressed to total obedience. As officers Dickson, Anderson, and I all had full right to kill anyone who set himself against us. Then considering that both the others were capable of acting in a blind rage, it's understandable that the situation gave me a feeling of great loneliness.

Nor was there anyone among the crew on whom I could wholly rely. Even the intelligent, balanced Arrowsmith had once or twice lost his self-control and attacked and provoked Captain Anderson beyond the limits of the latter's endurance. Tai-Foon hardly spoke any more, just looked at me now and then with those black, fathomless eyes.

When all was said and done, perhaps — or quite certainly — the helpless, useless Pat was my only consolation. I noted that I had begun to miss him if he was away for long. In reality I myself had gradually become just as dependent on Pat has he was on me. But I didn't understand that then.

Besides, it was Pat who told me the truth about the situation as it was.

One day when he was down in my cabin, he said:

'Hey, mister?'

'Yes?'

'Did you know Captain Anderson killed Arrowsmith's brother?'

'Where did you get that, Pat?' I replied.

'Stavros told me,' he said; 'but a lot of them know about it.'

For awhile I sat in total silence, just collecting my thoughts. Then I said:

'Have you heard about the pearls, Pat?'

'Yes,' he said; 'everyone has. They say he has pearls on board worth over half a million dollars.'

It was a long time before either of us spoke. Then Pat took my hand.

'Mister,' he said; 'I'm kind of scared.'

And before I knew what I was doing, I had answered him:

'Don't be afraid, Pat; I'll take care of you. You know you can count on me. Sometimes I'd like to throw you overboard, but I doubt that I ever shall.'

Pat squeezed my hand more tightly, and his smile broadened.

'No,' he said; 'because you're my father.'

For a moment I was utterly speechless. I couldn't find an answer. Pat just smiled, with his thin face and his bad teeth.

'Listen, Pat,' I said presently: 'I'm not your father, I'm not your big brother, I'm not your teacher. Not your pastor. I'm nothing to you. And at the next port I'll join a shop where you aren't on board. We'll part in Rio or Marseilles. I'm not your adoptive father!'

Pat was totally unmoved. He smiled on:

'But you're all of those, just the same!'

After a pause he went on:

'You can't ever leave me. Because you can't.'

I looked at him. There was a strange mixture of triumph and near-scorn in the child's poor, ruined face. It was impossible to answer him. He smiled again, almost like an angel. Then he repeated:

'Because you can't, mister.'

These words made me stand up. In the low, cramped cabin I rose to my full height, and my head bumped the ceiling. The usual cabin height was about six feet. I felt like hitting someone.

But I couldn't hit Pat. The truth was that he had become my son. However, we soon had other things to think about. But before I go on, I must correct a sin of omission. Of the whole crew on the bark *Neptune* there's but one man whom I've not yet mentioned, and it's not because — as is the case with the two twenty-year-old Malay ordinaries — I've forgotten his name. Quite the contrary; I remember him all too well. He was the oldest man on board, a little over sixty. His sinewy chest was always bared to the sunshine; he was slightly humpbacked and walked with a stoop, his arms rather bowed. His skin was as dark as any mulatto's, but from his tanned, freckled face shone two eyes of as light a blue as I've ever seen in a human being. His hair was as blond as oats, barely streaked with white. He was still both strong and spry, and if needful could go aloft with just as much ease as any of the youngest. By origin he was Low German; his parents came from the flat coastal plain behind the dunes of the North Sea, somewhere between Friesland and Holstein. But they had emigrated from the poverty at home, and their son was born in South America. His name was Christian Hellmuth and he was the boatswain on the *Neptune*. His mother tongue was German, but he spoke Spanish and English well —

191

though with the weakness which so many Germans have: He couldn't pronounce 'th', but said 's' instead.

His temper was just as calm and gentle as his clear, light-blue eyes. He had spent many years on German ships, but I believe that for the last generation he had sailed almost solely in the tropics under the sun he loved and under which, despite his yellow hair and flower-blue eyes, he felt at home. By the way, he never said just 'the sun,' but 'God's sun.' And for him such things were no mere conventions or phrases; they expressed a deep intimacy with a thought-world into which he now and then allowed me glimpses.

Hellmuth was one of the few people I have met whom I should truly call a Christian. But he was neither Catholic nor Protestant; he belonged to what he called 'the third confession' — a tradition which descends from the old German mystics: from the doctor, great researcher, careful scientist, astrologer, dreamer, and prophet Paracelsus; from the monk and knight Meister Eckhart, the keen thinker and devout, sensitive mystic who was convicted of heresy — because he sought to learn more than befits mortal man to know. But perhaps even more from the shoemaker of Görlitz, the deep, pious, self-taught Bible-reader and scholar Jakob Boehme — who, more than anyone else, casts shame on the proverb 'Shoemaker, stick to your last!' Thank God that Jakob Boehme did not stick to his last.

Likewise Christian Rosenkreutz and his old-time Brotherhood of the Rosy Cross lived on in the boatswain's life. But I think that it was chiefly the American branch — the Rosicrucians of the seventeenth and eighteenth centuries — with which he had had contact.

Now, Christian Hellmuth was certainly no dogmatic adherent or blind disciple of any of these; like his goodness, his experience of life and his insights came from deep springs within his own soul. Of course he had learned much and taken much from the mystics, but his thoughts were part of his own blood, his own heart.

That he couldn't subscribe to either of the great confessions was not, God knows, due to spiritual pride, but quite simply because neither of the ironclad theologies — the Catholic or the Protestant — could be reconciled with his devoutness and his experience of people. To him the notion that a single confession or church could set itself up as intermediary between God and man was an impossibility, a matchless arrogance. A churchly 'remission of sins' was to Hellmuth unthinkable and blasphemous — not least when one's absolver was just any priest from a seminary, perchance knowing no more of life than a little bad Latin. He saw the Roman Church's centralism and greed for power as an affront to human dignity and to that freedom which was the first prerequisite for approaching God. The idea that man is sinful and evil by nature was, to the boatswain, blasphemy.

Even more false, perhaps, did he find the Lutheran doctrine of the unbridgeable abyss between God and man: that man is, as it were, the antithesis of God — that God and man are enemies.

Here Hellmuth built rather on a teaching which is the opposite of the churches', namely the Gospel which proclaims: 'I have said, ye are gods!'

From one of my conversations with our boatswain I remember his saying that God and existence, or God and Being, are one and the same thing; all reality, including God, consists of evil and good. In this eternal struggle between the forces of light and darkness man can be redeemed through Christ, the perfect realization of the divine-human unity. Man must thus renounce everything, forsake himself — he must give away all, desiring *nothing* in return — simply in order to *become God.*

The thought reminded me greatly of my own thoughts about love, but Hellmuth broadened the perspective by applying it to all humanity. We had no trouble understanding one another, even though he was a Christian and I a heathen.

Another cause of his absolute break with the churches was that, in his own way, he was a socialist; he believed that the great churches had laid up treasures on earth, broken the Master's word, allied themselves with the princes and the rich and mighty of this world; they sought to defend the *status quo* instead of finding their place among the weak, the humble, the oppressed and exploited — among the sinners and the poor.

It's funny to think that the German knight and Dominican monk Meister Eckhart — who, with the shoemaker Boehme, had been one of our aging boatswain's mentors — had also been a mentor to Hegel, who had in turn been mentor to the German socialist and philosopher Karl Marx, dead in smoke-poisoned London sixteen years before *Neptune's* final voyage. Surely there must have been times when Tai-Foon sat in his cabin reading Marx while on deck Christian Hellmuth was telling me of the knight who had lived six hundred years before.

It's strange to see the rings widen in the water.

Yes, all has a meaning.

Hellmuth was an outstanding seaman, not least because of his vast knowledge of tropical storms and weather conditions. Until the mutiny began, his gentle and soft-spoken authority was unchallenged among the men in the forecastle. He excelled in everything: He could go aloft like a young boy, and did carpentry and made sails just as well as the craftsmen themselves.

After the death of the first mate, Mr. Cox, Captain Anderson asked Hellmuth to take over as 'best man' — that is: to sail as first mate, and for a first mate's pay, without having the papers. But Hellmuth refused; he belonged in the forecastle. Which shows that, despite his devoutness and his modesty, he by no means undervalued himself; he know who he was, and he knew his task. That task he never performed by talk or pedagogy, but by his way of *being* — by his soft-spoken manner and the great sense of peace which he radiated. The only ones who hated him were the two half-castes, the sailmaker and knife-wielder Pete Davis from Australia and the carpenter van Harden from Java; both of whom felt demeaned because their fathers had committed the infamy of siring them on coloured women, thus leaving them rootless — shunned and despised by the whites, yet feeling themselves above the coloured. They were homeless and hated everyone. But they fell outside Christian Hellmuth's gentle jurisdiction, and were spared having to obey him. They were their own executioners.

Of Hellmuth's personal life I knew only that he had lost his wife and two small children during a yellow-fever epidemic almost thirty years before. But in forty-five years at sea he had met with so much else that now no more could happen to him save death — which he saw not as an enemy, but as a faithful friend who awaited him.

One evening a strange incident occurred on the main deck. The men danced and played the guitar. The guitarists were Juan Cortez, the Cuban able, and Taddeo, the ordinary from Brazil. They improvised together, and both played splendidly, a wild, savage, hate-filled music, but lovely. Burning oil lamps hung from the foremast and the main yard, and at first the crew stood in a ring around the musicians, clapping. The mestizo Carlos began to sing, and soon they all joined in — in a kind of wordless *Ursprache*, since only the Spanish-speaking could follow the text. Then they began to dance, singly or in pairs. Soon the deck was a chaos of dancing men. Where they got the liquor I don't know, but I suppose that the steward, la Fontaine, had a cache down in the hold which had now been passed out to the crew. The dance lasted until late evening. And in the yellow half-light of the lanterns it was an innocent and wonderful sight.

We had several thoughtful and responsible men on board, and indeed it was difficult to grasp that the outbreak, when it came, could be so savage and so focused as it was. It must have stemmed from the bottomless, passionate hate which dwelt in men like Arrowsmith, Lee, Huang, and black André Legrand from the Congo; in the mestizo Carlos, in Lilly, in Julian, Taddeo, Tronchet, and the rest: It was the hate and vengefulness of generations, and nothing could stop it — nothing save force against force.

The Mutiny

Nothing could befall him save what each must
be prepared for: namely, defeat and death.

—J. C.

The attack came at night. I was off-watch and asleep below; but I
had on my trousers and shirt, and my revolver lay beside me. The
instant I heard the shots from the poop, I was awake and on my feet.
Up on deck all hell was loose. The first thing I saw was a figure
lying athwart the exit from the charthouse. It was Edgar Danson,
the white South African — shot or knocked down. Pete Davis, the
Australian half-caste, lay prone a few yards away. Against the railing
over the main deck Juan Cortez half lay, half sat, his face covered
with blood.

By the ladder up from the deck stood the third mate and the
captain, both with revolvers in hand. No one was at the helm, but
the wind was just a moderate breeze and the ship had swung around
and was rocking gently in the long swells. On the deck under the
ladder two more men lay motionless, but in the faint light of the
petroleum lamps I couldn't see who they were. A little further
forward stood a form which I recognized only by its size: It was
Arrowsmith.

Up the ladder a man came climbing; he had a knife in his right hand. The third mate did not shoot, but kicked him in the face. For a moment the man stood still, holding on with his left hand; the next kick caught him under the chin, and he raised both arms, stood poised for half a second and then fell backward, out into the gloom on the main deck.

Almost at once a new man ascended the ladder, and two swung themselves over the railing on either side. The attack was well-planned and went like lightning. I saw Anderson seize one of them and literally fold him double—he also hit him a couple of times; but straightaway the man who had come up the ladder fell upon the captain from behind. Then I heard Dickson fire, and saw the flash from his gun. I noticed, too, that something was happening behind me; there was a sound of something soft and at the same time heavy. Turning, I saw the big Chinese sailor Lee and the Algerian Ahmed on the poop; both had plumped down unseen from the spanker boom.

Now, I'd seen them in fights before and knew that both were dangerous at close range. At the same time I could see that they were surprised to find three men on the poop instead of two.

The plan had been well thought out; several men would attack Captain Anderson and Dickson from the front — and two from behind, by dropping from the spanker boom. But here I was in the way. Ahmed came at me at once, but I'd seen his running butts before and could easily defend myself against them. He hit only my forearm; I fired two shots at his feet. He ran across the poop, hopped over the railing and down onto the deck. I caught just a glimpse of his white pantleg and one foot up against the lamplight. Then came Arrowsmith tiger-swift up the ladder and attacked Anderson, whose neck already had two arms around it from behind. The captain fell backward under the mulatto's well over two hundred pounds. I heard a couple of oaths and some gurgling, then I felt the stab of Lee's knife in my left upper arm. I fired instantly. But I didn't aim at his body, just at his legs. Oddly enough I felt no

197

pain from the knife thrust, only a curious indignation: I'd never done anything to Lee, never harmed him. So why the hell was he sticking a knife in my arm? — The arm was not so badly hurt that I couldn't use it. I hit him hard from below — under the nose and upward — a blow which can drive the whole bridge of the nose up into the brain. And as he tottered back a few yards, I fired. I aimed only at his legs, and I hit him in the left calf.

I still see the scene before me: faint, yellowish light — and under this light, folk are busy killing each other. My shot went straight through his calf. Later, when as medicine man I was patching up the wounds, I saw that the bullet had miraculously passed between the fibula and the shinbone; no bones were shattered; the projectile had simply gone through his muscles and out the other side. Of course he felt that he had been hit, and began to roar as he limped backward. I pursued him until I had him with his back to the railing, then I hit him twice in the face. He went backward over the railing and fell with his full weight down to the main deck.

Behind me the third mate and the captain were busy with the four who had attacked from the front. One already lay senseless from Anderson's blow. Beneath Anderson lay the man with his arms around the captain's throat, and Arrowsmith was on top with one fist clutching Anderson's ear and cheek. In the other hand he held a long, slender knife.

What amazed me most was the sight of Dickson; perhaps the third mate was still afraid, but he didn't show it. His face wasn't red and it wasn't white. He was as calm as if he were making tea. Somewhat the same was the case with me; I felt no real terror any longer; the dread of recent days had found an aim and a meaning. Besides, only two of the mutineers were left on the poop. Captain Anderson got up with no help from Dickson or me. But the two remaining assailants — one of the hands and Arrowsmith himself — still hung on his neck. He scarcely troubled himself about the man on his back, and Dickson and I removed him easily. We hit him in the face a few times and threw him down the ladder. Then

198

Anderson seized Arrowsmith by the crotch with his right hand and by the throat with his left; a yell of pain sounded from the mulatto, I saw both of his feet up against one of the sails, and the man fell two yards from the poop to the deck.

On the poop only Dickson, Anderson, and I remained. The ship drifted in the moonlight, broadside to the wind. We had cleared the afterdeck.

But it all depended on the following: There was but one ladder from the main deck up to the poop. The attackers had been drinking before they went into action. In the forecastle they had knives and clubs, but no firearms. The provisions were aft with us. They outnumbered us several times over, but we were superior in material and weaponry. We were still masters of *Neptune*, we thought.

While all this was happening, Mrs. Anderson had stayed below with the children Mary and Bobby. They had heard the shooting and the blows and yells. But she had kept them quiet. Of course they were afraid, of course they had cried — but she had sung to them, talked to them, quieted them down.

The other children on board — the fourteen-year-olds Pat and Moses and the fifteen-year-old Elias, the latter two both from the States — had crept down into the anchor-cable bin and hidden there. Even for our beauteous, vulgar, and fallen angel, sixteen-year-old Greek Stavros, it had been too much. Despite his well-rounded muscular body, he had hidden both himself and his yellow curls in Tai-Foon's cabin, while the cook with his narrow black eyes stood out in the galley with the shark knife in his belt. Not a soul on *Neptune* would have ventured into the galley so long as Tai-Foon stood in the doorway in his pyjamas and his paper shoes. I understand it well; we were all children compared to him. His only equal was Christian Hellmuth, but God! — how different they were!

Well, so we had managed to clear the afterdeck that night when the mutiny broke out. But it was only a provisional victory. We all knew that the final reckoning was yet to come.

199

I was still the medicine man on board. I was an officer, and had helped put down the mutiny in the first round. Yet when folk lay bleeding and senseless on the decks, my next duty was to keep them alive. They were no longer my enemies; they were my children, my patients. Of course I was a ship's officer, but once I had knocked down, roughed up, or shot any of them, then I was their doctor and nurse. Strictly speaking I don't know which side I belonged on. Probably nowhere.

There's something called loneliness.

I don't know quite what it signifies, but I think it means feeling responsible. One can perhaps set up a kind of mathematic equation: Responsibility = Loneliness.

I suppose I felt quite lonely during those days.

I know of no one to whom I could have turned for support or solace. It would have had to be Christian Hellmuth or Tai-Foon, but neither showed his face. On the second day Pat came crawling up from the anchor-cable bin, pale, scared witless, and hungry. He crossed the main deck and came straight up the ladder to the poop. I don't think that either of the others took it amiss, but I felt as if life had returned; I put my arms around Pat, lifted him off the deck, and laid my cheek against his head.

This, then, was the first attack, the first serious attempt at organized mutiny.

It was just the beginning.

Two days later came the next attack.

In all fairness it must be said that none of us tried to draw the children into it, the adults' hell and world. Moses and Elias, our two little blacks of fourteen and fifteen respectively, moved freely all over the ship; they came aft to get food with no harassment from anyone in the forecastle. Pat was usually aft when he wasn't with Tai-Foon, and slept in my bunk. I myself spent the whole following time up on the afterdeck, where we three officers stood watch. We were there constantly; if one of us had to sleep, he did it either on the deck or on the sofa in the small wardroom next to the charthouse. We rationed sleep among us and never slept more than a couple of hours at a time, and never below deck.

It was obvious that James Arrowsmith was sole master of deck and forecastle. None of the hands obeyed orders; all refused as one to do ship's work. And with no hands on deck the vessel couldn't be manoeuvred. We couldn't tack, and so kept changing course: We sailed westward with the trades. Back again. We were all three getting too little sleep. To be sure, we had the provisions aft and could starve the rebels of food, but in return they could, by keeping us constantly on the defensive, starve us of sleep. In the long run three men — even though we were armed — couldn't keep control of developments. When all is said and done, one can manage longer without food than without sleep. Strictly speaking we couldn't afford to sleep; two men on a watch were all too few, especially when one of them had to stand at the helm.

Add to this that because of the lack of food in the forecastle, the next attack would come quite soon.

The morning after the mutiny I had to see to the wounded. It was simple enough to deal with the three who lay on the poop: Juan Cortez, Edgar Danson, and Pete Davis. None had gunshot wounds; they had merely been beaten half to death by Captain Anderson. All three were still disabled and harmless. Both Danson and Davis had severe concussions, and Cortez had had a great deal of skin scraped off his forehead by the captain's knocking him against the iron railing. He was nearly scalped, and I had to take several stitches and wrap a huge, antiseptic bandage around his head. The others each received a glass of brandy with orders to lay forward, turn in, and lie quiet. Since none of the three could walk normally, we had our green hands — Moses, Stavros, Elias, and Pat — help them down the ladder and across the deck to the forecastle while the third mate, the captain, and I stood along the railing with revolvers unsecured, waiting for a new offensive.

But it didn't come.

Below us, on the main deck before the poop, lay four men. There was one of the two Malay boys whose names I've forgotten; the second was Lee, whom I'd shot in the leg; the third was the ordinary Carlos, again badly roughed up. Oddly enough the fourth was our poor delirious steward, la Fontaine. He most certainly hadn't taken part in the mutiny; he was quite simply in no condition to grasp external things — but I suppose he had noticed that something was happening aft, and so had headed that way, into the throng. Perhaps he had unsuspectingly tried to climb the ladder and had been knocked down by the third mate or the captain. Lord knows. In any case there he lay, shamefully battered — conscious, but unable to move.

It was amazing how lightly we three on the afterdeck had escaped from the clash. I had only the stab in my left upper arm, and could plaster it myself. The third mate had taken some knocks and was stabbed in the leg. When I bandaged his thigh I saw how strong he was. He was just muscles, the whole man. Yet I had knocked him down when he was brutal to Pat. Probably it's all a question of awareness and concentration, of striking fast and in the right place.

But the fact is that after the mutiny we were good friends. I had a good deal of pain from the stab in my arm. At bottom we had no choice; we were forced to bear with each other. Apart from the knife thrust he had at least two broken ribs, which I covered with plaster.

Captain Anderson had been considerably more roughed up. He had two deep knife wounds; neither had pierced the gut or the lung. Probably both stabs came from Arrowsmith. The mulatto was out to kill, and gave not a damn about pearls or other possible treasures. Most of the hands were simply bent on murder for gain; it was the pearls and the money they wanted. The struggle in the forecastle had turned on this: On one side were the Marxist Tai-Foon and the anarcho-socialist Christian Hellmuth; for both it was a question of conscious organization — for Tai-Foon of organized revolution, for Hellmuth of the solidaric general strike which would destroy the

202

whole of existing society — the general strike which would alter all our forms into a Christian community of persons; make the earth our common property.

On the other side was chaos — the slaves' rebellion, the opposite of anarchy.

As for Captain Anderson's wounds, it was as if nothing really fazed him. He had the physique of a jaguar. All healed of itself, and he was clearly insensible to pain. Whether it was genuine insensibility or merely a boundless self-discipline I don't know; but I sewed him together myself, and not once would he let me inject him with Dr. Schleich's local anaesthetic.

Regarding the wounded on the deck, we disagreed. The others thought I should let them lie there. I replied:

'Captain Anderson, it is I who keep the log, and if you refuse to let me treat the sick, I must enter it in the journal. I must write that you have denied me permission to try to save the lives of dying men.'

'So?' he said.

'Well,' said I; 'after this business — if we ever reach land — there will be a trial, and I shall have to tell the truth as it is, just as I enter it in the log.'

'So?' he repeated. He took a couple of turns on the poop, stopped, and looked at me with his small, grey-blue eyes.

'If I don't receive your orders to see to the wounded, then it is you who have killed them, captain. I don't know if you can afford any more deaths on your record, Mr. Anderson.'

He stood perfectly still.

'No,' he said slowly; 'I can hardly afford more deaths. You're right, Mr. Jensen. You saw how careful I was last night.'

'Yes,' I replied; 'so I have the captain's orders to gather up the wounded?'

He didn't reply, just nodded.

I went forward on the poop and shouted for Arrowsmith. Presently he came out of the forecastle and stopped on the deck.

'What is it?' he shouted.

'Do you give me safe-conduct on deck to take care of the sick?'

It was a few seconds before he replied, and I saw that he moved with difficulty, always with a slight stoop; doubtless his neck and abdomen still pained him after the treatment he had received from the captain the night before.

'The bosun can do it!' he shouted.

'No,' I replied; 'he certainly could, but I have the medicine chest aft — sterile bandages, anaesthetics, instruments — and I can't let it out of my hands.'

He paused, then he said:

'All right, Mr. Jensen. You have safe-conduct on deck to take care of the sick. But come without your gun and don't go amidships!'

I gave my revolver to Dickson and went down the ladder. He stood at the rail with the gun while I examined the injured men. Three of them had gunshot wounds. The able seaman Lee had the shot through his left calf, a badly beaten face, and a concussion after his fall from the poop. I had knocked him over the railing while he stood on one leg and couldn't defend himself. The ordinary, the young Malay, was practically mincemeat after a hand-to-hand fight with Captain Anderson and then being thrown from the poop down to the deck. His left arm was broken and he had a severe concussion. He couldn't stand and was only half conscious. Poor la Fontaine was conscious — in his way, that is: He was talking to himself about something to do with confectioner's sugar and sugar sacks. He had ruined his back, probably in a fall from the ladder, and had been shot in the thigh as well. The bullet was lodged somewhere inside the leg.

The night had been hardest on the mestizo from Peru, the ordinary Carlos — who had already been badly roughed up earlier by the carpenter van Harden. He had been shot in the right ankle, where the bones were shattered. In addition he had a broken jaw with attendant brain concussion.

All this was far beyond my resources as medicine man; still, I could bandage and tend them. But it would have to be on the poop, not on the main deck. Both the ordinaries, the Malay and Carlos, I managed to carry up alone, but Lee and la Fontaine were too heavy for me. I shouted forward and asked Christian Hellmuth to come and help. He came, as always with his dark-brown chest naked and his improbably light eyes. But he didn't shine with his usual devout peace. He was troubled, sorrow-laden. Together we took the two men up the ladder and laid them on the poop.

Then he said: 'Grüß Gott!' and went forward again. It seemed that the whole mutiny had become a personal martyrdom for him. His idea was the great, peaceful general strike, but it would have to take place on shore; the hands must refuse to sign on. At sea there is legally no such thing as a strike; refusal to obey orders or to do ship's work is mutiny. Life at sea is indeed a military world, built on total obedience and submission on the crew's part. The captain is the government's deputy, he has the law on his side, and he is absolute dictator in his little society. He can be brought to trial for brutality or abuse of power, but only when he is back on land. Until then he is sovereign and must be obeyed.

The class difference between officers and crew is an unbridgeable gulf. In return all responsibility lies with the captain, and in a mishap he is duty bound to be the last to abandon ship. The vessel's sacred object — the log book — he must salvage even at the risk of his life.

Each has his precisely allotted rank and role. Their dictates are harsh, both for crew and command.

Carlos was in terrible pain from his shattered ankle and fractured lower jaw. At the outset all I could do was to pump him full of morphine. Then I cleaned the bullet wound, fashioned a splint of thick, stiff wire, and lashed the foot and leg securely with gauze to immobilize them. What to do with the broken jaw I didn't know, but I bandaged it so firmly that the mouth couldn't be opened. Until it began to heal he could be doubtless be fed with a tube somehow, either through the corner of his mouth or through the nostril.

Then I took on la Fontaine. He appeared to be dying. The back injury was probably due to several broken ribs. From my own experience I knew that rib fracture can be very painful; all I could do was to place long strips of plaster around his chest. As for the leg, I could only clean the wound and lay a compress over it to prevent inflammation. The worst was that he seemed about to die of heart failure; his breathing was heavy and rapid, and now and then his heart stopped altogether. We — the third mate and I — carried him down to the sick bay.

When I examined Lee, I found that the bullet had gone through his calf, between the fibula and the shinbone, and out the other side. I splinted the leg to keep it quiet, then saw to his face wounds and the injuries from the fall. The left shoulder seemed paralysed, but I found no evidence of fracture. My hitting him under the nose had not driven the nasal bone up into his brain; but the bridge was broken, and his face was dark-blue and violet.

I took a couple of stitches by the corner of his mouth, without local anaesthetic. I had no qualms of conscience; yes, I had shot him in the leg and hit him while he couldn't defend himself; but he had stabbed me in the arm first, though I had done him no wrong. He was lying in the bed he had made.

That left the young Malay. His head wasn't clear, and he was raving. His left upper arm was broken, and I put splints and a cast on it. Beyond that he had blue marks all over his body; Captain Anderson seemed to have used the boy rather roughly. About his head injury there was nothing to be done.

Of the wounded I let only la Fontaine remain aft. The others were sent forward. The boys' aid was indispensable. Elias, Pat, and Moses helped get the sick down to the deck. And not least did our degenerate angel, Stavros, who was strong as a grown man, put his best into getting them forward.

Around noon the steward died. Not from his injuries or the bullet in his thigh, but because his heart failed. The delirium, with its incessant wakefulness and activity, had at last been too much for him. Of course I entered the broken ribs and the gunshot wound in the log, but I gave delirium as the cause of death. With no formalities we threw the body overboard the same afternoon. All we did was to tie an iron weight to his feet, so that he sank instead of going to the sharks.

Now that I think of it, the night ended with no one's having been shot elsewhere than in the leg. And considering that the third mate, the captain, and I had all acted while in mortal danger, one must admit that all three of us had used our guns cautiously and responsibly. Indeed we had been no rougher than circumstances required.

During the next phase things got worse.

That day nothing happened. The night was quiet. The next day was likewise quiet. First on the following night came the main attack. And it was very well planned.

One circumstance was the weather. The wind steadily abated. At last we were just drifting, without steerage way. We were all three on the bridge at once, each with an unsecured revolver in his jacket pocket. All that last day we lay with limp, dead sails in the calm. No one was at the helm.

In the afternoon the captain approached me. Once again he spoke Norwegian.

'Jensen,' he said; 'I know just what's going on. Revenge and planned murder for gain. It concerns the valuables I carry with me, and the fact that I killed Arrowsmith's brother.'

'Everybody knows that, captain,' I replied.

'Well,' he said; 'in case Arrowsmith should succeed in killing me, I have a question for you.'

'Yes, captain.'

'Jensen, you will then be first in command, with all responsibility for further developments.'

'I'm aware of that, captain.'

'I shall also leave a wife and two children.'

'I've thought of that, captain.'

'Will you assume responsibility for my survivors?'

'So long as I'm alive, no evil shall come to them.'

He didn't reply, just nodded.

In the afternoon I realized that I must see to the sick, and I shouted to Arrowsmith. He came out.

'What is it?' he called.

'May I come forward and see to the wounded?'

'If you come without a gun, it's all right.'

'Well, I'll be there presently.'

From the sick bay I fetched opium, brandy, and morphine. At all events Carlos and the scalped Juan Cortez must be in terrible pain by now. I gave my revolver to the third mate and went unarmed down to the deck, forward, and into the forecastle. I was vastly afraid. But when all was said and done, they could do no more than kill me. Still, they had good reason; with me out of the way there would be only two on the poop at the next attack, and they could be certain of gaining the ship. On the other hand: Had I had my revolver with me, I could have shot Arrowsmith and thereby deprived the mutiny of its leadership. It was naturally this that they expected.

He stood by the door to the forecastle and felt my pockets before admitting me. Inside hardly a word was spoken; the men just sat mute and stared at me as I looked to the wounded.

My supposition proved correct; Carlos and Cortez were half beside themselves with pain. The young Malay with the broken arm and Lee with his fractured nose were likewise suffering greatly. Carlos, of course, had the worst of it. A crushed foot and a broken jawbone are no joke. He was fully conscious, and shone with hate when I sat down beside him. Because of his jaw he couldn't speak, but so strong was the emanation that I felt he would have killed me on the spot had he had the slightest chance of doing so.

I gave him a shot, and it was a liberation, presently, to see the effect; the soft, pain-free warmth which morphine gives. He quieted, and his muscles relaxed. He was in a world of gold and clouds and dreams.

Juan Cortez was crazed with pain from his flayed scalp, and I gave morphine to him too. When it began to take effect, he smiled at me.

To Lee and the young Malay I gave 'aurum,' my special blend of opium and alcohol. It's a potent anodyne and sedative, and is also — especially in England — rather much abused as an intoxicant. The effect, however, is not so strong as that of morphine, and one does not so easily become addicted to it.

Of course there was no question of treatment; one could only deaden the pain. All happened in total silence; nobody said a word. When I had finished, I nodded to Arrowsmith and went aft, indeed rather amazed that I was still alive.

The day passed slowly. We were all three on the poop and napped by turns on a blanket on the deck. We lay drifting in the calm all the while, and the sea grew smooth and shiny like oil. The sky was yellowish. Around the sun there was a kind of mist.

Later that afternoon I told Pat about Odysseus and his fabulous journeys. Pat loved to hear stories.

Toward four in the morning the attack came, and it was splendidly prepared. But we had already disabled six men; they were no longer so many. And it was we who had the firearms.

They came from all sides at once; some up from the deck, some outboard from the bulwarks. A couple of them came from the mizzenmast. It happened noiselessly, under the cloak of darkness. James Arrowsmith sprang like a panther over the railing and went for the captain, backed by two others. He was at once knocked to the deck, before he could use his knife. It all happened so fast that I don't remember particulars. But we battled for our lives. Again the third mate was a surprise; Dickson was calm and deliberate and fought like a lion. I was the first who managed to draw his revolver, and I fired at once. To be sure, I hit no one, but the flash and the report of a gun have a great psychological effect. Then I was hit in the face with some object, and partly lost consciousness: I went on defending myself, but I don't remember it. In a flash I realized that this time both the cannibal Lilly and the Greek Stavros were taking part in the attack. Lilly had been shot in the leg, but it made no difference, for he was so good at standing on one leg that he managed just as well as others do on two. Stavros was felled by Dickson and stayed down. In only a few seconds after the lightning attack we all three had our guns out of our pockets and the situation under control. One by one the men jumped down to the main deck. Only Stavros and Arrowsmith remained lying there.

When my head grew clear again, it was daybreak. All of us — the captain, the third mate, and I — were in bad shape. We were terribly beaten and we all had knife wounds, but strangely enough not in the chest or belly.

Stavros had been tossed down to the main deck, but Arrowsmith still lay on the poop.

Captain Anderson bent over him. Then he turned to me:

'Mr. Jensen,' he said; 'now I'm going to throw him overboard.'

'You can't do that, captain.'

'He's the brain behind the whole mutiny. Without Arrowsmith the men have no leadership.'

'Captain Anderson, it is I who keep the log. And I should have to write in it that you had drowned an unconscious man. You've been acquitted of manslaughter three times; this time you would be convicted. It would be patent wilful murder, and the maritime court will convict you.'

Anderson looked at me with a strange expression of hopelessness and despair.

'What on earth shall I do?' he said. 'Both you and Dickson are bloody and battered. We won't survive a third attack. You two can hardly stand on your feet.'

'It's not certain that there will be any third attack.'

'Oh, yes. They've begun the mutiny, and they have no choice. They'll have to continue. They can't sail into port with us. They *must* kill us all.'

Neither of us spoke for awhile. Then he went on:

'I shall be obliged to take upon myself the responsibility of killing Arrowsmith.'

'And I shall be obliged to witness against you in the maritime court.'

Strangely enough, Arrowsmith came to his senses just as we stood talking about him. And he awoke like a cat; the instant he opened his eyes he was wide awake. He rose with difficulty and staggered across the deck and down the ladder. Then he went forward.

The captain went to the railing and called after him:

'Arrowsmith, I could have killed you tonight!'

The mulatto didn't reply, but went into the forecastle.

The morning around us was strange. It was dead calm; not a breath of wind. The sea was smooth and shiny, around the sun there was a sort of mist, and the sky was yellow.

Then a man came walking across the deck. Very calmly he strolled over and came up the ladder. It was Christian Hellmuth. He went up to the captain:

'In an hour we'll have a full typhoon, sir.'

Anderson looked out over the sea, then nodded.

'Dickson!' he called: 'Read the barometer!'

Dickson went into the charthouse. When he came out again, his battered face was pale.

'It's not the lowest reading I've ever seen,' he said; 'but it's very, very low.'

Then I went into the charthouse myself, and when I looked at the barometer I felt the fear of death like a cold hand around my heart. Neither Hellmuth nor the captain troubled to look; they knew what was coming.

'If we don't get the sails taken in, none of us will be alive in two hours,' said Hellmuth.

'They won't obey orders,' replied Anderson. He looked up at the full spread of canvas. All the sails hung lifeless from the yards.

'All right,' he went on; 'I'll talk with them.'

Then he gave me his revolver and went forward, into the forecastle.

Toward the End

After about half an hour Anderson emerged from the forecastle again, unharmed. He came calmly across the waist and up to the afterdeck. His face was expressionless, and he turned directly to the boatswain.

'Mr. Hellmuth,' he said quietly, 'I can't get them to obey. Will you go forward and talk with them?'

'Aye, aye, sir.'

'Explain to them that to refuse to shorten sail is pure suicide.'

'Yes, sir.'

'If we can get the right spread of canvas, we may manage to keep her on the cyclone's periphery and out of the worst.'

Hellmuth nodded, went down the ladder and across the deck, into the forecastle.

What he said or did I don't know, but after about twenty minutes the men came out and went aloft. But it was too late; the heavy, coal-black clouds had already gathered in the north. It was as if night itself was coming over us, full of a thousand devils. Now all that mattered was to get the crew down from the rigging. No one could have stayed aloft in such a wind as now set in. It must have been up to around 130 feet.per second or close to eighty knots; on land that would be almost ninety miles an hour. We hadn't taken in much more than half the sail that we should have. When the wind reached us, the sails banged like cannon shots. Almost instantly half the deck lay under water. Then came the waves. They were close to sixty feet high and came at a furious speed. One of the first casualties was the foresail, blown out of its bolt ropes. Only shreds were left hanging. Then came one of those huge waves and beat over the whole ship.

Indeed I still don't know how *Sancta Vénere* stood the strain for as long as she did. The sea was no longer of water; it was no more an element, but a raging, conscious wild beast with but one aim: to destroy and kill us. The masses of water were heavy and hard as a rockslip. Truly a conscious, evil will to destroy stood behind them. That she managed so well was probably due to three things: She was light, supple, and graceful; she was a composite vessel with iron ribs under her wooden planking; and it was Christian Hellmuth who stood at the helm — assisted by the third mate, to be sure, but it was Hellmuth who steered her.

The first full-sized wave to come over us smashed one of the lifeboats on the weather side. It was broken athwart the middle, and both davits bent inward toward the deck. The whole waist was under water, and pieces of the lifeboat washed over the deck like battering rams.

Then the sea came in on the starboard quarter, and the next moment the poop was flooded. I lost my footing and landed against the railing on the lee side, wet as a drowned cat. Captain Anderson clung to the railing facing the main deck and stayed on his feet. Both helmsmen had also kept their footing.

After the first violent, stormy gusts the wind seemed to fall off somewhat. That was because we had got control of the vessel. She was making headway now, and we kept clear of the wind. But all was still a hell of sound and sea.

Anderson clung to the binnacle, occasionally bellowing a few words to Dickson and Hellmuth, who bellowed in return. The galley and foremast hands were all below now, down in the forecastle.

I said that *Neptune* was making headway, but that's a very mild expression. I don't know how many knots we were doing, but never in my life have I experienced a sail like that. Most of the time the whole lee side was submerged. She went like a bullet through foam and masses of water.

Because we were going so fast, the waves beating upon us aft no longer had such a violent impact. Though presently the jolly-boat was smashed and the other weather lifeboat then gradually beaten to splinters, it dawned on me for the first time that we still had a tiny chance to survive.

The plan was simple and obvious: to keep clear of the wind while heading her as far up to windward as she could stand, so as to avoid the eye of the cyclone and if possible get out to the periphery. That, of course, was our only chance. To sail downwind would take us into the typhoon's centre, where we should be blown and beaten to matchwood. To tack up into the wind was impossible; we couldn't have stood the waves against us, for our own speed against theirs would have increased their impact. We could only choose a middle course: to emulate the tough, elastic birch tree — not to resist the hurricane, but to follow it and simply try to ease over to the side.

At the same time every gust and each larger wave was a problem in itself. Each new attack of that savage beast, the Sea, must be met with cool calculation and calm by navigators and helmsmen. Turning the wheel just a couple of inches too far could mean that she would founder. I stood on the port side of the wheel with the boatswain. There were now three of us at the helm. Directly before us stood the captain, clutching the binnacle. While we three mostly kept our eyes on the sails so as to read from them the gusts of wind and the vessel's movements, he surveyed everything, forward and aft.

He turned his round, expressionless face aft, then shouted:
'Look out! Hold on!'

I turned my head, and behind me saw the highest wave I've ever seen. It stood plumb like a brick wall behind the stern frame. Then it came over us full force. For a moment all four of us were wholly under water. I clung to the wheel with all my might, half-drowned. Had I been knocked overboard, I should scarcely have noticed anything more. I was not fully conscious after the weight and the force in that mass of water. But I contrived to hold on.

When I could see again, the first thing I understood was that both the captain and the binnacle were gone, though Hellmuth and Dickson still stood at the helm. The binnacle had been knocked overboard, but Anderson himself lay on the port side of the poop, clinging to the railing. The door to the charthouse was staved in.

The waves which followed were nothing to that one giant; it was like coming into a sunset breeze after that wave. The whole sea and the sky felt calm and peaceful. Then the captain came crawling over the deck. To walk upright was out of the question. But he caught hold of the wheel and pulled himself up.

'Mr. Jensen,' he shouted: 'I'll take over here. Go below and see how things are with my wife and children!'

I crept over to the smashed door and made my way into the charthouse. All loose objects lay on the floor, tossing back and forth — log book, chart, instruments. It was almost impossible to move. One was thrown from bulkhead to bulkhead, and I clambered down the companionway like a man dead drunk. Below, all was as I had expected: The water was over my knees. I went through the wardroom, lurched between the table and the bulkhead and into Anderson's private cabin without knocking.

There too the water was high over the floor. In one of the bunks both children lay crying. On the other side sat Mrs. Anderson, trying to comfort them. She looked up and attempted to smile.

'We have a chance to make it,' I said; 'on deck it's going relatively well. We have a full typhoon, but we're on the way out to the periphery.'

She nodded.

I staggered out again, lurched through the wardroom, and climbed up the companionway. When I reached the deck the fierce wind took away my breath. For the first time I wished that *Sancta Vénere* had been a steel vessel; no wooden craft could stand this stress for hours on end without springing a leak. A ship which is built and welded of steel hasn't the same grace as a wooden one, but will take far more sea in the case of a prolonged hurricane. On a ship with wooden planking, after several hours of such waves with their savage blows and buffets, the topsides — even with an iron frame — will begin to work their fastenings, and the leaking begins. In a storm a wooden vessel can hold for weeks before springing a leak; but in what we were faced with now, it would be a matter of hours.

I scrambled over the slanting deck and hauled myself up on the helm.

'Everything's fine below!' I shouted into Anderson's ear: 'Of course they're terribly anxious, but nobody's hurt!'

He nodded.

At that instant the mizzenmast went overboard. Despite the wind we clearly heard the bang when the huge mast broke. For awhile it hung from the shrouds like a kind of sea anchor on the lee quarter; then the stays tore loose from the top, and the ship could again be navigated freely. Only the shrouds dangled behind us in the water.

Of course it had damaged the mainmast by falling with the wind, and the main topgallant sail tore right after. That too we could hear very clearly. In a few minutes only shreds remained, banging in the wind. At the same time I sensed that the typhoon was abating somewhat.

'Two men forward to see how things are in the forecastle!' roared Anderson. 'Mr. Hellmuth and I stay here at the helm, and the second and third mates go forward!'

I went numb with rage.

217

'How the hell shall we get across the main deck?' I shrieked: 'It's under water all the time!'

'You'll manage!' he shrieked back. 'And besides, as second mate you're responsible for the health conditions on board. There are several sick men in the forecastle. It's your duty, Mr. Jensen!'

I scrambled up the deck and made it into the charthouse, climbed down the companionway and waded through sea water, reeling and lurching, to the sick bay. It was in pitch-darkness, but I knew where things were; blindly I found the morphine and the syringe and stuck both, along with the opium and a bottle of brandy, into my jacket pocket. Of course there was no question of sterilizing the needle.

Back on deck I yelled to the captain and Hellmuth:

'We'll cross the deck if you'll lay her a bit further down to port, so we don't get the heaviest sea over us!'

'Of course!' roared Anderson: 'You won't even get your feet wet!'

They put the helm several inches alee.

Then Dickson and I crawled down the ladder. The minute I had the deck planks under my feet the first breaker came. I was lifted up, totally submerged; then my shoulders and head struck the hatch coamings. A moment later I was floating in the opposite direction, but I felt that my feet were out of water. I caught hold of the ladder, but lost it and was thrown against the hatch once again. Then I drifted off toward the bulwarks on the weather side and met something big and heavy and firm. It was Dickson. A second later the deck was clear. In deadly terror I clung to the third mate, who pulled both of us up to the weather bulwarks. He clutched me with his left hand and caught hold of the rail with his right. When we were slightly more than halfway we caught the next breaker, and once more floated about the deck; but Dickson didn't get let go of me. We clung to each other, and were in fact washed forward toward the forecastle. Then the deck was again above water.

The door to the forecastle was pounded to matchwood. Everything was afloat, but oddly enough a petroleum lamp burned from the ceiling. The sea washed back and forth over the floor. Carlos and Cortez were half-crazed with pain, nor were Lee and the young Malay very well off either. James Arrowsmith sat in his bunk, his upper body bare, and the huge chest, shoulders, and musculature stood in bold relief from the sharp shadows of the lamplight. All the way forward lay the children: The four green hands Pat, Moses, Elias, and Stavros. They were half dead with fright; as soon as Pat caught sight of me, he threw himself on my neck. Moses took my hand, and even our ruined sixteen-year-old angel Stavros tried to cling to me. I gave each boy a large cup of brandy, so large that the bottle was empty afterward. And through it all the water washed high over my knees, and it was almost impossible to keep my balance.

Then I gave Carlos a shot of morphine, and one to Juan Cortez. To the two others — Lee and the Malay boy — I also gave morphine, but in a lower dosage. During all this it was well-nigh impossible to stay on my feet, and more sea water kept coming through the smashed door. Pat was crying. Then we heard a violent crack from above our heads, and the vessel righted herself somewhat. When Dickson and I came out on deck, we saw what had happened: The foremast had blown overboard. It beat against the ship's side for awhile, then it was gone.

That was in the afternoon.

The wind had indeed fallen off somewhat, and we were clearly on our way out to the periphery; but the situation was more perilous than ever, for the vessel had had more than she could take. The foremast had gone overboard because the step and the wood of the mast had begun to soften. The shrouds and stays had become looser on their fastenings.

As Dickson and I stood outside the forecastle, Arrowsmith emerged with a huge coil of thick hempen rope over his shoulder.

'We'll stretch the line between the forecastle deck and the poop,' he shouted; 'it'll make it easier to cross the deck!'

Together, under cascades of foam and water, we got the one end anchored forward, then began to pull the rope aft. The idea was to fasten it to the iron ladder of the poop. When we were amidships a new wall of sea rose up to windward, and the next moment we were under water. My last glimpse before the wave buried me was of the third mate's arms reaching skyward. Then I knew that I was drowning. My hold on the rope I lost at once. Under the sea I felt myself beaten against something hard, which would have to be some kind of wall. It proved to be the bulkhead to the deckhouse. Again I was washed in the opposite direction, still with my head under water. Then I was thrown back again. My back struck something hard and sharp, and suddenly I found myself in total darkness. But the water around me was calm, and I gained a footing and got my head above water and could breathe once again. With my hands I caught hold of some iron object and hauled myself up. The sea around me was full of splintered planks.

I was standing in the galley inside the deckhouse, clutching the stove. The door had been staved in long since, and it was the remains which floated around me in the water. Before me I could make out the doorway against the faint daylight outside. I staggered the few paces to the high threshold and looked out. The deck had drained, and the ship was not heeling much. The third mate lay by the rail, and Arrowsmith in the middle of the deck; both were on all fours, in the process of rising. How they had managed I have no idea. Arrowsmith still had hold of the rope.

'Now let's run for it!' he shouted.

And we all three dashed over the relatively calm deck before the next wave should come. In the ladder we had something to hold on to, and could stand in the lee of the poop. We drew the rope as taut as we could and made it fast a good four feet above the deck.

As we stood there the next big breaker came in from windward. The whole main deck was under six feet of gushing, foaming water.

Then I saw something I had never met with before: The deckhouse with the galley and cabins for the cook and steward stood up. It rose on the masses of water, stood on end for an instant, then collapsed like a house of cards. A moment later it was washed to the lee side, where the whole house went overboard with a crash.

Almost happily I reflected that poor la Fontaine was already dead, and Tai-Foon, with his parchment face and his narrow black eyes, was in the forecastle. If there was light enough, he would doubtless be sitting and reading some work of social science or criticism — or possibly Karl Marx. But the light in the forecastle was faint and yellowish-brown, and in all likelihood he was just sitting quietly in thought. He had long since grown reconciled to the fact that no one can live forever, not even he.

As I stood with James Arrowsmith and Dickson and clung to the ladder — sheltered by the poop, but still bathed in foam and water up to my chest — I recalled some lines from one of the old Norse bards:

> Never, old man, you cry,
> Wet though the shower may be.
> You knew the love of maidens.
> For all of us death is waiting.

At the same time I pitied the captain's children and the four ship's boys who would die so young. I felt with a strange calm that for the rest of us it didn't matter. We had lived. But I didn't like the thought of dead children sinking and sinking, down into the infinite depths of Neptune's realm, into the timeless dark beneath us.

The hawser we had stretched between the two decks had held. It was still fast and taut and made communication possible between poop and forecastle.

Dickson, Arrowsmith, and I now climbed to the afterdeck, and were buried in a cascade which had washed in over the taffrail. Hellmuth and the captain still stood at the helm. Dickson and

221

Arrowsmith crept over the poop and pulled themselves up on the wheel to help the exhausted men. I crawled into the charthouse, where all was chaos. In the dark I fumbled my way to the shelf where the matches were kept. I found them, and I well knew where the barometer hung on the bulkhead. By dint of striking five or six matches I was able to read it. It had risen slightly. We were on our way out of the cyclone.

That gave hope. But on the other hand, the mainmast alone bore all the forces driving the vessel forward through the heavy seas, and with our reduced speed the waves beat over us with greater might than before the foremast snapped. The mainmast couldn't hold for long, but so far the ship could be manoeuvred.

The prognosis was clear. If she hadn't sprung a real leak, we might be able to keep afloat until we were out of the hurricane area. Both boats on the port side appeared to be intact. Sink she would sooner or later; but if we got out of the typhoon, we could still get twenty-eight people into the two lifeboats — fourteen in each boat.

But *Sancta Vénere* had lost speed, and little by little she was plucked of all her attributes. All her spars were washed away. But the mainmast held. It held for more than an hour. Then it snapped forward toward the port bow; for a while it lay across the deck and forecastle, hanging by the wires of the backstays and shrouds. Then it rose on an enormous wave and went overboard. It hung off the lee side for a long time, thumping like a giant battering ram against the wooden planking.

Therewith the vessel was fully dismasted and couldn't be manoeuvred. We bobbed about like a cork, while one wave after another came over us — from stern to stem. All we could do was to keep below and hope that the leaks weren't too great. She was more or less under water the whole time.

From below the afterdeck Arrowsmith and I went into the hold. It was full of water, but it was only chest-deep. Of course she was leaking, but less than I had expected. If it didn't get worse, she would float for many hours yet.

As we kept below in the darkness of the wardroom, we noted that something was happening on the poop. First there were a number of creaking, grating sounds of wood being broken to pieces. Then followed a couple of violent crashes, and a cascade of water descended on us. The deckhouse on the poop with the charthouse, the first mate's quarters, and the small saloon had gone overboard. Several hundred of those huge waves with hundreds of tons of brine had struck the house, and now it gave way. It was washed overboard, went to sea in all its glory, with instruments and the ship's memory — the log book — after first smashing the port railing.

Both the capstan forward and the wheel on the poop were gone now. The only thing intact was the rope we had stretched between the forecastle and the steel ladder to the poop. The port lifeboats hung there still, but they were damaged, probably unusable.

In the darkness I felt an iron grip on my arm. It was Captain Anderson.

'Mr. Jensen,' he said; 'we must go forward and see how things are.'

'Aye, aye, sir.'

'You take the morphine, and I'll go down to the galley stores and get brandy. There's nothing else we can do.'

'No, sir.'

I tottered and lurched into the sick bay, filled my jacket pocket with opium and morphine plus the dirty, unsterilized needle; Dickson went with Anderson to the galley stores, and between them they crept up with eight bottles of cognac. In our pockets we each found room for four bottles. When we crawled up on deck the wind had fallen off even more, though we still had a storm and tower-high waves. Before our eyes there occurred a miracle: The cloud cover was rent and the moon appeared. The wild, tattered clouds formed strange black figures against the lighter sky. The crescent moon lay on its back, perfectly horizontal, and cast a sort of half-light over the decks. What we saw was only water and foam.

Beneath us, on the main deck, it looked like a cataract during the spring thaw.

We climbed down the ladder and took hold of the hawser. During the clambering which followed, I found that my fingers weren't strong enough to keep a grip; so I bent my elbows and got the rope in the crook of my arms. Thus I managed. Two or three times we were under water, but we reached the forecastle. Down inside it was all afloat, but to my great amazement there was still light in the kerosene lamp under the ceiling. We were in water almost up to our waists. All the way forward lay the four boys, paralysed with terror. Pat threw his arms around my neck and kissed me. And the eighteen-year-old apprentices, Julian and Taddeo, had now joined them. The adults weren't much better off. Fear of death filled the forecastle. It was no cheerier here than aft. Pat called to me, and I returned to the boys and poured them each a big mug of brandy. I explained that the barometer had risen, the wind had fallen off more, and that if the ship didn't sink we still had a chance to survive.

Of course I didn't believe it myself. But in the back of my mind I knew that in theory it was yet possible. Having tried to comfort the boys, I went to Carlos, Cortez, Lee, and the young Malay and gave an injection to each in turn. Lilly, the other Malay boy, Ahmed, Huang, André Legrand, Danson, van Harden, Davis, and Tronchet got their brandy with opium.

When we came up on deck again, the wind had fallen off even more. It wasn't a lie, what I'd said to the men: We *did* still have a chance.

Then happened the thing which, all along, I had feared the most: A new sound mingled with the thunder of the waves and the howls of the storm. It was the accursed, hideous roar of surf against a coast. In the moonlight we could see nothing, but there was land to leeward. Anderson and I heard it both at once, and looked at each other. We were now drifting toward the coast; I've seen the foam of surf rise up almost fifty yards and strike a couple of hundred yards inland. The deep, roaring sound was perfectly distinct, and despite the fact that we were dismasted and rode deep in the water, the wind was driving us slowly toward the coast.

It was probably a coral reef we were being blown toward. Anderson and I crossed the main deck with relative ease; only when we lay on the poop did I catch, in the light of the half moon, the first glimpse of something white to leeward.

Behind the outer reef there would be a lagoon and an island. But inside the reef we could never come; there all would end. The ship had been drubbed soundly and was coming apart at the seams.

When we arrived below, we found Arrowsmith and Dickson in the darkness. Hellmuth was there too, but he was physically exhausted from the day's labours.

'Dickson and Arrowsmith,' said Anderson; 'go down to the hold and find a manila rope at least forty fathoms long and an inch thick.'

The two of them went.

While they were gone, the sound of the surf became even more distinct. Soon it drowned out the storm.

The Rope (II)

We neared the reef faster than I had expected. And the moon now and then shed a beam of light over what awaited us. The surf and the spray were like a snowscape in a storm to look into: white and very dark at the same time.

'Mr. Jensen,' said the captain; 'you must go forward and tell the crew, so that when we strike they'll be ready to try to go ashore. First we must get the injured men aft.'

With fair ease I made it across the main deck and into the dark forecastle.

The water stood high above the floor.

'Listen!' I shouted: 'We have land to our lee. It's probably an outer coral reef; we'll be up in the surf very soon.'

For a moment there was total silence; then came the shrieks from the boys and prayers, oaths, and curses from the men.

'Is it hard by?' called someone.

'Yes,' I replied; 'we can see the surf already.'

'I've heard it for a long time,' said Tai-Foon.

'There's no point in going aft,' shouted another; 'we no longer have a chance anyhow. We're going to drown like cats.'

'It's captain's orders.'

'Tell him to kiss his arse! We have no captain here.'

'You can do as you like, but at least we must have the youngest and the sick aft,' I shouted.

There was only the sound of mumbling and grumbling in reply. Then I felt something clinging to me. It was Pat. He was howling with the terror of death — as were the other three boys. I took Pat on my back and went out on deck.

The vessel was under water; then the deck cleared. She was a sorry sight now, plucked of everything. Only the heavy, lifeless hull — only the corpse — remained of *Neptune*. The wind and the sound of the waves were fierce, but all was drowned out by the thunder from the surf. The moment the deck was bare, I took hold of the rope and bounded across with Pat on my back. A wave stuck us, but we were half in the lee of the poop and came through all right.

Then the deck was under water again. Right after came Huang with Moses and André Legrand, the Congolese, with Elias. Stavros managed alone — as did both apprentices, the Brazilian Taddeo and Julian, the boy from Dixie.

Of the ordinaries — Carlos, Lilly, and the two Malays — only the one Malay boy was well. He managed splendidly by himself. A strange figure came hopping across the deck with a good grip on the line. For a few seconds he was hidden by water, then he stood there once again and hopped onward. It was the cannibal Lilly, hobbling aft on one leg. He came up the ladder to the poop, and like all the others was sent below, down into water and darkness.

Then came the Algerian Ahmed with the wounded Malay boy. At the same time Arrowsmith went forward. He returned with the totally helpless Carlos, the mestizo from Peru, on his back. Right after him came the cook Tai-Foon, helping Jan Cortez aft. The two half-castes, the carpenter van Harden and the sailmaker Davis, made the afterdeck on their own. Arrowsmith went forward again. He met the Canadian, Tronchet, struggling aft by himself. Once or twice they were both under water, but they got across.

Inside the forecastle a man lay screaming. He was well-nigh senseless with terror. It was the white South African, Edgar Danson.

227

He clung to the bunkside and was dragged out on deck by force. There Arrowsmith helped him on as he clung fast, partly to the mulatto, partly to the rope. At least once a breaker beat over them, but they reached their goal, and Danson was sent below.

Up on the poop only Captain Anderson, the third mate, Arrowsmith, and I now remained. Anderson gripped the iron railing, minding the manila rope fetched up by Dickson and the mulatto.

The clouds raced across the sky, and when the moon shone through the rifts we could see the sorry sight of what had once been *Sancta Vénere*. I recall thinking that she and I had begun life the same year; we were both thirty-three years old, and now we should die together.

To leeward we could see the foamy spray, and now the thunder of the surf drowned out all else; it was one continuous roar. And the reef was but a couple of hundred yards away. It would be a matter of minutes. The ship lay fairly stable in the sea, but even the afterdeck was occasionally under water. Captain Anderson posted me by the companionway down to the wardroom and the cabins, which were full of water and people. Arrowsmith and Dickson he kept on the lee side as he fastened the manila rope around his waist. Dickson held a coil of thinner rope.

'Listen!' yelled the captain: 'As soon as we're on the reef I'll go overboard. Then you, Arrowsmith, let out the line fathom by fathom. Don't hold it back, but keep the rope fairly taut. Understand?'

'Aye, aye, sir.'

'If I can, I'll go through the surf and in to land. And there I'll anchor the rope to something or other. A palm or something which will hold.'

'Yes.'

'When it's done, I'll fire a shot. That means I have the rope ashore and tied to something. Once you hear the report or see the flash, pull the rope taut and fasten it. Then I'll come out again. Is that clear?'

We were nearing the reef now. The noise of the surf was as from a great waterfall, ceaseless. And this massive roaring hell of churning water was but fifty yards away. Then there were thirty, twenty yards left. To say that I was afraid is far too mild an expression. I was numb and rigid with dread of this frothing inferno which was nearing.

Now no more than fifteen yards divided us from the reef. Yet another few minutes passed. Then we took the land with our whole port side. There was a violent crash of shattered planks and splintered wood. We on deck knew what was happening and held on. The wardroom below must have been an utter chaos of water and darkness and of folk hurtling against each other. We were cast back and forth a few times, then the soulless body of *Sancta Vénere* came to rest on her port side, canted so strongly that her deck was halfway vertical. The waves still beat over us, but it was chiefly foam and spray which came down over our lee. *Sancta Vénere* was a wreck now, and bit by bit would be smashed and ground to splinters.

Captain Anderson went off the lower rail and straight out into the water. For a brief moment we still saw his back and his bull neck, then they were gone into black water and foam. Now and then we glimpsed him in the moonlight. He was half creeping and climbing, half swimming between the reefs. Presently he vanished altogether, but Arrowsmith lowered more line. For an instant we saw him again.

Then he disappeared for a few minutes which seemed an eternity, but soon Arrowsmith had to let out more rope. After yet a few endless minutes, during which the mulatto kept feeding more line, we heard the report and saw the flash from shore. Now Dickson and Arrowsmith tautened the hawser and made it fast.

The ship was being pummelled by the waves, and she creaked and screamed in her joints, but she held — so far. The port side, on which she lay, must be crushed by now; only her composite build with the steel ribs held the remains of her together. The beautiful

229

Sancta Vénere was a total wreck. But she sheltered us still, and functioned to some degree as a breakwater as well.

Out of the surf came a round head and two brawny shoulders. He was gripping the taut hawser, and Arrowsmith and Dickson pulled him aboard. Anderson was breathing hard, and his face and hands were bleeding.

'Mr. Jensen!' he shouted: 'Get the girl up here — Mary!'

I called down to Christian Hellmuth, and soon had the child in my arms. She was screaming with terror, but calmed down once she was on her father's back. There Dickson lashed her securely.

'Arrowsmith, will you go in first and receive them as they come?' said the captain: 'It's not so easy to crawl ashore in there. And you'll manage just fine now that the rope is stretched fast.'

Without a word Arrowsmith took hold of the hawser and vanished down into the excited sea. Then he was gone in the surf. At once Anderson slid out into the water with the child on his back. In a short while he too was invisible.

Now I went down to join the third mate, and Tai-Foon and Huang took my place by the companionway leading to the wardroom.

'Get the boy ready!' I called to them: 'Bobby is next!'

They got him up, and he lay screaming in the arms of Tai-Foon, who talked to him soothingly.

Then Anderson emerged from the surf once again. He wasn't so spent this time. The first trip in, when he hadn't had the hawser to hold onto but was dragging it after him, had of course been the most arduous. He had with him the rope with which Mary had been tied on. Bobby was squalling.

This time he had no need to shout to anyone; we had the boy ready, and bound him securely to his father's back. Then he went down into the water again. One of the waves lifted them high, but he kept his grip on the rope. After that they vanished into foam and sea.

Next in line was the captain's wife, Margaret Anderson. When he returned we lashed her to his back, and once more he glided out into the surf. All the while *Sancta Vénere* was moving under the waves which beat upon her amidships and forward. She had entered the last phase of destruction now, and I was only waiting for her to break in two. Judging from the sounds in her hull, it wouldn't take much longer.

It was the boatswain, Christian Hellmuth, who was making the selection below, and he did it strictly according to the principle: Youngest first.

Moses was next. He went mute with terror at the sight of the sea and the surf around us. And Anderson kept us waiting a long time. But he emerged anew from the foaming spray and took Moses on his back. Again he vanished down into the churning sea.

Then it was Pat's turn. He was anything but mute; he cried and clung to my neck.

When the captain came back, and the boy was to be tied on, he shrieked:

'No! I want to stay with the second mate! Peder's going to take me ashore!'

'It won't do, Pat!' I shouted back: 'I'm second in command and can't leave the ship until the whole crew is safe on land!'

'No, no! I want to stay with Mister Peder!'

Explanations were of no avail. Only by force did the third mate and I get him tied to Anderson's back. He howled with fright as they slid down into the surf. And he had good reason, for they were both instantly covered with spray. On the way in they must have been as often under water as above it. But inshore they were received by the iron grip of Arrowsmith's hands. He pulled them up from the surf and the waves' undertow.

Then Anderson fetched Elias, and after him Stavros. The Greek was a sturdy lad, but absolutely not strong enough to manage the trip alone.

The sky was changing now. More and more often the moon appeared between the ravelled black clouds, and at times we could see all the way in to the surf on the beach. Unhappily we also had a vista over the wreck of *Neptune*. It was only the vessel's corpse which lay being smashed, plank by plank. The forecastle appeared to be half torn away. The wind had indeed fallen off somewhat; but the sea was as heavy still, and each wave hit with a boom against the weather side. Never have I received such a convincing impression of what a well-built vessel can take.

When Dickson and I had pulled Anderson out yet again, he stood for a moment and wiped the brine from his face and eyes.

'Mr. Dickson,' he said; 'you must go in and help Arrowsmith. He could barely pull us up from the undertow this time.'

The third mate nodded and went out into the sea. He was lifted up at once, followed the wave, but didn't lose the rope. Then he was under for awhile, but surfaced again. Indeed I think that all seamen suffer from hydrophobia. We have all — sooner or later — witnessed the sea in its full fury, and we never forget it. The sight of the ocean roused, breaking to a depth of ten or fifteen fathoms and revealing its secret bottom naked in all its malignant hideous obscenity, is more than a human being can stand. Some Frenchman has said that there's one thing he thanks God for: To have been spared the sight of the naked human soul. The sight of the ocean bottom is worse.

For the human being there's hope.

Of course destruction dwells in us all. In each there lives a murderer. But there also dwells a saviour and rescuer in us.

In the course of that night of death on the coral reef this became clear to me: We're willing to kill one another, but we're also willing to risk our lives for each other.

'What shall we do, Mr. Jensen?' the captain roared: 'Shall we take the sick or the youngest first?'

'Which is worse?' I screamed back: 'To be sick or to be young?'

'You're loony, Mr. Jensen!' he replied: 'I've known it all along.'

'I'm staying here!' I shouted. 'I want André Legrand to help me, and you can decide who shall die and who shall live. It's not my job to condemn people to life or to death. I'm not the captain here.'

He crawled up to the aperture leading down to the wardroom, and bellowed a few words. In a moment the ebony-black athlete stood beside me.

'Who shall we take first, Legrand?' I called: 'The youngest or the sick?'

'We'll take the weakest first,' he replied.

'Who's that?'

He named the name of the Malay boy with the broken arm, then he named Carlos with his shattered ankle and broken jaw, and after that Juan Cortez with his flayed scalp. Then he named the apprentices, both eighteen-year-olds: the criminal Julian from Dixie, the guitarist Taddeo from Brazil; and the other Malay boy, who hadn't been wounded.

'Then we'll take the youngest first,' yelled Anderson.

'And let the dying bury the dying!' I replied.

Just then came the crash as the vessel broke athwart the waist. With that the wreck no longer functioned as a breakwater, and the waves washed full force in over the reefs. Now the whole was a boiling, seething witch-cauldron.

Both apprentices were nimble and mobile; but as it looked now between the wreck and land, neither could possibly manage the trip alone. The Malay was light and agile, but nowhere near strong enough to hold fast to the hawser by his own power.

Anderson took them ashore one by one, bound securely to his back by Legrand and me.

Lilly, despite his ruined leg, made the beach alone. There he was pulled from the undertow by Arrowsmith and the third mate. The captain came back yet again. He resembled a kind of bloody sea monster when the Congolese and I pulled him aboard; a walrus or a sea elephant. We lashed the other Malay boy — the one with the broken arm — to his back, and he returned to the foaming eddies.

233

When he came back, we tied on the last ordinary — Carlos from Peru, with the smashed ankle and the broken jawbone. Then he went out into the sea anew. We could see nothing of them; all resembled a hell of dirty snow.

In my judgment it was now a matter of getting those ashore who might be able to do it on their own; so I ordered Huang, Ahmed, Edgar Danson, and Pierre Tronchet out into the sea in turn. One by one they went; they had the rope to hold onto. And they were all strong, mature seamen, used to hanging on the yards and reefing sails in all kinds of weather — hardy, practised men with heavy fists and ruined nails.

Then came the big, brawny Chinese sailor Lee, with the flesh wound in this thigh and the broken nose. I knew that he would manage.

After that Captain Anderson emerged from the sea again. Where he was concerned, nothing could surprise me any longer. Legrand and I pulled him up onto what remained of the afterdeck.

'Cortez!' he shouted: 'Where's that goddamned Cuban?'

We found him — the good seaman, fine-limbed and elegant, still in terrible pain from his flayed scalp. And we tied him to Anderson's back. Then both went overboard and vanished into foam and darkness.

Next I called for Tai-Foon; he slid down the deck, light and supple as a cat.

'Can you make the shore alone?' I yelled.

He stood before me — as always in paper slippers and pyjamas, and with that dreadful shark knife on his left hip. Tai-Foon did not reply, but his black Asiatic eyes narrowed to dashes. He smiled with his whole parchment face. Then he went calmly down into the witch-cauldron and disappeared. It must be said that the whole crew had reacted with the greatest self-possession. There was no hysteria, no rampant outburst of terror. None tried to save himself at others' expense.

Aside from André Legrand and me, only three men remained on board. There were the two half-castes, the carpenter van Harden and the knife-wielder Davis from Australia. And then there was Christian Hellmuth, the boatswain — sinewy and practised, but still over sixty years old.

Van Harden and Davis had to fend for themselves, and disappeared into eddies of foam and waves. Then the captain came out again. Hellmuth protested, but Anderson took him on his back and I bound him fast. He well knew that he couldn't make the shore alone, but I sensed that he would prefer to die — after what had happened.

They went down into the churning sea, and I was alone on board. I went below and clambered through the upended interior. In blackest darkness I found my way to the sick bay and stuffed my pockets full of morphine plus the needle in its case, opium, and bandages and dressings.

When I was on deck again, Anderson returned. I pulled him aboard.

'Mr. Jensen,' he said: 'Now you go ashore!'

'I'll wait for you, sir.'

'You'll go ashore now! That's an order.'

'To hell with orders. I'm not the one with a wife and children!'

'You're a fine mate!' he yelled.

'I do as I think right!' I replied.

'I should have thrown you overboard long ago!'

'It's never too late, sir.'

He shrugged his enormous shoulders.

'I have to make a trip below,' he went on.

'Is it necessary?' I shouted: 'She won't hold for many more minutes!'

'I must go below!' he yelled: 'It's absolutely necessary!'

He climbed up to where the charthouse had been, and descended into the darkness. After a long time he returned with a case of cartridges under his arm. I tied it to his back.

'Now you go out!' he roared.

I grasped the rope and went down into the roaring masses of water. It's probably the worst thing I've experienced. The pain of hitting against the corals I didn't feel, but I was oftener under than above water, and several times had the sensation of drowning. Then, too, I was still weak from the savage blow to my face and from three days and nights without sleep. Not until I felt the sandy bottom under my feet and got into the six-foot waves against the beach with their fierce undertow, did I lose hold of the rope. I washed helplessly to and fro, swept almost up onto dry land, dragged out by the waves again. For a time I was unconscious, tossed back and forth; then I felt that someone was clutching me. It was the captain, coming from the sea; and Arrowsmith had caught hold of me from land. Right afterward the third mate Dickson too seized one of my arms, and together they pulled me ashore. But I still had the bandages, the morphine, and the needle in my jacket pockets.

On the other hand my revolver was gone.

The Island — Epilogue

Next morning we surveyed the desolation. Of the bark *Neptune* not a splinter remained. The wind had died completely, the sky was blue, though the swells were still heavy. In the lagoon and along the beach lay a good deal of debris from the wreck, but nothing of value. Surely all of us were in a state of shock after the night, but none had perished. I myself had great difficulty walking. Even Arrowsmith was a wreck, but he smiled with his white teeth in his handsome brown face.

Most devastated was Captain Anderson. He lay up there in some bushes, surrounded by his wife and children. But he couldn't rise, he stammered when he talked, and his hands shook like those of a drinker in abstinence. He was badly bruised and cut up as well.

'Fetch Arrowsmith, Mr. Jensen!' he said, when I approached him with Pat by the hand. The boy, by the way, had come through it very well — as had the other children.

James Arrowsmith came and sat on the ground beside Anderson. Then Dickson and Hellmuth were fetched too.

'If this island is inhabited,' said Anderson; 'then the population is probably hostile — most likely cannibals. I know these waters very well. But we can assume that they've had contact with seamen, and that they know what firearms are. We have only two revolvers, but a good deal of ammunition. The essential thing is that the natives get the impression that we're all armed. So the guns must be passed around, with each in turn bearing one of the revolvers.'

With trembling hand he gave his Colt to Arrowmith.

'You have to arrange this yourselves,' he went on; 'I'm not equal to anything. I can't even get up. But most important now is to keep the natives at a distance, if they're hostile. Then there's making a fire and getting food. The fire Lilly can certainly make. Coconuts we have enough of, and in the lagoon and on the reef there are oysters and mussels and shellfish. I can do no more.'

We had practically nothing; beyond the two guns and Tai-Foon's shark knife, there wasn't a match, not a pot to cook in. The Malay boy who was well quickly climbed one of the palms and cut down nuts with the knife. It turned out too that we had a couple of ordinary knives — clasp-knives and pocket knives.

A bit further in on the island we found a brook with fresh water. There later proved to be other fruits too besides coconuts. And here of course the Malays and the non-whites were invaluable. Not least Lilly, who had grown up in such surroundings. He knew every edible plant. For a cannibal he was amazingly vegetarian-oriented.

Already that first day a group formed of the fittest went out to gather oysters, mussels, and snails. The reef was still inaccessible, but in the lagoon quite a bit was to be found. We arranged it from the beginning so that those staying home in 'camp' kept one of the revolvers, while the food-gathering expedition had the other. Since we had nothing to carry our booty in, we used shirts, jackets, and trousers; tying knots in the sleeves and legs gave us very usable 'sacks' in which to collect shellfish.

In the time which lay ahead, finding food would be our main occupation.

That first day we began too to build huts, so as to get some kind of roof over our heads. Tai-Foon made a fire without help from Lilly.

Among our most important finds in the debris from the wreck were a couple of bales of manila rope and an empty iron kerosene drum. With the latter a major problem was solved; we had a cooking pot. That very afternoon we had our first meal: Shellfish roasted in the coals at the edge of the fire.

Anderson had to be fed like a child. He was very weak, and during the months we spent on the island he was never again what he had been, though he eventually walked around a bit and swam a good deal in the lagoon. However, he had been right: The island was inhabited, and the natives were most unfriendly. In a couple of days we had our first meeting with them.

The first time it was only men who came.

They were armed with spears and clubs. None of them was tall. They were very dark and very muscular, with the Australoid's beetling forehead and totally flat nose. By race they were related to Lilly. They had teeth filed to points and were thoroughly tattooed. But Lilly didn't understand their language.

They brought us no gifts, and we had nothing to give them.

Arrowsmith performed a stroke of genius by shooting a gull in flight, just above their heads. And the effect was tremendous; they saw that we had firearms, and they saw that we could use them.

Thereupon they retired. They would have preferred to eat us.

Later we encountered them now and then. We also met the women and children. But all our relations took the form of a kind of armed neutrality.

Of course we were intruders; we were not welcome. We dug clams and caught fish in their lagoon, and we ate their coconuts and fruit and vegetables from the forest.

The island itself was of volcanic origin, with a high, forest-clad mountain, but ringed by coral reefs.

Gradually we formed a society in which none were masters and none servants.

It contrasted strongly with the natives' society of chieftains, under-chieftains, medicine men, and subjects. Our revolvers made

239

the rounds; even the ship's boys went armed now and then. Occasionally we shot something. There were wild boars in the forest, and when we shot them the natives heard the shots.

From the hempen ropes the sailmaker and Christian Hellmuth made, with endless patience, fishing lines, setlines, and fishnets. Our efforts to get food were our chief concern. We also found plenty of those small wild bananas, not much bigger than your middle finger, which must be roasted before they can be eaten.

Our boys, Elias, Moses, Stavros, and Pat, proved to be good fishermen and collected great quantities of shellfish. I taught Pat to swim, and in the five months we spent on the island he developed. He grew bigger and much stronger, he turned fifteen, his whole body became copper-brown, and the diet — fish, shellfish, fruit, and vegetables — made his teeth better.

Soon he came almost to my shoulder.

At the same time he was still wholly a child. When we went strolling along the beach he still held my hand, and at night he slept beside me in one of the huts. He had never really had parents; and now he'd found Second Mate Jensen.

We also held a kind of school for the youngest and for those of the men who wished to take part. Tai-Foon, the third mate, Hellmuth, and I were the teachers. The chief subject was reading and writing English, then mathematics and history. Christian Hellmuth, the Rosicrucian and mystic, proved to be a fount of myths, legends, and fables. We had no books and nothing to write on; we had to content ourselves with writing in the sand.

Our rescuers were the crew from a Polish steamer.

We saw the column of smoke from the funnel in the morning, and a couple of hours later the ship lay outside the reef. Two lifeboats were sent out, and we met them. They had come in for fruit and fresh water. By the end of the afternoon we were all on board. We got vodka and cigarettes.

The vessel was bound for Manila.

We had now entered upon a new century and a new voyage; we were at the beginning of the nineteen-hundreds. In the evening I walked alone on the forecastle and looked out over the placid swells.

Then someone came and took me by the hand. I knew who it was.

For awhile I stood thus, looking into an unclear future, into a new and unknown century, which nobody knew what would bring.

I stood with Pat's brown hand in mine and my own unquiet heart in my breast.